DATE			

Evan Blessed

Also by Rhys Bowen

Evan
Blessed

Rhys Bowen

ST. MARTIN'S MINOTAUR ❧ NEW YORK

www.minotaurbooks.com

Library of Congress Cataloging-in-Publication Data

Bowen, Rhys.
    Evan blessed / Rhys Bowen.— 1st St. Martin's Minotaur ed., 1st U.S. ed.
      p. cm.
    ISBN 0-312-33206-8
    EAN 978-0-312-33206-8
    1. Evans, Evan (Fictitious character)—Fiction. 2. Young
women—Crimes against—Fiction. 3. Missing persons—Fiction.
4. Police—Wales—Fiction. 5. Hiking—Fiction. 6. Wales—Fiction.
I. Title.

  PR6052.O848E755   2005
  823'.914—dc22

                        2005042962

First Edition: August 2005

10 9 8 7 6 5 4 3 2 1

This book is dedicated to the amazing Henoeds—Alice, Pat, Dee, Maxine, Leslie, Cecile, Doreen—and our conquest of Mount Snowdon. And also to our faithful driver John, who steered us ably around all those hairpin bends and along the driveway of death!

It is also dedicated to my friend Millie Sattler, who has supported my books from the very beginning and made me the beautiful stained-glass Welsh dragon.

Thanks, as always, to my brilliant critique team, John, Jane, and Clare, to whom I owe an additional debt of gratitude for coming up with the idea of musical clues in the first place.

Glossary of Welsh Words

bach—little, a term of endearment (pronounced like the composer's name)

bore da—good day (*booray dah*)

cariad—darling (*car-ee-ad*)

cawl—thick broth, usually lamb (*cowl*)

Cor Meibion—male voice choir, literally choir of sons (*core meye-beeon*)

Diolch yn fawr—thank you very much (*dee-olch en vower*)

escob annwyl—literally dear bishop. Good heavens! (*escobe ann-wheel*)

fach—feminine of *bach* (*vuch* with the *ch* like the gutteral in *loch*)

iechyd da—cheers (*yacky da*)

mam—mom

nain—granny (*nine*)

tippen bach—a little (*tippin bach*)

Yr Wyddfa—Welsh name for Mt. Snowdon (*Ur wuthva*)

ysbety—hospital (*isbetty*)

Evan Blessed

Chapter 1

He knew he shouldn't play the piano but he couldn't help himself. That last doctor at the hospital had suggested that it probably wasn't wise when he was in this frame of mind and the old cow next door had made it clear that she didn't appreciate noise after nine o'clock. But it was calling to him, drawing him as certainly as if he was a hooked fish. He had to feel the cool ivory under his fingers and fill the room with enough music to drown out the blackness.

He pushed open the door and fumbled for a light switch. The grand piano took up almost the whole front parlor. It was a magnificent instrument and deserved a room to itself. Giving it up would have been unthinkable. So what if the other downstairs room was uncomfortably cramped—it wasn't as if he entertained.

He rummaged in the piano bench and extracted the first music book his fingers closed around. Chopin, *Selected Pianoforte Works*. He couldn't have chosen anything more technically challenging. He opened the book at a random page and began to play. It had fallen open at a piece he knew well and he breezed through it, lingering notes of longing and passion that hung in the air after the Étude was finished. Then he turned the page and winced as he saw what lay before him. The Nocturne in F sharp, written by a virtuoso to show

1

off his own talent. He attacked it anyway. He had been able to cheat on the slow piece, by playing with incorrect fingering. Now he ordered his fingers to obey him and they flew up the keyboard in an effortless run until they came to the gap where his fourth finger should have been. A wrong note sounded. He slammed shut the keyboard and burst into tears.

"Is this the last of it, Evan *bach*?" Charlie Hopkins lowered the box to the flagstone path outside the cottage door and stood with his hand on his chest, breathing heavily. It took a lot to make Charlie Hopkins pant, even at the age of seventy-two, but the tenth trip up the mountainside had been too much on a hot afternoon.

"I think it is, Charlie," Evan Evans said, also breathing heavily even though he was half Charlie's age and in good shape. "I can't thank you enough for helping me out like this. I hadn't quite realized what a trek this would be."

"What else can you expect when you choose to go and live halfway up a bloody mountain?" Charlie demanded. He took out a large handkerchief and mopped his brow with it.

Evan smiled. "Bronwen wanted to call in a moving company."

Charlie snorted. "You'd never have got a moving van up here. I'd like to have seen her find movers willing to carry furniture like we did. You'd have had a strike on your hands."

"That's what I told her," Evan said. He hoisted a box with a grunt and kicked open the cottage door. Charlie followed with a second box.

"Where do you want me to put this then?" he asked. His gaze went around the small living room that was already piled with furniture and boxes.

"Anywhere on the floor will do, thanks," Evan said, dropping his own box beside several others. "How can one woman have so many things?"

"This all belongs to her, does it?"

"It does. She has to be out of the schoolhouse this week."

Charlie Hopkins sucked through his teeth. "Ah, so it's true then. They're definitely closing the school."

2

"They are. They've offered Bron a job at the new primary on the Caernarfon road. Five hundred children there will be at that school. All glass and modern looking. Quite a shock for our kids, I expect."

"I don't see why they had to change things," Charlie said. "This school was good enough for me and my boys."

"I'm sure it worked just fine with a teacher like Bronwen," Evan said. "But I can understand that she can't give a bright ten-year-old and a slow six-year-old all the individual attention they deserve."

Charlie nodded. "Maybe you're right. Education is different these days. When I was in school we got a cane across the knuckles for each word we got wrong on our spelling tests."

Evan laughed. "I bet you're a good speller."

"I am too." Charlie smiled, revealing a mouth with several gaps where teeth were missing. "So it's lucky for your Bronwen that you're getting married right now and moving into this place, or she'd have been hunting for digs."

"Don't make it sound as though she's only marrying me because she's losing the schoolhouse."

Charlie chuckled. "No, I suppose she could do worse for herself. So you'll be giving up that cottage that you're renting from Mrs. Howells?"

"Not until the wedding. Bronwen doesn't think it's right that I should move in with her. Not with my mother coming. She's rather old-fashioned about that kind of thing."

Charlie grinned again. "Quite right. No hanky-panky allowed. So the wedding's going to be a big shindig, is it? I heard you weren't getting married in chapel." He followed Evan out into the light afternoon breeze that had sprung up from the ocean.

Evan hoisted another box of kitchen equipment and staggered through into the cottage with it. "Bron and I wanted to, but her mother made a fuss. She'd been raised Church of Wales, you see, like all posh people. Her mother couldn't stand the thought of her daughter being married in a chapel." He balanced the box on top of a kitchen chair. "If it was up to me, I'd be all for running off to a

3

registry office, but it seems that weddings are a big deal for women. And Bronwen didn't get a proper wedding last time, you see."

"She's been married before? I didn't know that."

"Well, she didn't exactly go around broadcasting it, did she? She got married right after leaving university."

"Just a minute—so how can the two of you get married in church then?"

"Because the first marriage was annulled. Her husband . . . wasn't very satisfactory." He felt himself blushing.

Charlie grinned at his discomfort. "I don't suppose she'll have any complaints in that department this time around."

Evan looked away. "We'll have to wait and see about that," he said. "But as I was saying, it turns out that she wants a proper wedding with all the trimmings."

"Most women do."

Evan shook his head. "I hadn't realized. Suddenly I find myself involved in discussions about bouquets and what kind of champagne and how many tiers for the cake and what size marquee."

"*Escob annwyl!* Don't tell me you're having a marquee?" Charlie looked impressed.

"On the lawn beside the church. Her parents insist on paying so they're turning it into a big production. I rather wish now that we'd got married on the quiet and told them afterwards."

"Welcome to the wonderful world of in-laws, boyo. This is only the beginning."

"Luckily they live far enough away." Evan looked up with a grin. "So does my mother. I can't say I'm too thrilled about her arrival either."

"Will she be staying with you?"

"I've only got the one single bed, haven't I? So I'm putting her up with Mrs. Williams. They'll have a grand old time, comparing my faults and nattering to each other in Welsh. She doesn't have too many Welsh speakers where she lives in Swansea."

"Not many Welsh speakers? Fancy that. I'm glad I live up here then." He followed Evan into the cottage with the last box. "If that's all, then I'd better be heading down then, Evan *bach*. The wife will have my dinner waiting and she doesn't like it getting cold."

"Of course. Off you go then, Charlie, and thanks again for your help. I couldn't have done it alone."

"We don't want you knackered before the wedding, do we?" Charlie dug him in the side, giving a wheezing laugh. Then he came out of the cottage, blinking in the bright sunlight, and stood there for a moment, taking in the scene with sigh of satisfaction. It was one of those perfect summer days so rare in this part of Wales. The sky was like a clear blue glass dome over a landscape of mountains glowing with purple heather, sparkling streams, and deep valleys. The village of Llanfair below them basked in the afternoon sunshine, its row of neat whitewashed cottages looking like a doll's town. Seagulls wheeled overhead, sheep bleated on high meadows. The air was scented with heather and just a tang of the ocean.

"On the other hand," Charlie said slowly, "I can see why you'd want to live here. You couldn't buy a view like this for a million pounds, could you?"

Evan nodded. "That's what we think. Best view on earth, isn't it?"

"You may change your mind when the winter gales come," Charlie said. "I'll see you at the Red Dragon tonight then, eh, boyo? You can treat me to a pint for my services."

"I'll do that, Charlie," Evan said, "if we get back in time, that is. I'm joining Bronwen in Caernarfon this afternoon. Meeting with the bank manager to set up joint accounts, then on to an antiques shop. Bronwen's set her heart on furnishing the place with antiques and she's seen the perfect Welsh dresser for the kitchen." Evan made a face and Charlie laughed.

"Say goodbye to freedom and evenings at the pub, boy," he said.

"You go to the pub every evening," Evan pointed out.

"Ah, but then I've got her licked into shape after fifty years, haven't I?" he said. "If you want a word of advice, you have to start off on the right foot, so to speak. Show her who's boss and how it's going to be. None of this sensitive rubbish that you hear about on the telly these days. Men weren't born to decorate houses and choose curtains. We're the hunters, boy. They are supposed to be the bloody gatherers."

Evan laughed, pushing his dark curls from his face. "I'm afraid times have changed, Charlie. And if fixing up the place makes Bronwen happy, then I'm happy to help her with it."

Charlie shook his head. "You'll be wearing a pinny next. You mark my words, boy."

"No, I think we've agreed that Bron should do the cooking. I'm hopeless at it. *Diolch yn fawr*. Thanks again then, Charlie." He shook the old man's hand and stood watching as Charlie negotiated the steep track down to the village. Like all men born and bred in the mountains, he walked up and down them as if they were flat fields. In a few minutes he had disappeared among the first houses of the village. Evan turned and went back into the cottage.

It felt dark inside and he wondered if he should try to enlarge the windows. I'm getting into the do-it-yourself mode already, he thought, alarmed, and experienced a fleeting regret for the free, unencumbered life when he used to spend his weekends hiking and climbing and his evenings at the Red Dragon. He thought about carrying some of the boxes through to the bedroom, then decided that he had no idea where Bronwen wanted anything. Better to wait for her.

As he came out into the sunlight again he was startled by the figure of a man, right outside his front door.

"Oh—hello," Evan stammered. "Can I help you?"

"I hope so." He was a slim, angular young man with neatly parted dark hair and wire-rimmed spectacles. His boyish face was tense with concern. "You are the policeman, aren't you? They said in the village that I'd find you here."

"I'm Detective Constable Evans, but officially I'm off duty today. What do you need?"

"It's my girlfriend, she's lost." The young man sounded close to tears. He spoke with an accent that hinted at Manchester, or maybe even Liverpool. Certainly not Welsh.

"Lost. Where?"

"Somewhere up there." He pointed at the wall of mountains that rose on the other side of the valley, culminating in the great peak of Snowdon.

"On Snowdon, you mean?"

The young man nodded. "That's right. We took the trail up from the youth hostel where we're staying. Then we had lunch overlooking a little lake."

"The Pyg Track, and the lake would be Glaslyn." Evan nodded.

"On the way back we got separated, so I thought we'd meet up at the trailhead. But she didn't come and didn't come. I went back looking for her, then I went to the youth hostel to see if she'd maybe come down another way and got a lift back there, but she hadn't. I'm scared something has happened to her."

"How long ago was this?" Evan asked.

"We'd just had lunch," the young man said. "Finished our picnic and then started down. What time is it now?"

Evan glanced at his watch. "Quarter to four." He winced. He was supposed to be meeting with the bank manager at four-fifteen. He'd need to get down the hill and change out of his sweaty clothes right away. Then he reminded himself of what he'd told Bronwen so often—a police job is twenty-four hours, seven days a week.

"Then she's been missing for three hours."

"Does she have a mobile phone on her?" Evan asked.

"Yes, she does. That's why it's odd she hasn't called me if she's lost."

"Reception isn't always the greatest up here," Evan said. "Look, I can't really do anything yet unless it's a perceived dangerous situation. It may be that she's taken another path down and she'll have to find her way back."

"But what if she's fallen and broken a leg or something?" The young man sounded desperate.

"You said you went back along the path and looked, didn't you?"

"Yes, but you said she may have taken the wrong path by mistake."

Evan put his hand on the young man's shoulder. "What's your name?"

"Paul. Paul Upfield. My girlfriend's name is Shannon—Shannon Parkinson."

"All right, Paul," Evan said. "Come on. Let's go down to the village. I'll put in a call to HQ and alert them to the fact that we might have a potential problem. That way they can have the mountain rescue squad on alert. If it starts getting dark and she hasn't shown up, then they'll start a search."

The young man bit his lip. "Starts getting dark?"

"We can't send out search parties every time someone is an hour or two late. We'd be spending half our lives on the mountain."

The young man nodded, trying to accept that this was reasonable.

Evan patted his shoulder. "It's fine weather. And there are plenty of other ramblers out there. Chances are she's already been found and someone's driving her back to the youth hostel."

"Oh, I hope so."

He fell into step beside Evan down the mountain. Evan's conscience was nagging at him to call Bronwen and go with Paul Upfield to look for his girlfriend right now. He knew how frantic he had felt the one time he lost Bronwen. But he had to remind himself it wasn't even his job anymore. He was in the plainclothes division. If the uniformed branch called him in, he'd respond. Otherwise he'd be stepping on toes again and he'd certainly done enough of that since he joined the force.

"How did you become separated?" Evan asked the question that had been troubling him. When you went out hiking with just one other person, it wasn't exactly easy to lose track of each other. Especially not on a bleak, exposed mountain like Snowdon.

The young man's face flushed bright crimson. "We had a bit of a row. She's not much of a hiker, see, and I told her she was going too slowly. She was scared going down, you see. I thought she was being too cautious. She said, 'Fine. Go on ahead then. Don't wait for me.' We said a few stupid things about being selfish to each other and I stumped off. Well, I cooled down pretty quickly and felt bad about the way I'd behaved, so I waited for her. Then I went back and there was no sign of her."

No wonder he was looking so upset, Evan thought. He was battling a guilty conscience in addition to the worry. He nodded with sympathy. "I'll see what I can do about getting someone out to look for her. I hope you've learned a lesson about sticking together when you're out in wild parts."

"Oh, I have," the young man said. "I feel terrible. I promised her mum I'd take good care of her. She was against letting us go on this holiday together in the first place."

"How old is Shannon?"

"Seventeen."

"Well, that's good news, isn't it?" Evan said. "She's still a minor. Makes it easier to send out a search party right away."

They reached the bottom of the hill and came out onto Llanfair's main street—actually Llanfair's only street.

"Where did you leave your car?" Evan asked.

"I don't have a car. We've been taking the little Sherpa bus to the youth hostel."

"You better come to my place," he said. "I'll put in the call to HQ for you and they'll send out a squad car."

"Your place?" Paul looked confused. "So you don't live up there?" His eyes scanned upward to the gray stone shape of the cottage, perched halfway up the mountain slope.

"Not yet. I'm getting married and we're moving up there."

"Rather you than me, mate," Paul Upfield said. "I like the outdoors, but I don't think I'd fancy that trek every time I came home from work."

This seemed to be the universal response to the former shepherd's cottage he and Bronwen had bought. It had seemed like such a romantic place to live, with its stunning view and solid stone walls.

Chapter 2

"Sorry I'm late." Evan took a deep breath as he was ushered into the bank manager's office.

He noticed that Bronwen's lips were set in a prim, straight line—the closest she would come to showing her disapproval of his being twenty minutes late for an appointment.

"Do come in and take a seat." The bank manager indicated the leather chair beside Bronwen. "Your fiancée and I have been having a nice chat. I'm Neville Shorecross and I've been told that you're a policeman, Mr. Evans, which I'm sure explains your tardy arrival."

"It does," Evan said. "I was just about to leave home when I had to deal with a young chap who lost his girlfriend."

"Honestly, Evan," Bronwen said, "don't tell me you're playing agony aunt now."

"No, I mean really lost his girlfriend." Evan pulled up a chair beside Bronwen. "They were hiking together and became separated. He's hunted all over and he can't find her. He was very distraught so I had to stay with him until the squad car arrived."

"Oh dear, I hope nothing's happened to her," Neville Shorecross said. "Where exactly were they hiking?"

"The usual thing. Up to the top of Snowdon and back."

"Do you happen to know which path they took?"

"It sounded like the Pyg Track from the youth hostel, but I suppose she could have opted for an easier way down. The Pyg does get pretty steep."

The bank manager frowned. "If you need more members for your search party, I'd be happy to round up some of my boys. I run a local Scout troop, you know, and we've practiced mountain rescue exercises. We know the area well. They'd be thrilled to participate in the real thing."

"Thank you, that's very kind of you," Evan said. "I'm not the one organizing the search but I'll pass on the information."

"It is the summer holidays, isn't it?" Bronwen said. "There are loads of people out on the hills. I expect she'll be found quickly enough."

"One hopes so." Shorecross shook his head. "We seem to read about so many bad things happening to young girls these days." Evan looked at him with interest. He was the archetypal bank manager, a prim, neatly dressed little man with just the hint of a mustache, a signet ring on the little finger of his left hand, and a silk handkerchief in his top pocket. But when Evan studied his face, he wasn't that old. Around forty maybe. Yet he spoke as if he came from a bygone generation, already frozen in time.

"Yes, there are some strange people around, I'll grant you that," Evan agreed.

"Too much disgusting stuff on television," Shorecross said. "It puts ideas into twisted minds. Even our Miss Jones has had problems with a Peeping Tom recently."

"She's told the police, I hope?"

"Oh yes. They've had men out there, but they haven't managed to catch anybody. I have my suspicions, but you can't slander somebody without proof, can you?" He looked up, suddenly cheerful and businesslike. "Ah well. We'd better get through this paperwork as quickly as possible, hadn't we? Just in case you are called out again, Mr. Evans."

Half an hour later Mr. Shorecross escorted them from his office. "I look forward to having you as our customers, Mr. and Mrs.

Evans-to-be. And may I be the first to extend my best wishes for your upcoming marriage."

As they passed through the bank, Evan noticed an attractive girl in one teller's booth, chatting animatedly with a customer, while in another booth a sallow-faced young man eyed them warily from behind heavy-rimmed spectacles.

Evan took Bronwen's arm as they stepped out into the warm sunshine. Caernarfon was bustling with tourists. They crowded the narrow pavements, dragging children dripping melting ice cream cones, while others cruised the narrow streets looking hopefully for parking places that didn't exist.

"Everyone else in the world seems to be on holiday except us," Evan said to Bronwen.

"In two weeks, we'll be on our honeymoon in Switzerland," Bronwen reminded him. "Besides, all these wedding preparations are as good as a holiday, aren't they?"

"Oh lovely," Evan said, deadpan. "Never had more fun in my life."

Bronwen looked up at him and laughed. "You make the whole thing sound like a visit to the dentist."

"Just a little overwhelming," Evan said. "You forget you've got school holidays at the moment. I'm trying to fit all this in and do my job properly. I really felt bad about leaving that boy to a couple of uniform blokes who seemed totally disinterested. I think I might call Inspector Watkins and see if a search party has been sent out yet."

"Don't you think you may be overreacting?" Bronwen took his arm as they threaded their way through the stalled traffic in Castle Square to where their car was parked. "I mean, what's the terrible rush? If she's lost her way, she's bound to bump into someone sooner or later and get down to a road. It's not as if they were climbing, is it? She's not likely to have fallen and hurt herself badly."

"No, I suppose you're right," Evan agreed. "It's just that the young kid was so worried. They'd had a bit of a tiff, you see, so he was feeling guilty. He'd stalked off because she wasn't walking fast enough."

"Typical male," Bronwen muttered. "So he went back to look for her and couldn't find her?"

"Apparently."

"That explains it, then. My guess is that she's not lost at all. She was angry with him, so she's taken another route down. She may even have given up on the hike and ridden down on the railway. She's probably sitting in a café right now feeling sorry for herself."

Evan's face lit up. "Bron, you're a genius. I bet that's what's happened."

"And sooner or later she'll go back to where they are staying and they'll hug and make up and it will all be forgotten."

"Do you think I should call HQ and suggest that they check the cafés in Llanberis?"

She put a firm hand on his arm. "I'd suggest you do nothing. This isn't your problem, is it? The plainclothes division hasn't been called in."

Evan sighed. "You're right. And it is my day off."

"And if we get to that antiques shop and find that they've sold my Welsh dresser, you'll have a seriously miffed fiancée to deal with."

"Right. Welsh dressers, here we come!" Evan took her hand and pulled her across the square between two tour buses.

The shop was in a narrow back street opposite the castle. It looked like nothing special from the outside, but once inside it opened into a treasure trove of antiques. Classical music was playing softly in the background. The air was heavy with the smell of old wood and furniture polish, and shafts of late afternoon sunlight shone through a casement window. It was like stepping back into Dickens.

"I didn't even know this place existed," Evan commented to Bronwen as they stood alone, waiting for a shopkeeper to appear.

"Well, you're not exactly the type who goes antique browsing in your spare time, are you?" Bronwen teased. "And besides, I only found it by accident when it started to rain one day and I took shelter on the porch."

"Oh dear, that doesn't say much for my advertising skills, does

14

it?" A tall, skinny man stepped out of the shadows at the back of the store. He had a hollow, rather frail look about him and wore his hair somewhat longer than is fashionable today. He spoke with a cultured English voice with no trace of Welshness. "I've placed ads in the local newspapers and the free tourist literature. But I suppose it takes a while to generate business, doesn't it?"

"You're newly opened, then, are you?" Evan asked.

"I came here in April. That means four months now. I can't say that business is booming yet."

"You have some lovely things," Bronwen said. "Once word gets out about you, I'm sure you'll do very well."

Evan had noted some prices and privately wondered if the folk around Caernarfon could be persuaded to shell out that much for objects that had once sat in their grandparents' cottages.

"I hope so," the shopowner said. His voice was light and slightly tremulous. "Coming here was a big risk in the first place. When I had to give up my job, I asked myself what I really wanted to do with my life and the answer was to own an antiques shop. It's always been a hobby of mine. Well, to cut a long story short, I found out that I couldn't afford the property prices in the most desirable places—the Cotswolds, Devon—way out of my price range. Then I discovered that Wales was still affordable. I came to look and liked what I saw."

"So you're not from Wales, then?" Evan asked.

"Do I sound as if I am?" The man laughed. "I came here once on holiday when I was a boy. It rained the whole bloody time, I seem to remember."

"I hope you like it here," Bronwen said.

"As long as I don't have to learn the language." He made a face. "How does anyone get their tongues around all those hissing and spitting sounds?"

"Born to it," Evan said. "But you'll be able to survive here without speaking Welsh. Everybody speaks both languages."

"You're most reassuring." The man smiled. "I recognize the young lady, of course. You've been in here before, haven't you? Is there anything particular I can help you with today?"

"This." Bronwen went over to a handsome dark oak Welsh dresser and stroked it lovingly. Evan watched with apprehension. He didn't know much about bargaining but he did know that rule number one was not to show how keen you were on the item you wanted. Now here was Bronwen almost drooling over it.

"Ah yes. A very fine piece." The shopkeeper nodded with enthusiasm.

"We're getting married and moving into a restored shepherd's cottage," Bronwen said. "This will fit perfectly into our kitchen."

"How splendid," the man said. "A restored shepherd's cottage. I love the sound of that. Do they come up often for sale? I'm stuck in a miserable flat over the shop at the moment."

"I don't think they do," Evan said. "We were lucky because we were able to buy one cheaply from the insurers after a fire. But miner's cottages in the villages come on the market quite often at a good price."

"Excellent. If I can make a go of this shop, then I'll want to buy my own place. I hate the idea of paying rent."

"That's exactly what Bronwen has been telling me," Evan said.

The man turned sharply to her. "Bronwen? What a pretty name."

Bronwen blushed. "It's fairly common in Wales."

"It suits you perfectly." He smiled at her.

"Do you think you can lower the price a little for someone with a pretty name who's about to get married?" Bronwen asked him sweetly. "I'm afraid it's just out of our price range as it stands."

Evan looked at her in amazement. He hadn't thought of Bronwen as the type who used feminine wiles. The man was now smiling sheepishly and mumbled, "I'm sure for you, at this auspicious time, we can do something, fair lady."

"Mr. Cartwright is a nice man, don't you think?" Bronwen asked as they made their way back toward Castle Square. "Always so pleasant."

"I'm sure I could be pleasant if anyone had paid me that much money in one afternoon," Evan said.

"Ah, but you have to admit he did come down a lot when we started negotiating."

"When you turned on your feminine charms, you mean."

"Feminine charms?" Bronwen bristled. "I was just being nice to him."

"You barely stopped short of fluttering your eyelashes."

"I did not! You do exaggerate."

Evan grinned.

Bronwen had to smile too. "Well, anyway, it worked, didn't it?"

"It still cost an awful amount," Evan said. "I had no idea people paid that much for furniture."

"But it's a special piece, Evan. It's a part of our history and it's in beautiful condition."

"My *nain* used to have one in her kitchen," he said. "When she died I've no doubt it was thrown out as old junk."

"Most of them were," Bronwen said. "Luckily we've come to appreciate old things again. The next thing I want to find is a brass bed and an antique Welsh quilt for it."

"Hold on," Evan stammered. "I know we've just signed for a line of credit at the bank, but that doesn't mean we actually want to use it up."

"It's all right. Don't worry. Mummy is giving us some money to set up house."

Evan frowned. "You know I don't like accepting money from your parents. First they take over the wedding and now they're apparently furnishing our household for us."

Bronwen paused and turned to face him. She took his hands in hers. "They can afford it, Evan, and it gives Mummy pleasure. She's so delighted that her daughter, whom she considered to be a hopeless failure, is not going to wind up as an old maid after all."

Evan noted the touch of bitterness in her voice. He slipped his arm around her shoulder. "If furnishing the cottage the way you like it makes you happy, then I won't say another word," he said.

She wriggled away from him. "Oh, and how would you like it

furnished? A threadbare armchair, a couple of crates to put the TV and your beer on?"

"Sounds about right to me." He laughed and bent to give her a kiss.

Bronwen looked up at him. "It's going to be lovely, Evan. The cottage is going to be a perfect little home and we're going to have a beautiful wedding and a splendid honeymoon and everything's going to be absolutely bloody marvelous."

Chapter 3

The sun had dipped behind the mountains, plunging the narrow valley into deep twilight as Bronwen and Evan finally drove up the Llanberis Pass to Llanfair.

"It's later than I expected," Bronwen said.

Evan turned to glance at her. "I wasn't the one who had a wild impulse to stop off at the church and go over the service with the vicar for an hour."

"It had to be done," Bronwen said. "I wanted to make sure I knew what I was going to be asked and what I was agreeing to."

"I noticed you heaved a sigh of relief when the vicar said they'd cut out the honor and obey clause."

"He seemed a pleasant person, didn't he?"

Evan smiled. "You're finding everybody pleasant at the moment. It must be that pre-wedding glow. If you want to know, I thought he was a bit creepy. A little too gushy for my taste."

"But then you're used to the ministers at the two chapels, spouting hellfire and brimstone."

"And quite right too." Evan slowed the car to a halt outside a row of plain stone cottages, some whitewashed and some not. The one he was living in was not, but sported a red door, which the locals considered sinfully ostentatious.

19

"It's almost dark." Bronwen looked up the mountain. "I had planned to get one room of the cottage sorted out enough to sleep in. Now I'm not sure what I should do. I presume my bed is already up there?"

"It is, and you can't go up there tonight," Evan said. "It's a proper mess. Charlie Hopkins was a wonderful help in carrying stuff up the mountain, but it's all just dumped willy-nilly in the living room. I had planned to start getting things in order before I met you at the bank, but instead I had to deal with the hiker and his missing girlfriend."

"I hope he's found her by now," Bronwen said.

"I'll call HQ and see if there's any news," Evan said. "But first we've got to decide what to do with you. I've cleaned out the schoolhouse, which means you'd better stay here, I suppose."

"That's probably one of the most romantic proposals I've had in my life." Bronwen gave him a sardonic smile. "Is it my reputation you're thinking of, or yours?"

"Oh, come on, Bron." He turned his key in the lock. "You know what I mean. I've only got the one single bed, haven't I? You're welcome to take that and I'll sleep in my sleeping bag on the floor."

Bronwen slipped her arm around him as they went inside. "Don't be such a martyr. I'm sure it will be very cozy if we snuggle up." Then she went on down the hall into the kitchen. "More to the point, what are we going to eat? If I know you, you'll have one tin of baked beans and some cheese in the larder and that's it." She opened the fridge. "Oh, and some eggs. Amazing. Well, I can always whip us up an omelette then."

"I thought we might have something over at the Dragon," Evan said.

"Oh Evan. If we're going to eat out, let's splurge and go up to the Everest Inn. At least their food isn't reheated in microwaves."

"They do a decent bangers and chips at the Dragon. And the fish and chips isn't bad either," Evan defended. "And besides, I promised Charlie Hopkins that I'd treat him to a pint for helping me carry all of your possessions up the mountain today."

Bronwen shrugged. "In that case, I suppose I'd better admit defeat and resign myself to Betsy's microwaved shepherd's pie."

The Red Dragon's regular customers had been at the bar for an hour or more, enough time to create a thick tobacco fug. Bronwen stifled a cough.

"It will be better in the ladies' lounge," Evan whispered, knowing her feelings on smoke.

"If you think I'm being exiled while you stand around the bar chatting with your mates, you can think again," Bronwen whispered back.

Through the smoke haze the voices of the village butcher and milkman, both called Evans, rose above the low hum of conversation.

"Bloody tourists," Evans-the-Meat's loud baritone echoed back from the oak-beamed ceiling. "Don't tell me they're good for the local economy. And don't tell me you're getting rich by selling them ice creams either. I had some English yuppie type come into my shop today and ask if I had any marinades to go with the lamb she was buying. I looked her in the eye and told her it was best Welsh lamb, not your imported New Zealand rubbish. It didn't need marinades. It had flavor all by itself."

The other men at the bar chuckled and nodded agreement. As Evans-the-Meat finished his story, he looked up and spotted Evan and Bronwen in the doorway. "Well, would you look what we've got here," he exclaimed. "None other than the lovebirds. Is this the equivalent of the last phone call then, Evan *bach*? You're being allowed one final look at the inside of the pub before your marriage?"

"He won't have the strength to stagger up that mountain after he's been drinking," Evans-the-Milk dug the butcher in the ribs.

"And if he manages to get that far, he won't have enough strength for anything else that night," Evans-the-Meat retorted, and the group broke into noisy laughter.

"You two just keep quiet." Betsy the barmaid leaned out across the bar to deliver a slap on the closest arm. "I think it's lovely just that there's going to be a wedding in this place. So romantic. I can't wait to see Bronwen in her veil and her long white dress."

"And Evan in his top hat?" Evans-the-Meat quipped.

"Give over, Gareth," Evan said to the grinning butcher. "Can you see me in a top hat? I'm just going to be wearing a dark suit. None of this morning coat stuff, thank you."

"I think you'll look just fine," Betsy said, giving him a wistful smile.

"Where's Barry tonight then?" Evan asked, mentioning Betsy's current flame and hoping that Bronwen hadn't noticed Betsy's gaze.

"Out on the mountain looking for some stupid lost hiker," Betsy said. "Charlie's up there with him and a couple of other men from the village too."

"How long ago were they called out?"

"They've been gone a couple of hours, wouldn't you say?" Betsy asked.

There were several nods. "They had vans full of coppers. They even had dogs," Evans-the-Meat said. "Big-scale operation, I'd call it."

Evan turned to Bronwen. "So it looks like she hasn't been found yet. Maybe I should call in to see if they need me."

"Not until you've had a pint and something to eat," Bronwen said. She lowered her voice. "And now that we've found out that Charlie isn't here, maybe we could go up to the Everest Inn?"

"That would be rude, now that we're here," Evan said, "and I thought we were supposed to be saving up for the honeymoon." He turned back to Betsy. "What can you rustle up for dinner for two hungry people, Betsy *fach*?"

Betsy wrinkled her forehead. "I'm sorry, but we're not doing food tonight. Harry's away, you see, and it's just me holding the fort."

"Never mind." Bronwen gave Evan a quick glance. "Why don't we just have a quick drink then and I'll cook something at your place."

Evan managed a convincing smile and resigned himself to the omelette. Personally, he felt that eggs belonged on the breakfast table or hardboiled at a picnic. Definitely not a man's dinner.

"A pint of Guinness, is it then, Evan?" Betsy asked, already starting to draw it. "And for you, Miss Price?"

"Bron will have a shandy," Evan said before Bronwen could ask for a Perrier and thus embarrass him.

Betsy had just handed them their drinks when Evan's mobile phone rang. He excused himself and stepped out into the hallway to answer it.

"Evans, Watkins here," came the clipped voice of his inspector. "I want you to meet me at the Snowdon Railway. I've just had a call from the boys in the search party and you won't believe what they've found."

"They've found the missing girl?" Evan didn't dare to ask more.

"No, it's not the missing girl. I can't talk right now."

"Do you want me to bring any more men with me?" Evan asked.

"No, we certainly don't need any more men." Watkins's voice sounded tense. He lowered it. "This could be something rather nasty, Evans."

"I'll be right there, sir." Evan put the phone back in his pocket. "Sorry, *cariad*, but I've got to go." He gave Bronwen a kiss on the cheek. "I'll see you later. I'm needed with the search party."

"Oh, Evan. Haven't they got enough men searching so that you have time for dinner?"

"Inspector Watkins wants me there right away."

Bronwen's face fell. "Oh no. Something hasn't happened to that girl, has it?"

"I don't know yet, love. I honestly have no idea what it is. Only that the inspector sounded very upset. You've got a key to let yourself back in, haven't you?"

With that he pushed open the heavy oak door and stepped out into the cool night air. The evening star hung big and bright over the horizon and behind the peaks a glow hinted at a moon about to rise. At least it would be a good night for searching, if searching was what he was being called to do. He recalled the dread in the inspector's voice and shivered. It took a lot to rattle someone like Inspector Watkins, who had been on the force for almost twenty years now.

He made the journey down the pass to Llanberis in less than ten minutes and parked in front of the terminal of the little rack-railway

23

that ascended Mount Snowdon. Two white police vans were parked there, but no sign of any policemen. As he stepped out of his car, Inspector Watkins emerged from the shadows of the station porch, his hands thrust into his raincoat pockets.

"That was quick," he called.

"I was at the Dragon. It's only a ten-minute drive," Evan said. "I had to leave without having dinner, so I hope this is important."

Usually Watkins would have come back with some quip about Evan's waistline. Instead he muttered, "It's important all right," and led the way past the station platform where the little train sat silent and dark. "I hope we don't need hiking boots," he said. "I understand we've got a bit of a climb."

"And it's not the missing hiker, sir? What exactly is it?"

"I'm holding off judgment on that until I see for myself. Okay, Pritchard, D.C. Evans is here."

A uniformed figure rose from a bench beside the path. "This way, sir," he said, and set off, following the lane that ran beside the railway track. He carried a torch and the beam danced ahead of them.

"We thought she might have taken the Llanberis path down, because it's the easiest." The young constable turned back to Watkins as the lane began to climb steeply and then became a hiking track. "Sergeant Jones suggested we search that wood, just in case someone had been lurking and saw her coming down alone." He indicated the dark shape of a stand of trees ahead to the left of the path. "And we had the dogs with us and one of them led us right to it."

They left the main path and picked their way through heather, bracken, and rocks until they reached the wooded area. D.C. Pritchard shone his torch and led them among the trees.

"It's not that far," Pritchard said, his voice echoing unnaturally loud in the clear night air. Leaves and bracken crunched underfoot. Gnarled old oaks and giant conifers loomed up in front of them, looking like deformed monsters, reaching out clawed hands in the torchlight. They started to climb steeply as the wood ascended the slopes of the mountain. Evan felt his heart hammering, although he was used to walking up mountains. He sensed the urgency in the other men. He just wanted to know and to get it over with.

As they came out into a clearing, moonlight streamed down onto them, and a view opened up below them. Across the narrow valley they could see the thin ribbon of Llyn Padarrn, glistening in the moonlight. The slate cliffs rose in menacing tiers above it, looking like a forbidding fortress in the dark.

Then they plunged into thick woodland again. Brambles and twigs grabbed at their clothing as they pushed past. Ahead of them Evan could see lights bobbing among the trees and the murmur of voices.

"Here's Inspector Watkins now, sir," someone called out, and the beefy Sergeant Bill Jones stepped out from behind a large fir tree.

"Hello, sir. We thought you'd better take a look at this. I've also taken the liberty of calling forensics, just in case." He looked over at Evan and nodded hello. "This way, then. Mind your step in the dark. Davies, bring that torch here so I don't go arse-over-tip."

He bent down, pulled on something, and a trap door opened.

"We didn't go down, sir," he said, looking up at Watkins, "but we shone the torches around pretty thoroughly. It doesn't look as though anybody's there."

Watkins dropped to his knees and took the torch that the young policeman was holding. Evan knelt beside him and peered into the hole.

"Bloody 'ell," was all Watkins could say.

Evan looked and fought back the sick, sinking feeling in his stomach. The torchlight didn't illuminate the far corners but what he could see was enough. It was a complete bunker, furnished with a camp bed, camp stool, and foldout table.

"Did the owner leave a convenient ladder for us to get down, Jones?" Watkins asked.

"Not that we've found so far, sir."

"I want to get into that hole right now," Watkins said. "Any suggestions?"

"A good shove, sir?" came from the darkness, followed by a general chuckle.

"Most amusing, Roberts," Watkins said. "We're looking for a missing girl, for God's sake. Would you want your girlfriend down there?"

"No, sir."

"Then bloody well think of a way to get someone down to take a look."

It took all of Evan's willpower to speak. Being naturally claustrophobic he dreaded the thought of dropping into darkness. But the thought of a young girl, maybe still alive in one of those dark corners, drove him. "I could probably lower myself, sir, and then help you down."

"I'm not a decrepit old fogey, Evans," Watkins said. "And I don't want you breaking an ankle."

"It's not that far, sir. I'm over six foot and I'd say it wasn't much deeper than that. If you can come up with something for me to hang onto . . ." He lowered himself experimentally and sat with his legs dangling into the darkness.

"Here. Grab hold of my hand," Pritchard said.

"I didn't know you cared, Huwey," someone quipped.

"Too bad he's already engaged," another voice added, but the constable grinned and knelt down.

"Someone hold onto Pritchard. We don't want him tumbling in too," the sergeant commanded.

Evan turned onto his stomach and inched himself over the lip, just as he had done many times when climbing down a mountain. Hands grabbed at his wrists as he lowered himself until his voice echoed up, "Okay, let go."

There was a thud, the sound of something falling, and a muttered, "Bloody 'ell."

Watkins peered over the rim. "Are you okay, Evans?"

The damp, moldy, earthy smell was overpowering.

"I'm okay." Evan shivered in the miserable cold. As he moved around in the torch beam, grotesque shadows stretched across the walls and dirt floor. His hands reached out over the damp soil until he located what had fallen. "I knocked something over when I landed. It's all right. Just a stool. Are you ready to come down now, sir? The boys can lower you the way they lowered me."

"The big question is can we get you out again?" one of the young constables said and got a general laugh.

Evan felt cold sweat run down the back of his neck. He could never reveal that his darkest fear was being shut underground, or they'd kid him about it forever. He heaved a sigh of relief as Watkins's lean frame came down toward him and he reached up to guide the inspector to the ground. Watkins switched on his torch and Evan blinked, temporarily blinded by the powerful beam.

"Don't touch anything if you can help it, Evans. We'll want forensics to go over it," Watkins said. He covered one wall with the torch beam, then the next.

Seen from close up like this, the small room wasn't as frightening as it had seemed from above. It was a rectangle, about eight feet by six, well framed with sturdy timber. The camp bed took up most of one wall. Behind it was a bucket toilet. There was a camping lantern with extra batteries, a one-burner camp stove, and a supply of cans and dehydrated food. A personal CD player and some CDs were piled on another stool behind the bed.

Watkins picked up the top one with his handkerchief. "Bach's Brandenburg Concertos—highbrow stuff." He turned to Evan. "So what do you think?"

Evan looked around him. "I think that maybe we're dealing with some sort of survivalist, a crackpot who wants to be ready for the next nuclear war."

Watkins shook his head. "I don't think so," he said. "Look up there."

The torch beam picked out chains hanging from the beam at the top of the far wall. Chains with handcuffs attached to them.

Chapter 4

It was just before dawn when Evan's car finally drew up outside the red front door and he staggered up the stairs. He felt sick with hunger and tiredness and every muscle in his body ached. He told himself he should eat something before he went to sleep, but he was just too exhausted. He thought of waking Bronwen to cook him something, but when he saw her lying there, her long ash blond hair spread out over the pillow like a figure from a Renaissance painting, he hadn't the heart to disturb her. He took down his sleeping bag and spread it on the floor. He even started to wriggle into it. Then the desire to be close to her, to feel the warmth of her was too strong, and he slid into bed beside her, trying not to wake her.

She did wake, though, and turned to give him a sleepy smile. "Hello. What time is it?"

"Five o'clock," Evan said. "Sorry to disturb you. Go back to sleep."

"You're freezing," she said. "Have you been out on the mountain all night?"

"Pretty much."

"Did you find the girl?"

"No, not yet. They've still got teams out there."

28

"Perhaps she got fed up and went home to Mum. Has anybody thought of calling her home?"

"I don't think she did, Bron," Evan said. "We found something really horrible. An underground bunker, fully equipped with food and everything, as if it was ready and waiting for someone."

"You think someone might have been looking for a young girl to kidnap?"

"The thought did cross our minds."

"Are you sure it wasn't just boys building a secret clubhouse? Some kind of Scout project maybe?"

"There were chains on the wall, Bronwen. Chains and handcuffs."

Bronwen shivered. "How horrible. Some kind of proper psycho, then. Thank heavens you discovered it. At least now he won't be able to take anybody there."

"But he may already have her, Bron. He may have captured her and now not know what to do with her, and that's not good."

"No, you're right. If he's nowhere to put her, he either has to let her go or—" She couldn't complete the sentence.

"And he couldn't risk letting her go because she'd be able to identify him."

"So what are you going to do?"

"I'll find out what the overall plan is when I report back for work at eight o'clock. Between now and then I'd like to get a couple of hours of shuteye."

Bronwen wrapped her arms around him. "I suppose I'm now just learning what life as a policeman's wife is going to be like," she said. "At least I'm glad I'm here to get up and make you breakfast before you go."

Evan snuggled into her arms, enjoying the warm, sweet smell of her. Other thoughts crossed his mind but before he had time to decide whether to act on them, he had fallen asleep.

In his dream he was down in that bunker and looked up just in time to see the trap door being closed, plunging him into total darkness. He felt around for the stool, climbed on it, and started pounding on the trap door.

"Let me out!" he shouted. He thought he heard the sound of maniacal laughter. He went on pounding and pounding until . . . he opened his eyes to bright sunlight streaming in through the window. Birds were singing but their song was drowned out by the pounding that was still going on. Evan sat up, his heart hammering as loudly as the noise he could hear. He was alone in the bed and now that his senses were returning, he could smell coffee downstairs.

He jumped up, just as the pounding ceased. Downstairs, he heard voices. They had found the girl, he thought. He was being called to a murder scene. He ran down the stairs. Bronwen was standing at the half-open front door. She was wearing one of Evan's T-shirts, which came to mid-thigh on her, and nothing else. She looked up at the sound of Evan's feet on the stairs.

"I didn't want to wake you until seven-fifteen but we've got a visitor," she said, her voice unnaturally cheerful.

"I wasn't expecting to find you here, Miss Price," a voice said, and to Evan's horror, his mother stepped past Bronwen and into the front hall. "Hello, son," she said.

"Mother, what are you doing here?" Evan stammered. "We weren't expecting you until the weekend."

Mrs. Evans's face was a stone mask. "My next-door neighbor, Mrs. Gwynne, said her son was driving a furniture lorry up to Bangor. I thought to myself, why not surprise my son and save the money for the train fare too?"

"You certainly surprised me all right," Evan said.

The stony expression didn't waver. "I thought to myself that my boy might need some extra help in the busy time before the wedding and he might need someone to make sure he was eating properly. But I see you've already got extra help." Her gaze traveled over Bronwen. "But don't tell me you've already had the wedding?"

Bronwen flushed and went to say something. Evan put a hand around her shoulder. "No, Mother. The wedding is still two weeks away, as you very well know. And I've been out all night on a particularly nasty case, so Bronwen was making me some breakfast."

Mrs. Evans's face struggled, as if she wanted to believe this, but couldn't. "Well then," she said. "I could do with a cup of tea, after sitting in that bumpy old lorry all night. Evan can bring my case in for me."

"I'm afraid I was making coffee," Bronwen said. "Evan hardly got any sleep so I was helping him to stay awake. But I can put the kettle on for some tea."

"And maybe you'd like to pop upstairs and put your dressing gown on at the same time, Miss Price," Mrs. Evans said. "You'll catch your death of cold running around in your undies like that."

"All right." Bronwen kept her face composed until she was out of sight, then bounded up the stairs.

"Mother, now you've upset Bronwen," Evan hissed.

She stared at him with the same stony gaze. "I should hope it was her own conscience that upset her. What on earth do the neighbors say when the policeman brings women in for the night?"

"Women? Mother, she's my fiancée. And I'd like you to try and be nicer to her." He left his mother standing in the hallway and ran up the stairs. He found Bronwen standing at the window, staring out.

"I'm sorry, love," he said.

"I know she's your mother," Bronwen said in a low voice, "but she's a miserable old harpy."

Evan came up behind her and wrapped his arms around her. "You're right. She is."

"She's never going to accept me as a daughter-in-law." Bronwen's voice cracked. "She still calls me Miss Price, for God's sake. And the way she looked at me. You'd have thought I'd been entertaining an entire army regiment!"

Evan laughed and squeezed her to him. "I don't know what she can have against you, but I'm sure she'll improve."

"Of course we know what she's got against me. I'm taking her precious son away from her control."

Evan reached behind the door and took down a velour robe. "Here, put my dressing gown on, and as soon as we've given her a cup of tea, we're going to march her over to Mrs. Williams and get her settled in there."

"Lucky Mrs. Williams," Bronwen muttered as Evan led her downstairs.

"Hello, Evans, been oversleeping again?" Sergeant Howell Jones asked as Evan came into Inspector Watkins's office. "They've done studies, you know. Too much rest isn't good for you."

There was a general chuckle. Evan looked around to see that he was, indeed the last, although the clock on the wall only said 8:03.

"Sorry," he muttered as he pulled out a chair. "Last-minute complication. My mother arrived from Swansea—took us by surprise."

"If Bronwen was with you, I'd imagine it did give you a nasty shock." D.C. Glynis Davies gave Evan a knowing smile. Glynis was Evan's fellow detective constable and should have been his rival for promotion, except that a close friendship had developed between them—one that Bronwen didn't always understand, since Glynis was unattached, clever, and gorgeous. Today she was wearing an open-necked blue and white checked shirt that showed off her sleek copper hair and porcelain skin to perfection.

"Come on, folks. No time for chitchat, we've got serious business to attend to." Inspector Watkins clapped his hands like a schoolteacher quieting an unruly class. Evan remembered the time, not so long ago, when Watkins was a humble sergeant and always had a ready quip.

"Right." Watkins leaned forward over his desk. "For those of you who weren't in on last night's fun, we received a report of a missing hiker at around four p.m. Became separated from her boyfriend while coming down from the summit of Snowdon. He waited, then went back to look for her. No sign of her. Since she was seventeen and therefore still a minor, we sent out a search team. It was suggested that she may have found the Pyg Track or the Miner's Path too steep and elected to take the easy way down following the railway, so that area was also searched. A couple of dogs were brought in. One of them picked up a scent and led us to what turned out to be an underground bunker, in the woods just above the Llanberis station. Fully equipped with bed, provisions, and even a CD player."

"But not inhabited?" Glynis Davies asked.

"Not inhabited. The early forensic reports have come in. No traces of blood, which is good. The bed appears to have new sheets on it and not to have been slept in. No hairs or fibers gathered. The bucket toilet has not been used. The place is almost devoid of fingerprints. Obviously he used gloves or wiped things clean. We have managed to pick up some prints, however, and we're matching them now to our files."

Glynis raised a hand. "What reason do we have to think that this could have anything to do with the missing hiker, sir? There are all kinds of strange survivalists, or even a teenager who wanted a secret space away from home."

"If he's a teenager, then I'd say he's got a sick mind," Watkins replied. "One thing I didn't mention. Show her the photo, Dawson."

A gawky youngster who looked like an overgrown schoolboy sorted through a pile of photos and handed one to Glynis.

"Here you go. Take a look at that, then."

It was a close-up of the chains with handcuffs attached, high on the wall.

"Oh, goodness," Glynis said, glancing across at Evan. "So it looks as if we made a lucky discovery, doesn't it? Someone was planning to bring a victim to the bunker, but hadn't already done so."

"Or a willing participant," Sergeant Jones suggested. "There are those whose idea of kinky sex might involve being shut in a bunker and handcuffed to a wall."

"You're right, Howell," Watkins said. "As P.C. Davies says, this may have nothing at all to do with our missing hiker. It may be pure coincidence that we stumbled upon it when we did."

"On the other hand," Evan began, never comfortable at speaking out at meetings like this, "we do have a girl who vanished in good weather on a mountain that must have been crowded with other hikers. I agree there are some dangerous parts of the mountain where she could have slipped and gone over a cliff, but the paths are easy to follow when there are other hikers on them, and if she was injured, she would have been found by now."

"I agree with Evan," P.C. Dawson said. "I do a bit of climbing myself, but it's like a zoo out there in the summer holidays. Crawling with tourists. If you're a serious walker, you stay away from Snowdon in August."

"So you don't think it's possible that someone could have grabbed the girl and taken her off without being seen?" Watkins asked.

Evan considered this. "In that wooded area where we found the bunker, maybe," he said. "It was quite warm yesterday afternoon. If she went into the woods for some shade, and he was in there . . ."

"Then why not take her straight to the bunker, if it was all prepared and nearby?" Glynis asked.

There was silence as the group digested this.

"He was waiting until it was dark, and by then our men were out on the mountain?" someone suggested.

"So what's he done with her? Is she still alive? Is there any hope of rescuing her?"

Silence again, then Glynis said in a tight voice, "He may have more than one of these bunkers prepared, sir. He may have gone to plan B."

"So what do we do now, sir?" Sergeant Jones asked impatiently. "Have the girl's parents been called, just in case she's gone home or contacted them?"

Watkins nodded. "They were called last night. They hadn't heard from her then. We should check in again this morning before we do anything else."

"And if they still haven't heard from her?" Sergeant Jones continued. "It was sheer luck we stumbled upon that bunker last night. The chances of finding another one are pretty slim. But we should take another look at the whole area in daylight, just in case we've overlooked anything."

"Yes, we should definitely do that." Watkins looked strained—tired and old and strained. "Can you arrange a team, Howell? See if you can get help from the Parks Service again. Pay special attention to areas where she could have fallen as well as looking for any signs of a scuffle."

"And what's our next step with the bunker?" Glynis asked. She looked at the faces around the room. "Do you want me to check the national sex offenders database? Find out if anyone has been released from a mental facility and is now living in the area?"

"How about seeing whether the modus operandi has come up before?" Watkins suggested. "That would narrow it down for us. Any cases of girls abducted and taken to bunkers, bodies with signs of handcuffs on the wrists."

"The National Criminal Intelligence Service should have that kind of thing on file, shouldn't they?" Glynis looked up from the pad on which she was scribbling notes. "That would save contacting every regional police force."

"Start off with them, definitely, but I think we should double-check with the regions too, just in case something hasn't made it to the database yet. If they've got an ongoing investigation that's similar, it might not have been put into a database yet."

"So you want me to contact NCIS and all the regions?"

Watkins grinned at her. "You're our computer whiz."

"I wish I'd played the helpless female when I first arrived here," Glynis said. "And while I'm at it this morning, do we have access to a profiler, or should I check who does?"

"Excuse me, sir," Evan interrupted. "It seems to me that we're jumping the gun a bit with this sex offender database and profiler."

"The sooner someone can give us a profile on the type of man who might have built the bunker, the sooner we know who we're looking for," Glynis countered.

"What are you getting at, Evans?" Watkins asked.

"Well, sir, I was thinking that one of us should start with the boy who reported the missing girl. Maybe go over their route with him, and talk to the other hikers at the hostel. Something might have been going on there."

"Like what?" Watkins asked.

"All sorts of strange people stay in hostels, don't they? One of them may have had his eye on her and waited for an opportunity to get her alone. Perhaps someone overheard or noticed something out of the ordinary. We know she had a row with her boyfriend—"

"I didn't know that," Watkins interrupted. "Nobody told me that."

"That's how they became separated on the mountain. She wasn't as good a hiker as he was. He said she was going too slowly. They had words and she told him to go on ahead. He did, then felt guilty and came back to look for her."

"I see. Well, maybe you're right, Evans. We'd better go and question him again. And ask around at the hostel."

"A couple of other suggestions," Evan said. "Apparently she had a mobile phone on her. So why didn't she call if she was in trouble? We can check if any calls have been made from it since she disappeared."

"I can do that, I suppose," Glynis said, jotting down notes on a pad.

"And we can make sure your search team keeps an eye out for the phone, Jones," Inspector Watkins said. "If someone grabbed her, he may have discarded it."

"And check with the local police stations in case someone has found it and handed it in," Evan added. "And I think we should ask around Llanberis and higher up the pass too, just in case anyone saw her trying to hitch a ride."

Watkins nodded. "All worth doing. I'll drop all those in your lap, then. I'm going to meet the forensics team at the site and we're going to take another look at that bunker in daylight. Then maybe I'll catch up with you, Evans. At any rate, let's meet again down here at two o'clock."

Sergeant Jones got to his feet. "You plainclothes types can go to your computers and your forensics," he said slowly, "but there's one thing that seems obvious to me that nobody has mentioned."

Heads turned in his direction.

"What I want to know is how someone carried a bloody great shovel and all those supplies up a mountain path. Who could have done that without drawing attention to himself?"

Chapter 5

Red fury seethed inside his head. How could they possibly have stumbled upon his hideaway, after he'd put in so much effort and planned so well? Meddling, interfering little busybodies. Well, he'd show them. They weren't going to stop him now. He was going to go ahead in spite of them. Let them do their worst.

His breath came in rapid gasps as he opened the door to the piano room, sat down, and thumped out the somber chords of the Funeral March. Then a smile crossed his face as an idea came to him and he jumped up from the piano again.

"Maybe," he said to himself, a slow smile spreading across thin lips. "Their wits against mine. No challenge at all, really. Peasants, the lot of them."

He turned from the piano and began to write.

As Evan drove into the small tourist haven of Llanberis, he realized what a difficult task it would be to find anyone who had spotted the missing girl. On this sunny August morning, the town was crawling with tourists. Tour buses from strange corners of Europe belched diesel smoke as they disgorged their passengers. Families wandered across the road, trailing children and pushing prams. Serious climbers, with ropes slung over their shoulders and big, solid boots, seemed intent on getting out of the crush as quickly as possible. There was already a long line for the little train up Snowdon. If Paul Upwood's girlfriend had come down the mountain and into this town, she could have drifted unnoticed among the crowd. Even if she had walked alone down the pass, or tried hitch-hiking, she would have joined a procession of other young people doing the same thing. A hopeless task, really.

Anyway, first he needed to meet Paul Upwood again and get a detailed description of the girl from him, and hopefully a photo. Then they could make posters and he'd have a photo to show around on the Sherpa bus and in the cafés.

Evan stopped off at his house as he passed through Llanfair to change into hiking gear. Bronwen was nowhere in sight. He suspected she'd be up at the new cottage, trying to put her belongings into some kind of order. He grabbed his hiking boots and an anorak and raced out again before the bush telegraph which worked so efficiently in Llanfair could alert his mother to his presence. As he drove past the two chapels he noticed that the minister of Capel Bethel, the Rev. Parry Davies, was out pasting up a new biblical text on the billboard outside his chapel. It read: Faith without works is dead. St. James.

Evan couldn't resist looking across at the identical billboard outside Capel Beulah and saw instantly why Mr. Parry Davies had made his selection. The other minister, Rev. Powell Jones, had chosen as his text: St Paul says, "You will be saved by your faith."

In spite of the grimness of the day, he smiled as he drove on. By the time he reached the youth hostel at the top of the pass, the cloud had closed in, so that the young people who loitered smoking outside the door were huddled in little groups, shivering in the cold wind. Evan changed into his hiking boots in the car, then hurriedly put on his jacket as he got out. Cloud swirled, turning the hostel into a ghostly shadow in the mist and obliterating the peaks beyond. If it had been a day like this when Shannon disappeared, Evan could have understood it. He'd been on the mountain enough times himself when the world was suddenly swallowed up into the mist and one false step could have sent him tumbling over a cliff. But yesterday had been sparkling clear.

He paused on the gravel outside the hostel, thinking. If someone had kidnapped her, how could he have done it? Where could he have taken her without being noticed on such a bare and well-populated mountain? Then he reminded himself that the bunker had existed, unnoticed, almost within shouting distance of a well-traveled path and a railway. The person who dug it had taken a terrible risk by situating it there. Obviously a person who enjoyed taking risks. He'd remember to mention that to Glynis when she was making her profile.

Paul Upfield was sitting in the common room, halfheartedly flicking through a magazine, as Evan came in.

He jumped up, letting the magazine fall to the floor. "Any news yet?"

Evan shook his head and pulled up a chair beside the boy. "I'm afraid not. Have you been in touch with her family again this morning?"

"No, I've been putting off talking to them until I really have to. They don't like me very much," he said.

"Why's that?"

The boy's face flushed. "They don't approve of us going together. They told her she was too young for a serious boyfriend, and she's almost eighteen. Some people get married at eighteen, don't they?"

Evan nodded. The boy sighed and sank his head into his hands. "They'll probably blame me for this. Her mum didn't want her to go on this holiday with me, you know. She thought we'd get up to—you know. They keep her in a cocoon—don't let her go dancing or anything."

"So you don't know whether she's shown up at home this morning?"

Paul Upwood shook his head.

Evan pulled out his phone. "I think they'd like to hear from you, Paul. What's their number again?"

Paul Upwood winced as he gave Evan the numbers.

"Hello?" The woman's voice sounded tense.

"Mrs. Parkinson? It's D.C. Evans of the North Wales Police."

"You've found Shannon?"

"Not yet, I'm afraid. We still have men out there looking. I've got Paul Upwood here with me and—"

"I knew I should never have let her go with that boy," Mrs. Parkinson said bitterly. "She's never been allowed off on her own before and now look what happens."

"Accidents happen, Mrs. Parkinson. People get lost in the mountains all the time. The good thing is that it was a fine night and quite mild." Even as he said it he noticed Paul Upwood staring out of the window at the swirling mist.

"That no-good boy promised to take care of her." Her voice trembled this time.

There was no answer to that one.

"Please rest assured that we are doing our very best to locate her as quickly as possible, Mrs. Parkinson," Evan said. "You have our phone number and if you hear from her at all, please let us know."

"Why wouldn't she have called us before? That's what I want to know." The voice trembled. "If she's all right somewhere, she'd have been able to call home, wouldn't she?"

"There may be a simple explanation for all this," Evan said. "She could have dropped her phone, taken a wrong turn on the mountain, finally fallen asleep, and just now be making her way down to us."

"But why was she by herself? Why wasn't he looking after her?" Mrs. Parkinson insisted.

Evan decided not to mention the tiff they had had. No sense in putting the boy even deeper in their black books. "He feels as badly about this as you do, Mrs. Parkinson. In fact, he's waiting to tell you how sorry he is. But try not to worry too much. I'll call you again when I've got any news."

"All right." The voice sounded defeated, almost as if she suspected she wasn't going to hear from her daughter again.

Evan handed the phone to Paul, who took it reluctantly.

"Look, I'm really sorry, Mrs. Parkinson," Paul stammered. "I looked everywhere. I won't rest until we find her, I promise." Then he hung up quickly before anything else could be said and handed back the phone.

"All right. Let's get moving," Evan put a hand on Paul's shoulder.

"Moving?"

"That's right. You and I are going to retrace your steps up the mountain, exactly as you went yesterday, and you're going to look out for any clues—"

"Clues?"

"Anything she might have dropped along the way. Anything that might have belonged to her."

"In this weather?" Paul asked. He was wearing a T-shirt and his adam's apple danced up and down nervously. "Isn't it dangerous to go up there in weather like this?"

"You want to find her, don't you?" Evan asked. Then he took pity on the hunched shoulders and patted the boy's back. "Don't worry. I've been up and down that mountain so many times I can do it in my sleep. You won't come to grief if you're with me. Go up and put your boots and jacket on. And while you're about it—do you happen to have any photos of Shannon? I'd like to show one around and get it blown up into flyers."

"Just this one." Paul pulled out a wallet and extracted a snaphot. It was of him with his arm around a pretty, petite girl. They were gazing at each other, smiling. "It's not very clear, but it's better than nothing," he said as he handed it over.

"Good-looking girl," Evan commented as he took the picture.

"Yeah. Best-looking bird in her class at school."

"Are you still at school?"

"No, I'm at university, studying accountancy."

Evan wondered why a mother could possibly disapprove of a young man who hiked and studied accountancy. "Go on, get those boots on," he said.

The moment Paul had disappeared up the stairs, Evan went looking for the hostel warden. He found him in the kitchen, scraping out the last of a giant porridge pot. "The fun part of breakfast, and guess who gets stuck with it?" he said, looking up with a smile.

Evan explained why he was there and showed the warden the photo.

"What can you tell me about this couple?" he asked.

"Quiet. Keep themselves to themselves. You say she's missing?"

"Yes, she didn't come back from a hike yesterday."

"Is there a search team out looking for her?"

"Yes, we had men out there yesterday evening and more today."

"I could round up some additional chaps if you'd like," the warden said. "I'm sure everyone staying here would want to help find her."

"Thanks. You're very kind. I'll relay that message to the officer who's coordinating the search," Evan said. "I'm about to take Paul up to retrace their route. I just thought I'd ask whether anything might have happened here that was worth mentioning."

"What sort of thing?"

"I don't know, really. Paul says he and his girlfriend had a disagreement while they were hiking. Had they quarreled at all while they were here? Had there been anyone else staying here who might have tried to pick her up? Or given them a hard time? I'm just trying to come up with a reason why she didn't come down the mountain."

The warden scratched his luxuriant dark beard, then shook his head. "I can't say I noticed them interacting with any of the other hostelers. There is usually a lively group in the common room. Someone has a guitar. Lots of laughter. But as I told you, they kept themselves to themselves. I don't recall them in the common room at all in the evenings."

Evan thanked the warden and showed the photo to all the other young people he could find, but the response was shrugs and blank faces. Some of them remembered seeing them at breakfast, but that was all. Nobody had overheard any quarrels.

Paul Upwood clomped down the stairs in hiking boots, now wearing a dark green anorak and carrying a stick.

Evan grinned. "I must say, you're prepared for the worst, aren't you?" He led the way out of the hostel and across the car park to the start of the path up the mountain.

"Did you say you took the Miner's Path or the Pyg Track?" Evan asked as they reached the first grassy slopes beyond the car park.

Paul Upwood looked around uncertainly. "I'm not sure which is which. This path here." He indicated a well-defined trail going off to the right.

"That's the Pyg Track," Evan said. "The Miner's Path drops down to Llyn Llydaw. You'd remember if you'd taken that one because it crosses the lake on a causeway."

"Not that one, then," Paul said. "I didn't cross any causeways." He looked cold and miserable and a little scared. Well, who wouldn't, Evan thought. I'd be scared if Bronwen had vanished. I'd be out of my mind with worry.

They started up the track and instantly the youth hostel was swallowed into mist. The only world was a few tussocks of grass and rocks around their feet and their footsteps echoed from unseen crags. As they came to the top of the first crest, the wind hit them full in the face, swirling cloud around them. Paul Upwood stood breathing heavily, leaning on his stick.

Evan glanced in his direction. For someone who had criticized his girlfriend for her slow pace, Paul Upwood wasn't exactly in the greatest shape himself. The real ascent didn't even begin until they had passed the first lake, Llyn Llydaw, which now lay invisible below them. It suddenly occurred to Evan that perhaps they were both novice hikers and they hadn't made it to the summit at all.

"You said you parted company right after picnicking above a lake," Evan said. "You didn't mean the lake right here, did you? You went all the way up to the summit first?"

"Oh, are there two lakes?" Paul asked, then shook his head. "I'm getting confused. No, I must mean the lake below the summit. Little round lake, isn't it?"

"That's right," Evan said. "A little round lake. Okay, then you did make it all the way up, then. Come on, let's get cracking. We've got the hard slog ahead of us."

The path dipped slightly, then rose again, now narrow and rocky as it hugged the side of a steep slope. The clouds parted suddenly, revealing a long, thin lake below them. The water was so still that it looked like black marble. There was a sudden flapping sound, making both men start, and a pair of ducks rose from the smooth surface. Then the cloud closed in again, shutting them off into a private world.

After a while Paul Upwood was panting like the little steam engine that climbed the other flank of the mountain. "How much farther?" he gasped. Perspiration ran down his face.

Evan couldn't resist commenting this time. "I thought you said you were the great hiker and your girlfriend couldn't keep up with you?"

"I'm too tense to breathe properly today," Paul replied. "My legs feel like jelly. I'm so scared that we'll find her and. . . ." He let the rest of the sentence trail off.

"We had a team of men searching yesterday," Evan said, "and dogs, and there were hundreds of people out on the mountain. So it's hardly likely that she's just lying somewhere, waiting to be found."

He put a friendly hand on the boy's shoulder. "You are keeping your eyes open for any signs of her, aren't you?"

Paul nodded. "I'm not sure what signs of her we'd find. She isn't the sort of person who'd drop chocolate wrappers."

After a long, hard climb, during which they had to stop to rest several times, Evan pointed at a stone pillar beside the path. "This is where the Miner's Track comes up from Glaslyn to join this one," he said. "You didn't actually go down to the little lake for your picnic, did you?"

"No, we stopped and ate beside the track, looking down at the lake," Paul said.

"So you stuck to this route. You didn't do the circle like a lot of folk, up on the Pyg Track and back on the Miner's?"

"I didn't," Paul said slowly. "But we may have separated above this point. Might it be possible that she took the other route, by mistake?"

Evan stared down into swirling grayness. "I suppose if she saw other people taking that route, she might have followed them. So maybe we should go back that way, just to make sure."

"Is it longer?" Paul's voice sounded exhausted.

"About the same. A little steeper, especially the first part. In this kind of mist you have to make sure you follow the path exactly because there are abandoned mine shafts dotted all over the place."

"Mine shafts?" The words echoed back at them.

"There used to be copper mines all over the mountain. That's why it's called the Miner's Path."

"Mine shafts she could have fallen down, you mean?" Paul Upwood's voice quavered.

Evan was annoyed with himself for not considering this possibility. "I think they are well signed and blocked off, but—"

"But she could have slipped and fallen—if she was in a hurry. If she was trying to catch up with me and—it's all my fault. I should never have been so bloody stupid. I suppose I was tired and when I'm tired, I get cranky."

Evan looked at the serious, owlish face with more sympathy.

"We'll call out a team to check the mines. Watch your step." He grabbed at the young man's jacket as he slithered on the loose shale. "We don't want you disappearing over the edge." It came to him that Paul Upwood was completely ill at ease in such conditions. Not a hiker, then. Shannon must indeed have been a delicate flower if she had seemed slow to Paul.

"I'll go first," he said, "then you can grab onto me if you feel yourself slipping. Watch where I put my feet."

He started off again, stepping down from rock to rock. The round outline of Glaslyn became visible through the cloud, then disappeared again. Suddenly Paul shouted, "Wait. What's that?"

Evan stopped. Paul was staring down a steep face of loose scree. "There. Down by the water's edge."

Evan had to wait until the clouds parted again before he saw what Paul was pointing at. A tiny patch of red, close to the waterline.

"She had red gloves with her," Paul said.

"Stay there," Evan commanded, and started to pick his way down the slope. Of all the things he disliked most, maneuvering across scree was one of them. With every footfall it was possible to set off a miniature avalanche that would gather momentum and send him plummeting downward, unable to stop. He slid, clambered, slid some more, until at last he was standing at the lakeshore. Then he picked his way across the scree slope to retrieve the red object. It was indeed a glove. He piled a cairn of stones to mark its position and started the long, treacherous ascent back up to Paul. Thoughts buzzed inside his head. Had she stumbled, stepped off the path, and slid down out of control toward the lake? In which case, had she gone in? Wouldn't someone have noticed or at least heard her cries? Would someone have heard the splash? And, unless she was first unconscious, why hadn't she been able to scream for help? If she had been wearing a heavy backpack, would it have dragged her under?

Evan regained the path and handed Paul the glove. The latter let out a sob when he saw it. "It's hers. It's Shannon's glove. Then she did come back this way. But what was it doing down by the lake?" He peered downward. Strands of mist hid the surface again. "You don't think she fell in, do you?"

"I don't know," Evan said. "Was she wearing a backpack?"

"Yes, she was. It was quite heavy, too. You don't know Shannon. She always has to have her makeup and hairbrush and then she had her jacket and a camera. I carried it for her for a while, but I gave it back to her after lunch, because I thought it would be lighter after we'd eaten the food."

Evan took out his mobile phone. "I'll call my boss and let him know what we've found. He'll take it from there. I just hope the phone works up here."

"Watkins here," came the voice on the other end.

"Sir, it's Evans. We've found the girl's glove. At the bottom of a steep slope beside Glaslyn. It looks as if she could have fallen down the scree and gone in."

"Bloody hell," Watkins said. "Right. I'll get men onto it. And how fast can you get down here, Evans?"

"Down where, sir?"

"My office. Forensics was able to match one set of fingerprints on a can of baked beans we found in the bunker. Young bloke who was arrested last year for beating up his girlfriend. He's being brought in as we speak. I'd like you present when I question him."

Chapter 6

It took a frustratingly long time to get Paul Upwood back to the youth hostel. He was so tired that he stumbled frequently and seemed close to tears.

"Sorry to rush you like this," Evan said, "but my boss wants me down at the station right away."

Paul looked up sharply. "Have they found something you're not telling me?"

"It's someone they've brought in for questioning," Evan said. "Nothing to do with this."

"You mean finding Shannon isn't even your number one priority? You've got other cases?"

"We're doing all we can to find Shannon, trust me," Evan said. "We've got men out on the other side of the mountain right now . . ."

"Why would they be looking on the other side?" Paul asked. "She wouldn't have gone back to the summit and then down that way, would she?"

"You can't think of any reason why she would?" Evan asked, looking directly at the young man.

"Such as what?"

"If she was really upset after your row and decided to go home without you?"

"Shannon wouldn't do that," Paul said, but Evan could see the doubt written on his face.

"Maybe she was just too tired to walk down and decided to take the railway," Evan suggested.

"In which case, why would they be looking for her on the mountain. She'd catch the train and it would take her all the way to Llanberis, wouldn't it?"

Evan sighed. "I don't know the answer any more than you do, Paul. I just know that they gave this side a pretty good going over yesterday."

"But they missed her glove, didn't they?"

"That's true. We'll know more when they bring in a team of divers."

Paul stood shivering. "I just wish I knew, one way or the other. Not knowing is the worst."

"You're right. Not knowing is the worst."

The indistinct black humps of cars in the car park loomed ahead of them. "Do you want to ride down to Caernarfon with me?" Evan asked. "At least you can get a cup of coffee and wander around a bit—better than sitting and biting your nails at the hostel."

"Yeah, thanks," Paul said.

"And you'll be on hand in case Inspector Watkins wants to talk to you."

"Inspector Watkins?" The boy looked startled.

"He may want to talk to you himself. After all, he's only had all the information secondhand so far. Hop in." He opened the car door and the young man climbed in. They set off down the pass. Just as they reached Llanfair, they saw the Sherpa bus groaning its way up the pass. Evan stopped, got out, flagged it down, and climbed on board.

"Hello, Constable Evans," the driver said. "Got car trouble, have you?"

49

"No, I just wanted to show you a photo," Evan said. "We've got a young girl missing on Yr Wyddfa. I just wondered if you remembered giving her a ride yesterday."

The driver took the snapshot and looked at it carefully. "I think I recognize her," he said. "Yes, I'm pretty sure she's ridden on my bus before, with the young man. I recognize him too."

"But not yesterday? Not on her own?"

The driver chewed on his lip. "Not that I can remember," he said. "But it was a sunny day yesterday. We were chock ablock full all day. Standing room only, so I probably wouldn't have noticed her."

"Right. Thanks again. And if you do see her, or you can think of anything that might be useful to us, give me a call, will you?"

"I'll do that, Constable Evans. And I hear you have a wedding coming up?"

"I do, but I can't stop to talk now. I'm wanted down at the station."

"Looks like you're also wanted up here," the driver said, glancing in his rearview mirror. "There's an elderly lady running up the street waving her arms."

Evan turned around to see his mother making a beeline for the parked car.

"Oh no," he groaned and sprinted across the street. "All settled in, Ma?" he called as he put the car into gear and pulled away.

"Yes, but I need to talk to you about—" Mrs. Evans shouted.

"Later, Ma. I've got a dangerous suspect here I'm taking into custody," he called back and drove away as fast as he dared.

"What was all that about?" Paul asked nervously. "You don't think I'm a suspect, do you?"

Evan laughed at his worried face. "That was my mother, and if I hadn't stopped her, she'd have kept us there for hours. She's been in the village all morning so she's probably already come up with at least twenty things to complain about."

"Sounds like Shannon's mother," Paul said. "Nothing's ever good enough for her."

"Mothers can be difficult," Evan agreed.

· · ·

50

"What have you been doing? Driving here by way of Scotland?" Inspector Watkins demanded as Evan finally entered the Caernarfon police station and found his boss pacing the reception area.

"When I talked to you I was halfway up a mountain," Evan said, "and since you didn't send a helicopter to pick me up, I had to get down on my own two feet."

"I've got an angry young man in the interview room, demanding to see his lawyer and threatening to tell the newspapers about police harassment."

"The one whose fingerprints were on the tin?"

Watkins nodded. "Name's Dave Matthews. We had him on file for an assault charge last year. He was never prosecuted because the girl withdrew her complaint, but he's a nasty piece of work. Works as a stockboy at Tesco's when he's not playing in a local garage band and riding around on a motorbike pretending to be a Hell's Angel."

"So we've brought him in just on the basis of his fingerprint on the tin?"

"It's the only match we've come up with. In fact, there were suspiciously few fingerprints, making me think that our man wore gloves most of the time, or wiped items clean after him."

"Someone who thinks ahead then—considers all possibilities."

"Right." Watkins nodded. "Ready to face the raging bull then?"

Evan grinned as Watkins pushed open the interview room door. The man sitting at the table was swarthy-complexioned, overweight, with a lot of unkempt black hair. He was wearing a black leather jacket with studs on it and he stood up immediately, almost knocking his chair over. "About bloody time," he said. "What have you been doing keeping me waiting like this? I've missed my effing lunch break. And I'd better not be docked any pay for this."

"Sit down and shut up," Watkins said. "We'll ask the questions. You give us the answers and you can go back to work. Start the machine please, Evans."

Evan saw the man react nervously at the mention of the word "machine". He walked across to the table and pressed the button on a tape recorder. "The date is August third. Time one forty-five p.m.

Present at the interview Inspector Watkins and D.C. Evans." He turned to the man, who was now glaring at them, elbows on the table. "Would you state your full name and address please?"

"David Merion Matthews. Twenty-five Bangor Street, Caernarfon."

"And your occupation, Mr. Matthews?"

"I play bass guitar with a rock band and I also work for Tesco."

Inspector Watkins moved in to take over from Evan. "And last year we had the pleasure of your company when you were involved in a case of domestic violence, Mr. Matthews. You came home drunk and knocked around your lady friend. Is that correct?"

"You can't hold that against me," Dave Matthews said, looking at them defiantly, "because she dropped the charges. It never got to court. So as far as you're concerned, it never happened."

"But one thing that did happen was that you were fingerprinted," Watkins said.

"So?"

"Would you mind telling us what you were doing yesterday?"

The reaction was complete surprise. "Yesterday? What the bloody hell is this about? Yesterday I was working the early shift at Tesco, mate, then I came home and had an afternoon kip because I'd been up since five, and then me and the band practiced over at Gareth's house in the evening. Not exactly the most thrilling day of my life."

"You ride a motorbike, is that correct?"

"That's right. A Harley. My pride and joy."

"Ever take it off road?"

"What's this all about? That old git down the street complaining about me revving the engine and waking him up late at night again?"

"Ever drive up Llanberis way and onto the mountain?"

"What on earth for?"

"So you've never ridden your bike through Llanberis?"

"I might have done, although I can't think why. Deader than a doornail once you get to those bloody villages, isn't it? Not recently anyway. And I don't take her off road. I'm not risking mud on the chrome."

"What time did you clock out yesterday?"

"Two o'clock."

"And you said you took a nap when you got home. Anyone vouch for that?"

"Yeah, I've got my harem waiting for me, haven't I? Of course nobody can bloody vouch for it."

"Your girlfriend? Are you still together?"

"We don't live together no more. She's a bloody pain in the arse, nagging about my smoking all the time."

"So nobody saw you come home yesterday and nobody saw you leave again?"

Matthews shrugged. "Someone on the street might have done," he said. "The old biddy opposite has got nothing better to do than sit behind her curtains."

Watkins glanced at Evan. "Anything you'd like to ask, Constable?"

Evan wasn't at all sure where this was going. He couldn't equate this unkempt, overweight individual with the builder of the bunker who had meticulously stacked supplies, made the bed with hospital corners, and who listened to Bach.

"Not really, sir," Evan replied.

Watkins gave him a swift look before he said, "All right, Matthews, you're free to go for now."

Dave got to his feet. "Are you going to tell me what this is all about?"

"Not at the moment. We may be calling on you again."

"Then do you mind calling my supervisor and telling him that I ain't done nothing wrong. I don't want him getting ideas about me when I'm a law-abiding citizen." The big man pushed his way past them and stumped out of the interview room.

"So what do you think?" Watkins asked when Matthews had been escorted out.

"If you want my opinion, he had nothing to do with it," Evan said.

"Why's that?"

"Wrong type," Evan said. "Men who bash their women around don't have to fantasize about keeping one of them in chains. And you saw how neat and ordered that bunker was. This bloke probably only takes a wash once a week."

Watkins pushed back his sandy hair, which was now showing the first signs of gray at the sides. "I can't disagree with that. But the fingerprint on the baked beans tin?"

"He does work at Tesco," Evan pointed out. "He was probably the one who put it on the shelf."

Watkins nodded again. "But why was there just this one clear set of prints and no others?"

"Because the man we are looking for is very meticulous. He wears gloves. He wipes things clean. He overlooked a couple of prints."

"Pity. It all fitted so nicely. Violent with women, rides a motorbike—"

"What's all this about the motorbike?"

"Oh sorry, I didn't get a chance to tell you. The team found bike tracks near the bunker. Someone might have carried stuff up there on the back of a bike. We'll have forensics look at Matthews's tires, but I suspect you're right and he's not the type we're looking for."

"We do know one thing," Evan said.

"What's that?"

"Our man shops at the local Tesco."

"And what help is that?" Watkins demanded. "Do you think we can go into Tesco and ask if they saw anybody suspicious buying a tin of baked beans recently?"

"It wasn't just one tin of baked beans. It was a good quantity of tins and packets. If he bought them all at once, one of the checkers might have remembered." Evan smiled. "And it does tell us one thing. It's more likely that he's a local and not someone from outside who came to the area looking for a remote spot."

"But that's just the point," Watkins said angrily. "It's not a remote spot. It's within a few yards of the most popular path up Snowdon. If I were going to capture a helpless female and hold her prisoner somewhere, there are plenty of really remote places."

"Perhaps he does have other bunkers in those more remote

places," Evan suggested. "Or perhaps he just enjoys taking risks. I get the feeling he probably does."

They both looked up at the tap of light feet on the vinyl floor and saw Glynis Davies coming down the hallway toward them.

"It's almost two. Where is the meeting going to be?" she asked.

"Almost two?" Watkins muttered. "I haven't even had lunch yet."

"Neither have I," Evan said.

Glynis smiled sweetly. "What a pity. I've just had rather a good salad at that new Greek place. Lots of lovely garlic and olives and feta cheese."

"Shut up." Watkins managed a smile. "Be an angel and go and stall Sergeant Jones and the others while Evan and I pop into the cafeteria to grab a quick sandwich, will you? Not for my own good, you understand—but this growing boy here has a wedding in a couple of weeks. We can't have him dropping dead from lack of nourishment, can we?"

There was a flicker of amusement in Glynis's eyes. "I'd have thought he'd welcome the chance to slim down so that he looks good in the wedding pictures," she said.

"Slim down?" Evan demanded. "Do you know I've lost over a stone since I've been cooking for myself? And I've been up Snowdon and back already today, and I don't mean by train."

Glynis nodded. "I'm impressed," she said. "What was that for?"

"I took Paul Upwood to retrace their route."

"That was smart. Did you learn anything?"

"We found her glove at the bottom of a nasty scree slope, right next to Glaslyn."

The smile had faded from Glynis's face. "Oh no. That doesn't look good, does it? Do you think she went into the lake?"

"I think there's a good possibility she did."

"I've already asked HQ for a team of divers," Watkins said, "although that lake's pretty deep, isn't it?"

Evan nodded. "But it's clear water. Although a day like today doesn't make for the best conditions up there. Very thick mist. We could hardly see more than a couple of feet in front of us."

"Lucky you found the glove then." Watkins said.

"Very lucky. The clouds just parted at the right moment."

Glynis looked from one to the other. "This rather changes everything, doesn't it? It looks as if the two cases aren't linked after all. She had an unlucky accident and maybe that bunker is just some poor twisted bloke's fantasy hideout. He never really intends to kidnap anybody, just fantasizes about it."

"What did your computer searches turn up?" Watkins asked. "Anything useful?"

"Not really. No patients recently released from psychiatric institutions who might behave in this way, but then, as the man at the NCIS told me, this kind of crime is almost impossible to spot in advance. Most serial killers are model citizens, quiet, well behaved, and smart enough not to do anything that might draw attention to themselves."

"Do we have any other missing girls on our files at the moment?" Evan asked.

Watkins nodded. "That's a good line to pursue. Not just on our files. He could have kidnapped girls from anywhere and brought them here, or he might have similar bunkers in other parts of the UK. Unless we're lucky enough to have caught him at the very start of his career, he's done exactly the same thing before somewhere." He glanced at his watch. "Five past two. Well, Evans, there goes our sandwich."

Evan sighed.

Chapter 7

It was five o'clock when Evan finally drove back up the pass with Paul Upwood in tow. He felt hollow with tiredness and it was all he could do to force his eyes to stay open. He was conscious of the long drop to the lake on his left and the tour coaches, belching diesel smoke, not to mention holiday drivers, who had little concept of the size of Welsh roads, plus the occasional stray sheep by the roadside, but sleep even fought against these hazards. Only ten minutes more, he told himself. He would drop Paul off at the hostel and then he could fall asleep.

Paul had been very quiet, sitting with shoulders hunched, staring straight ahead of him. Evan guessed that it had finally occurred to him that Shannon might not still be alive. He was probably going over and over that last argument in his mind and was slowly drowning in guilt.

"It wasn't your fault, you know," Evan said gently. "Every couple has ups and downs. My fiancée and I have some good old shouting matches at times, but we always make up afterwards and they're all over and forgotten. Couples fight about the silliest things. If something has happened to Shannon, you didn't make it happen."

"That's just not true," Paul said, still staring straight ahead. "I was supposed to be looking after her. You should have seen her on the mountain paths. She was scared silly, especially when there was a big drop on one side. I kept telling her she was perfectly safe, but she wouldn't listen to me. If she really fell into that lake and drowned, and I didn't even hear her calling for help, I'll never forgive myself. Never."

Evan couldn't come up with an answer to that one. He thought that he'd probably never forgive himself if anything happened to Bronwen.

"How long do you think I have to stay here?" Paul asked as they approached the hostel. "I mean, I want to know what's happened to her. I'll do anything I can to help find her, but it's really getting me down, staying alone at the hostel, having the other hikers looking at me and whispering about me."

"You're free to go when you want to, of course," Evan said. "It doesn't appear that we're dealing with a crime scene. But we might still need your help, so I'd stick around for a few more days, if you can bear it. Get out and do some walking if you can. It will be good for you."

"In this bloody fog?" Paul asked.

"It will probably be better tomorrow. In fact, look, you can see the sun shining out over the sea already. You know what they say about Wales, don't you?"

"What?"

"If you don't like the weather, wait half an hour."

Paul attempted a smile as he left the car.

Fifteen minutes later, Evan pulled up outside his red front door. Cup of tea then bed, he thought. He didn't even have the strength to stagger over to the Dragon for a Guinness first. He opened the door and smelled onions frying.

"Bron?" he called hopefully.

Instead of Bronwen, his mother's face peeped out from the kitchen.

"Oh, there you are, son. Perfectly on time, just like your father was. I'm making your favorite, liver and onions."

"Where's Bronwen?" Evan asked suspiciously.

"At her own place, I should imagine." Mrs. Evans's face was stony once more. "She did stop by, talking about cooking you some kind of pasta for dinner, but I sent her off again. 'The boy needs good, wholesome Welsh food, not Italian muck,' I told her." She turned back to the stove and lifted several rashers of bacon onto a plate. "Mrs. Williams was just saying this morning that you haven't been eating properly ever since you left her. Going out without breakfast and then having to pop across to the public house for dinner. That's no way to live, Evan *bach*."

"Ma, I live perfectly well. I'm a grown man and I don't need my mother to look after me."

"Evidently you do," she said, lifting the lid on a saucepan that contained cauliflower by the smell of it. "I don't know when this place last had a good cleaning. Cobwebs behind the curtain rods, dust on the picture rails, and smutty windows. If that girl comes over here as often as I suspect she does, why doesn't she take care of the place—that's what I'd like to know."

"That girl, as you refer to her, is soon to be my wife. I've never asked her to clean my place because she has a full-time job and a house of her own to take care of. What's more, we've both been working in our spare time to get our own cottage finished before the wedding. Have you been up to take a look at it yet?"

"That place halfway up the mountain?" Mrs. Evans shook her head. "What on earth possessed you to think you'd want to live up there?"

Evan realized with a sudden flash of joy that the path to the cottage was too steep for his mother. He suspected that Bronwen had discovered the same thing and fled up there.

"I'm going to get Bronwen," he said, heading for the front door. "I expect she's starving. Be back in a minute." And he ran out before his mother could protest.

It was definitely a slog up the mountain path to the cottage. After the morning's jaunt up the Pyg Track, his muscles protested. He had just reached the flat area that surrounded the cottage and was pushing open the white front gate when Bronwen opened the door.

"Oh, there you are at last," she said. "I was wondering when you'd turn up."

Evan fought to give a measured response, but the tiredness won out. "Don't you start," he snapped. "I've had one hour's sleep in the past twenty-four, I've been up a mountain and down again, I've been in meetings all afternoon, and now I've come home to find my mother has taken over my house."

Bronwen looked at him and opened her arms to him. "Oh Evan, I'm sorry," she said. "I've been up here all day, lifting heavy boxes and feeling sorry for myself and angry at you for not coming home sooner to help me. And of course you've had to go all day without sleep."

He wrapped her in his arms and she nestled her head on his shoulder.

"You've had a bad day, have you?" he asked.

"Horrible. I worked like crazy up here all morning and came down to your place to make myself some lunch, only to find your mother in residence. How she had got in, I didn't ask. Anyway, she told me my services weren't needed and she was there to see her son got some proper food before his wedding. Then she went on to lecture me about how a man needed meat and two veg at every meal and if I wanted to make you happy, I'd better learn to cook. She even offered to give me some cooking lessons."

"Well, at least she was trying."

"You can say that again."

Evan laughed at the double meaning. "I meant she only had my welfare at heart, however annoying she was being."

Bronwen wriggled out of his embrace. "Anyway, since you are finally here. You can come and see the fruit of my labors." She took his hand and led him up the garden path and in through the front door.

"There," she said. "It's still lacking a lot but when that Welsh dresser is against the far wall and we find two nice armchairs, it will be quite cozy, won't it?"

Evan looked at the room, which had been piled high with boxes the day before. Now there was a rug on the floor, a little table and two chairs in the front window, a sofa facing the fireplace, and a low bookcase filled with books running along the side wall.

Bronwen slipped her arm through his. "I know it's your house too, so I don't want you to think I'm taking over, or anything. This is just temporary, because I wanted to establish some kind of order here. But of course we can rearrange things the way you'd like them."

"It looks lovely," Evan said. "You've been working miracles again."

Bronwen beamed. "It is beginning to look like a home, isn't it? And you know the very best thing about this place?"

"The view?"

Bronwen shook her head. "The hill is too steep for your mother to walk up it!"

They fell into each other's arms, laughing.

"We may have to do something about that steep hill, though," Evan said, becoming serious again.

"What can we do about it? It's steep. We can't change that."

"I meant we may have to bite the bullet and invest in another car. I really don't think my old bone-shaker can make it up here, and we can't always expect to go up and down on foot."

"We could never afford a Land Rover. They cost the earth," Bronwen said. "And the walk will be good for us. It will stop us from getting old and fat."

"But what about when it's raining or snowing? What about if we start having children?"

Bronwen thought about this and nodded. "I admit I don't fancy carrying the week's shopping up the hill."

"It doesn't have to be a Land Rover. Any four-wheel drive would do. Those English people who bought this as their summer cottage used to drive up in a Jag, didn't they? So we know it's doable."

"I'd imagine four-wheel drives don't come cheap."

"We are both working, and we're saving by living together, and we've just established that line of credit at the bank."

"Which you just said you didn't want to touch." Bronwen smiled at him.

"For a good cause."

"Oh I see. A car is always a good cause for a man."

"Bronwen!" Evan looked hurt. "You have to admit that my old thing is on its last legs. We need a vehicle that will make it up the hill. And a second car would be handy too, now that you'll be working at that new school. You won't really want to rely on the bus to take you up and down the hill every day, will you?"

"A car would be nice," Bronwen agreed.

"So I'll pick up the local papers and we'll take a look at second-hand cars, and if I have time, I'll pop in and see our friendly bank manager to find out how much he might want to loan us."

"All right." Bronwen looked around. "You weren't expecting me to have cooked you supper, were you? I'm almost out of supplies and of course I haven't had a chance to shop."

"Of course I didn't expect you to cook tonight. I came to get you. My mother's got liver and bacon waiting."

"I bet she only cooked enough for you." Bronwen gave a wry smile.

"We'll share." Evan took her hand. "Sooner or later she's going to have to get used to the idea that you are part of my life, whether she likes it or not."

He led her out of the cottage. The clouds that had blotted out the mountains all day had dispersed in a strong west wind. The peaks glowed in the clear air while occasional clouds sent shadows racing over the hillsides. A flock of seagulls rode the wind, their cries competing with the bleating of sheep. Evan and Bronwen paused to smile at each other in satisfaction.

"I think we've got the best view in the world," Bronwen said. "I can't wait for the wedding."

Evan slipped his arm around her waist. "I wish you had already bought that brass bed," he said.

"Bridegrooms aren't supposed to jump the gun," Bronwen said with mock severity. "You've only two more weeks to wait."

"No, that wasn't what I had in mind," Evan said. "I'm so tired that I could fall asleep this minute. I don't think I've got the strength to walk back down the hill."

Chapter 8

The next morning the morning paper displayed a picture of Shannon Parkinson on the front page. HAVE YOU SEEN THIS GIRL? the caption read. Evan resigned himself to having breakfast with his mother at Mrs. Williams's house. It was either that or have his mother come to his place and complain about his lack of cooking equipment, his inadequate stove, and the grease spatters on his walls. He even resigned himself to eating the full Welsh breakfast without which his mother and former landlady both felt that a man shouldn't start his day.

Evan was just using the fried bread to soak up the last of his egg yolk when he stopped with food poised on his fork, listening in amazement. The radio had been going in the background, along with the chatter of the two women, throughout breakfast. It was the morning show that Mrs. Williams always liked: Bore Da North Wales—a light mixture of music, local news, interviews with local celebrities, and bad jokes from the compère, comedian Dewi Lewis.

"I hear there's a wedding coming up in the village of Llanfair," Dewi said in conspiratorial tones. "Or at least so I'm told by the postcard that has been sent in, requesting some special music for the happy couple. So this is for Constable Evan Evans, of the North

63

Wales Police, and his lovely Bronwen. In honor of his upcoming nuptuals our listener has requested that we play a piece by Rimsky-Korsakov—and I hope I'm pronouncing that correctly, being one of those lowbrow types, you know. The piece requested for them is the Shipwreck sequence from *Sheherazade*. I don't know the piece myself, being more of a Beatles fan, but I'm sure it has special significance for the happy couple. So here's to you, Evan and Bronwen. *Iechyd da*. I'm raising my glass in a toast to your future life."

"Well now, wasn't that nice?" Mrs. Williams was beaming.

"Funny piece to choose, though," Evan's mother said. "Does it have a special meaning for you two? Did you meet on a boat?"

"I've never heard of the piece before in my life," Evan said. "I've no idea what they're talking about."

The music started, slow, ponderous chords of which Russian composers seem so fond.

"Dear me," Evan's mother said, shaking her head. "What a dreadful gloomy choice of music for a happy occasion. Who on earth would have chosen that for you?"

"They didn't say the name, did they?" Evan asked. "Maybe it's a joke. One of the blokes in the force having a laugh—you know, like I'm sailing into dangerous waters, getting married."

"That's not very nice," Mrs. Williams said.

Evan got up. "I expect I'll be in for more teasing by the time the event takes place," he said. "It's all in good fun, isn't it?"

"You haven't had your toast and marmalade yet," Mrs. Evans complained.

"Sorry, Ma, can't stop any longer. I'm due at the station at eight." Evan took his jacket from the back of his chair. "Thanks very much for the breakfast, Mrs. W. You do a lovely fried bread."

"I expect she could teach it to your future wife, if you asked her nicely," Mrs. Evans said, giving the other woman a knowing look.

As he went out he heard Mrs. Williams's soft high voice saying, in a stage whisper, "It's too bad he never really hit it off with our granddaughter I told you about. Lovely little homemaker she is."

Evan shuddered as he closed the door, remembering the overbearing personality and annoying laugh of her lovely little granddaughter.

"I heard you mentioned on the radio this morning," the receptionist greeted Evan as he pushed open the swing doors into the police station. "I didn't know you were a fan of classical music."

"I'm not," Evan said. "I suspect it was a joke. Probably one of the lads here."

The receptionist grinned. "I'll keep my ear to the ground and let you know which one if you like."

"Don't bother," Evan said. "It could have been worse. It could have been the Funeral March."

Inspector Watkins, Glynis, and the uniformed branch officers were already assembling in Watkins's office.

"Here he is, the household name," Pritchard commented as Evan walked in.

"So you were really on the radio this morning?" Glynis asked.

"I wasn't. Dewi Lewis played a piece of music for me on Bore Da North Wales, that's all."

"In honor of his upcoming nuptuals," Dawson commented and giggled.

"How sweet," Glynis said. "What was it?"

"Some classical piece," Evan said. "Something about a shipwreck by some Russian composer."

"A shipwreck. That's funny." The uniform branch constables dug each other in the side and chuckled. "Sailing into disaster."

"Are you sure that one of you didn't request it?" Evan asked.

"Look at them." Glynis gave them a scornful glance. "As if they'd know the name of a Russian composer. They don't even know the name of a Russian football player."

"Only because Russia doesn't produce any football players worth mentioning," Prichard said. "Ask me the name of a Brazilian and I can tell you."

"Right, everyone. Down to business." Watkins stopped conversation with one loud rap on his desk with his mug. "Let's get ourselves up to date. Still no sighting of the missing girl. I see they've run her picture in the paper as we requested. Sergeant Jones has put up flyers along the route she might have taken."

"And the divers, sir? Have they come up with anything?" Evan asked.

"They're going to have another shot at it today. The weather was so bad yesterday that they said there was almost zero visibility. And the spot where she might have gone in shelves steeply down a hundred feet or more."

"So we're no farther along?" Sergeant Jones asked.

"I have a list of psychiatric patients who have been treated at Ysbety Gwynneth over the past year or so," Glynis said. "I suggest we follow up on some of them."

"Any specific cases?" Watkins asked.

"I haven't had a chance to go through them yet. I've also talked to a local psychiatrist but he wasn't very cooperative. He kept mumbling about patient confidentiality, which I suppose is fair enough. I did ask him how he'd feel if a young girl was tortured and killed because he wouldn't share information with us. He then said he had no patients on his books at the moment who would pose that kind of threat."

She looked around the room, waiting for a response.

"He'd be able to guarantee that, would he?" Evan asked.

"He seemed to think so. He also said that the type of person we want had probably never visited a shrink and may have led an exemplary life so far."

"Which makes our job pretty damned impossible." Evan sighed. "We can hardly go door to door."

"If Glynis comes up with any possibles from her list, we can get them fingerprinted," Watkins said.

"I thought you said the place was almost clean of prints?" Glynis said.

"The tech boys managed to lift a couple here and there, apart from the very distinct ones that didn't pan out."

"So the bloke you brought in yesterday wasn't a possible suspect?" P.C. Pritchard asked.

"Negative. We've concluded he probably touched the tin when he was stocking shelves at Tesco."

"Too bad. He'd have been conveniently easy—with a prior woman-beating charge against him," Sergeant Jones muttered. "Right, so where do we go from here?"

"We need a profile," Glynis said. "We should have headquarters find a profiler for us and bring him to the scene. We need to know who we are looking for. Do you want me to send in the request, sir?"

"Hold on a minute," Watkins said. "I'd have to justify something fancy like a profiler with headquarters. They'll say we have no evidence so far that a crime has been committed."

"A young girl disappearing in broad daylight?" Glynis countered. "And a bunker with handcuffs in it? I'd say that sounded suspiciously like a crime to me."

"But we found her glove, didn't we?" Watkins countered. "At the bottom of a slope that indicated she must have fallen. And the divers haven't managed to search the lake properly yet. We have to give them a chance to find her body."

"Even if they do find her body, we have a duty to find the man who dug the bunker. If he hasn't kidnapped anyone yet, he will." Glynis was insistent.

"We don't know it will be a girl," Pritchard said suddenly. "He might go for boys."

"He might have a grudge against someone. He might want to string up his mother-in-law," Sergeant Jones said, producing a chuckle.

"True enough," Watkins said. "We don't know. We don't seem to know anything much, except that this man is pretty damn slick if he has managed to kidnap her and spirit her off a mountainside full of people."

"That's why a profiler is so important at this stage," Glynis said. "We need to know who we're dealing with."

Watkins nodded. "I'm not disagreeing with you. Just expecting a fight when I ask HQ for something that's not usually done and is over budget. Knowing them, they'll probably say we overspent on our tea money this month."

"And what about some kind of surveillance, sir?" Evan asked. "There is a possibility that the bloke who dug the bunker doesn't know we've found it. Or perhaps he feels he might have left something incriminating there. If we could leave it intact and set up some kind of camera or alarm system, we'd catch him going back there."

"That's not a bad idea, either," Watkins said, and Evan noted the general nods. "I'll ask the tech boys."

"A camera would be useful." Glynis agreed. "One of those security cameras like they have in car parks."

"Of course, ten to one he does know we've found his hidey-hole," Watkins said. "There was very little dust or mold down there, indicating that this had all been stocked recently. That's why the timing on this is so worrying. A girl vanishes the moment a bunker is ready? Has to be a connection, doesn't there?"

"He may have tossed the glove down that slope to throw us off the scent," Glynis suggested.

"Good point." Watkins nodded.

"And done it after the fact," Evan added, "or else why didn't Paul Upwood notice it when he went back to look for her the day before? A red glove is a pretty obvious clue."

"Which would mean he's got her somewhere close by." Watkins sucked air through his teeth. "Let's hope she's still alive. And with any luck this profiler can suggest where we should be looking for him." He looked around him. "Right. Assignments. Davies, you've got enough to do pursuing the leads you've already turned up. Sergeant Jones, can you still spare me some of your men?"

"What do you want done?" Jones asked. "I don't see any point in further searches at this stage on the mountain. We must have covered every inch of it."

"I agree."

"It might be useful to show that newspaper photograph around," Evan said. "In the cafés and at the Snowdon Railway station—and even the mainline station in Bangor, on the unlikely chance that Shannon left the area and didn't tell anyone."

"Right, Evans, I'll turn that over to you," Watkins said.

"I thought that perhaps some of Sergeant Jones's boys could do that for us, sir," Evan said, glancing across at the rotund sergeant. "It's routine stuff."

"I can't keep my lads off regular patrol indefinitely," Sergeant Jones said. "What did you have planned for yourself then, Evans? Using your little gray cells to come up with the villain single-handed while the rest of us poor suckers do the slog work?"

Evan chuckled with the rest of them. He knew only too well that there had been some resentment when he was selected for detective training, after he had been helpful in solving several big cases. "I didn't know if D.I. Watkins might need help with whatever he had planned for this morning," he said.

"I'm going to see D.C.I. Hughes to ask him about procuring a profiler," D.I. Watkins said. "Unless if you'd like to volunteer for that job instead of me?"

Evan maintained the smile. "No, that's all right, sir. I'll go and pound the beat."

Chapter 9

All in all it was a frustrating morning. The cafés and souvenir shops in Llanberis were so busy that those working had little chance to remember anybody. And Evan had to admit that Shannon probably looked a lot like a host of other young people. The Snowdon Railway station was equally busy and Evan had to wait until the next train set off up the mountain before the booking office clerk would even speak to him. He was a testy old Welshman and scowled at Evan. "Look you, boyo," he said, "I'm run ragged handing out tickets to bloody tourists. You don't think I have time to see who might be strolling past, do you?"

"No, I can see that you're busy," Evan agreed. "But another question. Earlier in the year, a couple of months ago, maybe. Did you ever happen to see someone going up the mountain carrying a shovel, or any building materials?"

"A shovel? Building materials?" He thought about this one. "I've seen National Parks workers driving up with tools in their vehicles when they have to do repairs to paths."

"Right. Brilliant. You can't remember any particular vehicle you've noticed recently?"

"Can't say I have."

That was all that Evan could get out of him, but at least he'd come away with one slim lead. Of course National Parks workers would arouse no suspicion if they were seen driving over mountain tracks with tools or wood. Definitely one thing worth pursuing.

He repeated the question about tools and building materials at businesses and homes with gardens that backed onto the mountain, but got no other tips. He stood looking up at the start of the Llanberis path up Snowdon and at the woodland where the bunker had been discovered. How did anyone manage to grab Shannon without being noticed? he wondered. How did anyone manage to dig the bunker without being noticed, and then stock it? And if the girl wasn't still hidden away somewhere on the mountain, how could anyone have brought her down into this hubbub of activity? Evan stood, letting the tide of humanity sweep around him, then finally shook his head and made his way back to his car. He would just have enough time to drive into Bangor and show the picture at the mainline station.

"All these young people look alike to me, mate," the sad-faced man at the ticket counter said. "We've got a constant stream of them coming through every day."

Evan called in his findings to Inspector Watkins, who jumped at once on the possibility of a National Parks vehicle being involved.

"Those ranger types are often social misfits and loners, aren't they?" he said. "I want you to go and talk to them, right after the two o'clock briefing this afternoon."

That gave Evan a precious hour of freedom. During his lunch break, he managed to visit a local car dealer and blanched at the price of a new four-wheel drive utility vehicle. Until he was made an inspector and Bronwen was a headmistress, it would definitely have to be secondhand. The dealer promised to keep his eyes open and Evan picked up a copy of the weekly free advertisements to study when he had a moment. He decided it might be wise to double-check what kind of payments they could expect on a car loan, glanced at his watch, and sprinted in the direction of the bank.

"I'm sorry, Mr. Shorecross isn't in his office. He's stepped out for a while," the pleasant-faced young teller called to Evan. "Is it anything I can help you with?"

"No thanks, it's about a car loan," Evan said. "Do you know when he'll be back?"

"He should be back soon. I think he's at a doctor's appointment," she said.

Evan turned to go and noticed the other teller—the silent, sallow fellow with the heavy specs. Suddenly he remembered the conversation with Mr. Shorecross and his mention of the Peeping Tom. Wouldn't someone who watched young women from the shadows be the kind of person who might have dug the bunker? Evan turned back to the young teller. "I wonder if I might have a word with you in private, Miss?"

"Jones. Hillary Jones," she said. "Isn't everyone called Jones around here?"

"Except for those who are called Evans, like me," Evan said.

"Or Williams or Davies." She smiled. "What's this about?"

"Nothing to do with banking. It's police business."

She looked wary. "Okay. We can use Mr. Shorecross's office, I suppose." She looked across. "Rhodri, can you handle things? I need to talk to this gentleman. Give me a call if you need me."

Her tone was completely relaxed and friendly, making Evan re-think the suspicions that were hovering in his brain. Hillary Jones led the way into the bank manager's office. Evan closed the door behind them.

"Miss Jones," he said, "Your manager mentioned that you'd had problems with a Peeping Tom."

"That's right, I did. A few months ago. Nothing recently. He seems to have given up on me because I invested in heavy curtains."

"Would you like to tell me about it?"

"Nothing much to tell, really. I have a ground-floor bedsitter. It faces the front of the house. There's quite a big front garden with a path up to the front door and laurel bushes on either side. I hadn't closed the curtains and one night I was watching telly and I got up to throw an apple core in the wastepaper basket and there was a man standing across the street. Just standing there. Not moving. When he saw me looking out, he took off. Then a few nights later I looked out and I saw the shrubbery moving. I thought it was a cat or a dog, but then I realized it was a person. He dodged behind a bush when I got a glimpse of him and I called the police that time."

"Did you see what he looked like?"

She shook her head. "Not really. Average height. He was wearing a long raincoat and some kind of cap on his head so I didn't have a chance to see his face or his hair color. The police came right away, but they were too late. They staked out the place for the next few nights but he didn't come back. And I went out and bought these really heavy curtains that you can't see through. So I suppose that solved that."

"And you have no idea who might have wanted to spy on you? No secret admirers?"

"If they were secret, I wouldn't know about them, would I?" she asked with a grin. Then she shook her head. "Honestly, I've no idea."

"Do you have a boyfriend?"

She nodded. "I've a very nice boyfriend."

"Any disgruntled former boyfriends?"

"No, I've been going out with Jeff for two years now."

"Any neighbors who have ever shown interest or acted strangely toward you?"

She shook her head. "I don't really know the neighbors much, but the ones I've met are nice enough."

"What about co-workers?" Evan tried to make it appear that he was just tossing off the question. "Get along well with them, do you?"

"Oh yes. Everyone here is very nice. I don't hang out with them in my spare time or anything, but they're friendly."

"The young man out there?"

"Rhodri?" She giggled. "I don't think he's the type who'd be interested in watching a young lady undress—if you know what I mean."

Evan wondered if she meant that Rhodri was gay or just not interested in women.

"Anyway, he's really sweet. He bought me flowers on my birthday."

"What's his last name?"

"Llewelyn. But he'd never do a thing like that."

"You'd be surprised at the things people do. Sometimes the most harmless, inoffensive person can commit the most unspeakable crimes."

He broke off and looked up as Mr. Shorecross came into his office. "What's this about, Miss Jones?" he asked in a clipped voice. Then he recognized Evan. "Constable Evans. It's you." He smiled and crossed to his desk. "Mr. Llewelyn said you were meeting with a young man in my office. I didn't quite know what to expect."

"Constable Evans wanted to question me about my prowler."

Mr. Shorecross frowned. "But I thought that all stopped months ago. Don't tell me he's returned?"

"No, he hasn't. At least I have no idea if he's outside or not. He certainly can't see much since I put in those new curtains."

"We still haven't located the girl who went missing on Mount Snowdon," Evan said. "Since she hasn't turned up after an extensive search, we can't rule out foul play. And since your Miss Jones is another pretty young girl who was stalked, I thought it might be wise to see if she could share any insights with us."

"But I'm afraid I couldn't be at all helpful," Hillary Jones looked up at Evan. "It was really too dark to see him clearly."

"Surely a prowler, a Peeping Tom, is usually a harmless kind of chap, isn't he?' Shorecross asked. "The type whose own life is boring and who seems to find watching young women take their clothes off exciting."

"You're probably correct," Evan said, "but we have to follow up any possible lead at the moment. Young girls don't just vanish in broad daylight on busy mountain paths."

"I did offer my senior Scouts to help you," Shorecross said in a slightly pained voice. "Maybe more people out searching on the mountain at an earlier stage might have been beneficial. My boys are well trained in rescue drills."

"I did pass along your kind offer. Unfortunately I'm not the one handling the search and frankly I don't think more manpower would have made any difference."

"Well, if you still need us, just let me know," Shorecross said. "Be Prepared is the scouting motto, after all. I can mobilize my troops fairly rapidly."

"Thanks. That's good of you," Evan said.

"Now, if you're finished with Miss Jones, I'd like her to get back to work. There was a line waiting at Mr. Llewelyn's counter and we hate to keep our customers waiting, don't we?"

"Very good, Mr. Shorecross." Hillary gave Evan a beaming smile with just a hint of flirtation to it and left the room.

"A bad business then, Constable?" Shorecross asked. "I didn't like to say what I was thinking in front of Miss Jones, but if your girl hasn't been found by now, then the outcome is probably not going to be favorable."

"I'm afraid you're right," Evan said. "We're doing everything we can. But it's hard to know what to do next."

"I don't envy you your job," Shorecross said.

Evan glanced at his watch. "And I should be getting back to it. I came here to ask your advice on a car loan, but I see my lunch hour is almost over, so it will have to be some other time."

"Very well then," Shorecross said. "I'm always here. Bring your delightful fiancée with you. I did enjoy talking with her. Such a well-educated young woman."

"She went to Cambridge."

"Did she really? Good God."

Evan read the thoughts—then why is she marrying a police constable and settling in a village? He occasionally had the same thoughts himself. It was still miraculous to him that anyone as bright and wonderful as Bronwen had chosen to share his life.

As he hurried out of the bank, he noticed the surly Rhodri Llewelyn watching him with apprehension. I'm definitely going to check on that one, Evan thought. He considered going back to Neville Shorecross and asking a few discreet questions there, but realized that this line of investigation should probably go through his chief first. He'd been in trouble before now for being the maverick and not working through the appropriate channels. He was, after all, a relatively new D.C., assigned to D.I. Watkins. It was not his investigation.

As he walked back to the station he remembered that Hillary had reported the Peeping Tom incidents to the police. Surely Rhodri's name must have come up in the process of that investigation?

It appeared that D.I. Watkins had stepped out when Evan returned to the station so he used the time to hunt through records. He found Hillary's complaint from last February. Rhodri Llewelyn's name was among those mentioned in the report, along with Hillary's other co-workers. But he had obviously been dismissed with the brief annotation: "Interviewed co-workers. Alibis check out."

"Hello, what are you up to?" Glynis's voice made Evan jump.

"Just searching through our records," Evan said.

Glynis laughed. "You must be doing something unapproved, you look like a guilty schoolboy caught raiding the biscuit barrel."

Evan grinned. "If you must know, I wanted to see what a previous investigation had turned up." He told her about the Peeping Tom.

"And what makes you suspect this chap?" she asked.

"Nothing except that he looks nervous every time I see him. And he looks like a Peeping Tom."

"He looks like a Peeping Tom? Evan, if everyone looked like the type of criminal they were, our job would be so much easier. We'd just have to say, 'All line up and the one who looks like a murderer probably did it.'"

"I know, but he has this guarded, secretive sort of look to him and I noticed him staring at Hillary Jones when he thought she was busy."

"So you think this incident may be linked to our current case?" she asked.

"Probably not, but it would be the same type of bloke, don't you think? Someone who lurks in the shadows to watch a girl undress? He might take his fantasies one stage further."

"Possibly." Glynis nodded. 'See what the D.I. thinks."

"What about you—have you come up with any leads?"

Glynis shrugged. "I've got a couple of male psychiatric patients we should take a look at. One has a huge grudge against women, the other likes to build things."

"Interesting."

"Ah, there you are, troops." D.I. Watkins came bursting into the room. "Good news. HQ have okayed our profiler. I'm picking him up and showing him our potential crime scene later this afternoon. Evans, you're going to tackle the National Park people. Smart observation that. Why didn't we think of it before? A Parks Service truck can go all over the mountain without drawing any special attention. Why, if she'd fallen and twisted her ankle, she'd have accepted a ride in a Parks Service vehicle, wouldn't she?"

Evan and Glynis exchanged a glance.

"No news from the divers yet, then?" Glynis asked.

"Not yet. But it's a very deep lake. It's probably not an easy assignment."

"Right, sir. I'll be off then," Evan said.

"Tread carefully, Evans. We don't want to put the wind up anybody. We're just wondering which of their men might have been working on the mountain and might have seen anything unusual. No hint of suspicion or accusation. Got it?"

"Yes, sir," Evan said, somewhat annoyed at being told what to say, especially in front of Glynis. "But before I go, I've come up with another lead we should look into." He recounted the Peeping Tom story.

"But you say the chap you suspect was investigated once before and apparently his alibi checked out in the incident?"

Evan nodded.

"But Evan thinks he looks suspicious." Glynis couldn't resist getting in the dig.

"I'd like the chance to question him, sir. He's definitely uneasy when he sees me. I just have a feeling that this is something we should follow up."

"When you're through with the National Parks then," Watkins said. "Worth keeping at the back of our minds."

"At the back of our minds," Evan muttered as he left the building. Pretentious git. Watkins was dismissing his suggestions as if they were of no importance. There had been a time, not too long ago, when he and Watkins had made a good team. They'd shared pints and laughs. Since Watkins had been promoted to detective inspector, he had to act the authority figure, firmly in charge all the time. Normally it didn't bug Evan. He supposed he was especially keyed up at the moment.

He signed out a police car and headed south to park headquarters just outside Porthmadog. The journey along the A487 took a frustrating hour as the road was full of slow-moving holidaymakers, many of them towing caravans, making passing impossible. At last he passed Porthmadog and drove over the shining tide pools and mud flats of the Glaslyn estuary on the toll bridge known as the Cob. It was with a sigh of relief that he finally came to a halt outside the headquarters building.

"Oh dear, so they never found the missing girl then," the slim, gray-haired woman at the reception desk said, when Evan announced the reason for his visit. "We sent out everybody available as soon as we got the call from the police."

"I know you did, and we're very grateful," Evan said. "I just wondered if I could speak with those involved in the search. We found the girl's glove the next day, you see. So they might be able to provide us with more clues."

The woman looked up at a white board. "We've got sixteen on call at the moment—most of them summer volunteers, of course. Our permanent staff is only four rangers—lack of budget these days, I'm afraid. They'd all be out on patrol right now. You couldn't imagine how many people get themselves into trouble and need rescuing in the tourist season."

"Oh, I could imagine it very well." Evan smiled. "I've been part of a mountain rescue team myself."

"Have you now?" She gave an approving nod. "Then you'll know what stupid risks tourists take. Going up Snowdon in their shorts and sandals and then finding themselves trapped when a storm comes in and snows on them."

"Where would I find your chaps on patrol then?" Evan asked.

"That's hard to say. They call in from time to time. Let's see. Eddie was last up near Cader Idris. Diana and Roger were investigating an illegal fire on the shore flats outside Harlech. I can call them on their mobiles if it's important—"

"That's all right. It can wait. If you could give me names and addresses, I can contact them when they're off duty," Evan said. He copied down names as she gave them to him. Of the four workers, two were women.

"So, who would have access to your vehicles?" he asked.

"Our vehicles?" A confused frown crossed her face. "Whoever is out on patrol. Usually one of our rangers will take one of the volunteers with them. The volunteers aren't supposed to take vehicles out alone. We have a mini-bus for transporting them around."

"But it doesn't go up mountains?"

"Of course not. What is all this about our vehicles? One hasn't been stolen, has it?"

"No, nothing like that." Evan tried to think quickly. "We're just checking on the report of a vehicle sighted on the mountain the day the girl vanished."

"Could have been one of ours. There's someone out on patrol all the time."

"Alone?" Evan asked.

"Usually they take a volunteer with them in the summer," the receptionist said. "In the off season, when things quieten down, then they're mostly out alone."

"So you can't tell me definitely whether any of your people was out alone on the day the girl vanished?"

"Why would that be important?" She was definitely looking suspicious now.

"Well now." Evan paused. "Because the vehicle reported seen on the mountain had just one person in it. I wanted to rule out whether it was one of yours."

"I can't think what other sort of vehicle might have been up there. It's off limits to traffic, even if someone did have a four-wheel drive capable of tackling that sort of terrain."

This wasn't going to lead anywhere productive, Evan decided. He might learn more from talking to the summer volunteers. He was told that they were out clearing brush. He drove to the spot where they were working and found a group of noisy, lively students busy hacking away at rampant brambles that threatened to cover a stile. They all knew about the missing girl and had all taken part in the search.

"How did you get up the mountain?" Evan asked. "Did you have to walk up?"

The students laughed. "Not bloody likely. We're not that fit."

"No, several of us piled into the back of Eddie Richards's Land Rover and you lot went with Jenny Henderson in hers, didn't you?"

"I didn't think it was going to make it up there with all our weight," one of the boys said.

"Speak for yourself." A slender girl tossed back long dark hair.

"So, Eddie Richards—who's he? One of the permanent employees?" Evan asked.

"Yeah, he's the head honcho. Old bloke. Like a bloody drill sergeant."

"Used to be in the army once, before he retired," someone else chimed in.

"And what are the others like?" Evan asked.

"Jenny's cool. Roger's all right."

"All right?" Evan asked.

"Quiet sort of bloke. Not too chatty. He's okay when he's not singing."

"Not singing?" Evan asked.

The students grinned. "He's in one of those male choirs and he

80

tends to practice a lot. Having Welsh hymns sung in your ear all day can get to be a bit much."

"And what about Diana?"

"Diana's a bit standoffish. Frightfully upper class. She went to a snobby girls' boarding school."

"So did I," the slender girl said, "but I don't act the way she does. She's just a cow."

"You lot all seem to get along really well," Evan said. "I suppose you have to enjoy being one of the gang if you choose summer work like this."

"You have to be a bloody masochist, mate," the chubby boy said gloomily. "I've lost over a stone since I started here."

"Not that anyone could tell!" They were laughing again.

"So you were all up on the mountain that day. And you didn't see anything suspicious?" Evan asked.

"Such as what?"

"We found the girl's glove yesterday. Which meant it had been overlooked the day before."

They now faced him with worried looks.

"We weren't told to look for gloves and things. People are always dropping stuff on the mountain paths. We were told that she might have wandered in the wrong direction or fallen and hurt herself."

"We searched, we didn't find her, and we piled in the vehicles again to ride down when it got dark," the chubby boy said.

"It seems really strange that she hasn't been found yet," one of the girls said. "I hope nothing's happened to her."

"Like what?" Evan asked.

"You never know who you'll meet on a mountain, do you?" the girl asked. "There are some weird types out there."

"Yeah, but look at all the people there were up there that day," a boy countered. "If you tried to drag someone away, she'd only have had to scream and tons of people would have heard her."

"We've got divers searching Glaslyn at the moment," Evan said. "She may have fallen in."

"Ooh, how terrible." The dark-haired girl shook her head. "Yes, I can see that might have happened. There are places on the Miner's Path where you could lose your footing if you weren't paying attention. Poor girl."

"So, nobody remembers seeing a red glove then?"

They looked at each other, then shook their heads.

"I'd have noticed a red glove, I'm sure," one of the girls spoke up at last. "Because it was a warm day. Who would be wearing gloves?"

Who indeed? Evan thought as he drove home. Unless it had fallen from her backpack as she slid down the screen slope. But why hadn't anyone noticed it sooner? Unless the man who had taken Shannon had planted it there after the search had concluded, to throw everyone off the scent. However much Evan wanted to believe that Shannon had fallen and drowned, he knew that in his heart, he didn't believe that at all.

Chapter 10

After leaving the volunteers, Evan drove to the first of the four addresses he had been given. It turned out that Eddie Richards lived in a National Parks bungalow, not far from Parks Headquarters. He wasn't there as Evan had expected, but his wife was preparing dinner.

"Yes, Eddie told me about this missing girl," she said, "and I saw her picture in the paper today. What a sad business. I hope she turns up safe and sound. Such a worry for her parents. Eddie was quite cut up about it. He used to worry about our two girls before they went off to university. If they weren't home the moment they said they'd be, he'd start pacing the floor."

Evan left with the feeling that he could probably rule out Mr. Richards as a suspect. Anyone who worried about his own daughters' welfare was not likely to have evil intentions about other young girls, he decided.

Jenny Henderson, the driver of the other vehicle that day, had the day off. She lived at home and Evan was told by her mother that she'd gone shopping. That left Roger and Diana, who were out on patrol together.

As he got back into the car, Evan decided that he should probably interview each of the rangers in person. Even a man who sang hymns all day! Of course the two women weren't likely to be suspects. But even if they weren't involved themselves, one of them might have seen evidence of the bunker being built. Or have glimpsed something that hadn't seemed suspicious at the time but had resulted in the disappearance of Shannon Parkinson. He went back to Parks Headquarters and had the receptionist call up the two park vehicles on the radio. Eddie Richards was on his way back to headquarters. Evan drove to intercept him. He saw immediately why the students referred to him as a drill sergeant. Short, buzzed hair. Lean. Sharp-eyed. No-nonsense sort of bloke. Quick on the uptake, too. After Evan had asked him a couple of questions, he demanded, "All right. What's behind all this? You don't think the girl met with an accident, do you?"

"Possibly not," Evan said.

"I don't know. There are still places it's impossible to check out properly. She could be lying at the bottom of a mine shaft. There are still a couple of those not properly sealed off."

"Possible, yes."

He regarded Evan with his sharp blue eyes. "In my business you go for the obvious, until it's been disproved." He paused. "Unless there are things you're not telling me, of course."

"We may have reason to believe that someone abducted the girl," Evan said.

"Ah. I see. So that's it."

"Were you in that area on the day she disappeared?"

"Tuesday, was it? Yes, I think I was. Not up on Snowdon, though. I was driving around, restocking our information centers with materials. I got the emergency call and took a carload of kids up with me to look for her. Believe me, we did a thorough job."

Evan left Richards feeling sure that he was not the kind of man they were looking for, a man of action, family man, not a secretive loner. It took him another half-hour to locate Roger Thomas and Diana on a nearby beach. He saw instantly that the students' assessment of Diana as a snobby, boarding school type had again been accurate. She had one of those lazy, upper-class drawls not often heard these days and she looked as if Evan might be a bad smell under her nose.

"Sorry," she drawled. "Tuesday was my day off, Roger's too, wasn't it?" She turned to him and he nodded, averting his eyes from Evan's gaze. Roger Thomas was not unlike Evan in build—big, dark-haired, but with a fresh, schoolboy's face that made him look much younger than he probably was. Like a schoolboy having been sent to the headmaster, he shifted nervously when Evan addressed him.

"Your day off too, sir? So you weren't involved in the search and rescue mission on the mountain that day."

"No, I'm afraid we missed all the excitement," Roger said. He had the slightest lilt of a Welsh accent, but with overtones that indicated a school or college education in England.

"And how did you spend your day off, Mr. Thomas?" Evan asked.

"Me? I was—my choir was practicing over in Bala for a concert we're going to give there next week. I sing with a *Cor Meibion,* you know."

"He never bloody well stops singing," Diana said dryly. "You should try driving around all day with hymns being sung at you."

Roger grinned sheepishly. "I can't help it," he said. "It's in the blood. My da sang with the chapel choir and his dad before him."

Diana made a snorting noise of derision.

"And you, miss. How did you spend your day off?" Evan asked.

She met his gaze with a cold, blank stare. "I was washing my hair," she said. "Any more silly questions? What exactly is this about?"

Evan repeated the suggestion that a vehicle had been sighted on the mountain and Shannon Parkinson might have been abducted.

"Sorry we can't help you," Diana said. "As I just told you, it was our day off."

"Have you noticed any suspicious vehicles on the mountain in the last few weeks?" Evan asked. "Our man may have been spying out the land."

"If we'd found any vehicle on National Park land, we'd have intercepted it and sent it back to the road," Diana said. "Wouldn't we, Roger?"

It was clear to Evan who gave the orders in that duo. Roger was staring at the ground, clearly wishing the interview would end. Why? Evan wondered. Because he was naturally shy, or was there a more sinister reason? Still, singing with a choir in Bala, some fifty miles away, was a pretty solid alibi. And Roger Thomas wouldn't have had use of a parks vehicle on his day off.

"Is that all, because we're rather busy at the moment," Diana said impatiently. "Come on, Roger. We need to get going." She turned her back on Evan. Roger hesitated, glanced up at Evan, then followed her back to their Land Rover. Evan couldn't think of any good reason to make them stay.

As he drove back to Caernarfon, he tried to assess what, if anything, he had gleaned from the afternoon's interviews. Roger Thomas was uncomfortable in his presence. Eddie Richards wasn't. Apart from that, the only useful piece of information that Evan had gleaned was that nobody he had interviewed that afternoon had seen a red glove when they were initially searching the mountain for signs of Shannon. He drove back fast, and pulled up at the same time as D.I. Watkins.

"I've just dropped off our profiler," Watkins said as he got out of his car. "Interesting bloke. Amazing what they can do."

"What did he say?"

"He took pictures, asked questions, and will send us a written profile," Watkins answered. "He didn't say a word when we were at the bunker, except to ask whether we moved anything. But he was telling me about other cases when we were driving together. Amazing that they can put together a whole personality and even a physical description based on one item of clothing that they find. What about you? Anything useful?"

"Nothing really. One of the rangers didn't enjoy talking to me, but he had the day off on Tuesday and was in Bala singing with his choir. It would seem that the red glove wasn't on the mountain during the original search. Oh, and one of the rangers suggested that we should double-check the mine shafts."

"I don't know how we can possibly do that—unless you're volunteering to be lowered down?" Watkins grinned.

"Oh, right. I'll definitely volunteer for that." Evan smiled. "But from my recollection, it's not very easy to fall down one of those shafts. The obvious ones are sealed off. And they're all fenced in, with plenty of warning signs."

"But still, it's a thought, isn't it? If someone wanted to dispose of a body in a hurry . . ." Watkins sighed. "I'll ask HQ if they can come up with a way to have them checked. I don't want any of our boys lowered down there. We'd need qualified cavers, or maybe the local army base can spare us a commando or two." He gave Evan a gentle shove. "Why don't you bugger off for the night. I'm sure your future wife has planned a hundred and one things for you to do."

"It's too late to look at antique furniture, thank God," Evan said. "That's her main occupation these days. The cottage has to be furnished with brass beds and Welsh dressers."

"That's going to cost you a pretty penny, isn't it?"

Evan grimaced. "Her parents are paying, apparently."

"Lucky you."

"I'm glad you think so. I'm not too thrilled with the idea myself. I sort of feel that we should furnish our own house, bit by bit as we can afford it."

"Don't like being beholden to the in-laws, eh?"

"Exactly. They've already taken over the wedding. Instead of a simple affair, it's now progressed to a marquee and a fancy caterer. I've more or less backed away at this stage. I'm leaving it to Bronwen."

"Wise man. I can see you'll have a long and happy life together if you let her take over."

"Bron's not like that," Evan said. "And I'm sure she'll do a great job with the wedding and the decorating."

"Go on, then. Off you go," Watkins said. "At least you can play the supportive groom."

"Wait a minute. What about that Peeping Tom I was telling you about? Don't you think we should be checking on that young chap at the bank?"

"He was investigated once before, and I've no reason to believe that our men didn't do a thorough job."

"Okay, so they found he had an alibi for the times when the Peeping Tom showed up, but—"

"There you are, then. What more do you want? Don't tell me you're turning someone into a suspect because he's got a shifty-looking face? That's not like you, boyo. You've been working too hard. Go on home."

Evan had no choice but to obey.

Chapter 11

"Constable Evans! A word, if you don't mind." Mrs. Powell-Jones, the wife of the minister of Capel Beulah, came bearing down the street toward Evan as he stepped out of his car. She was wearing a wide white cardigan that flapped out around her, giving her the appearance of a galleon under full sail. It was too late to get back in the car again. Evan took a deep breath and resigned himself to his fate. He wondered what she'd found to complain about this time. She usually found some small infraction in the village and didn't seem to understand that he was no longer the community policeman, in charge of such things. He was on the spot. That was all that mattered.

"What's the problem, Mrs. P-J?" he asked.

"You are, Constable. I've just heard the most distressing news."

"You have?"

"I understand that you are to be married shortly."

"That's hardly distressing news, is it?" Evan asked.

She ignored this. "Of course I had hoped—well, expected, really, that my husband, being the senior pastor in this place, would have the honor of performing the ceremony. But now I find that isn't to be so. I sincerely hope you have not asked that man to do it instead."

"Which man is that, Mrs. Powell-Jones?" Evan asked, even though he knew the answer.

"The minister of that inferior chapel across the street. The one who frequents public houses and other dens of vice."

"Oh, you mean Mr. Parry Davies?" Evan asked, with a grin. "No, you can rest assured he's not going to perform the ceremony."

Her face turned pale. "Surely you don't mean you're going to be married in a registry office? Not invoking the blessing of the Almighty?"

"Wrong again," Evan said, for once enjoying the confrontation with her. "We're getting married in the little church at Nant Peris."

"Anglican?" She clutched her ample bosom in dramatic fashion. "High Church, with incense and chanting and all that Papist nonsense? Mr. Evans—how could you?"

"Bronwen's choice, not mine," he said, "but I've nothing against it."

"That's even worse than a registry office. Incense and statues are tools of the devil. Your marriage will be doomed from the start."

"I don't think so. But cheer up, you'll be invited, of course. We're having a marquee and everyone is invited."

She drew herself up into her Queen Victoria imitation. "Mr. Evans, if you think I'll set foot in a Church of Wales establishment, then you can think again."

With that she turned on her heels and had started to walk back up the street when a loud popping noise echoed back from the mountainside. Evans-the-Post came roaring down Llanfair's main street on his motorbike. Mrs. Powell-Jones leaped for safety onto the pavement as the postman passed her, a look of half terror, half excitement in his eyes.

"You should never be allowed to ride that thing!" Mrs. Powell-Jones screamed after him. "You're a menace to society. I shall call the postmaster!"

As the postman drew level with Evan he didn't slow, but shouted out: "I left a letter for you at your house."

"Who's it from?" Evan shouted back.

Evans-the-Post was known for reading the mail before he delivered it.

"They didn't say. No signature. All typewritten. Boring." The words floated behind him as he shot over the hump-backed bridge and disappeared down the pass.

Evan grinned to himself. If Evans-the-Post could only deliver the mail to the whole of North Wales, there would be considerably fewer crimes. He certainly had the knack of reading the most amazing amount through sealed envelopes. In fact, if the whole world operated a bush telegraph system like the village of Llanfair, the police would have a far easier job of tracking criminal activity. Not much went on in the village that everyone didn't hear about within five minutes. If Evan had been to visit Bronwen when she lived in the schoolhouse, his time of arrival and departure were duly passed along to his landlady. Evan suspected the village probably even knew what he and Bronwen were doing behind closed doors. In fact—he stopped short as a thought struck him. Several local men had joined in the search that first afternoon. It would be worth asking them what they might have seen on the mountain. And if he had to have a pint of Guinness, just to keep them company—well, that was part of the job, wasn't it?

As he crossed the road to the Red Dragon, he admitted to himself that this was also a way of delaying another evening of confrontation with his mother and Bronwen. Evan couldn't understand why his mother was being so difficult. What was there not to like about Bronwen? If he had been about to marry a brassy, gum-chewing hussy, he could have understood her attitude. But Bronwen was everything a mother should wish in a daughter-in-law—intelligent, pretty, gentle, caring, well educated, well liked. What more did she bloody well want?

He pushed open the heavy oak door of the pub and marched inside.

"Watch out, here comes the future bridegroom, and from the look on his face, they've just had a tiff," Evans-the-Meat called out, giving Charlie Hopkins a dig in the ribs that almost made him spill his pint of Robinson's.

"We haven't had a tiff," Evan said. "I've just got things on my mind, that's all." It would have been disloyal to complain about his mother, however annoying she was being.

"It must be having his mother in the village, keeping an eye on him," Charlie Hopkins commented to the men gathered around the bar. "She makes sure Bronwen goes home by eight o'clock at night, and no creeping up the mountain when it gets dark, either."

Evan grinned.

"I'm glad you came in, Evan *bach*," Betsy said, pouring him a pint of Guinness without being asked. "I want to show you and Bronwen what I want to wear to the wedding. Barry thinks it's too revealing, but then you know what a fuddy-duddy he is."

"That's not being a fuddy-duddy, expecting my girl to look refined and classy and not all tarted up." Barry-the-Bucket, Betsy's current beau, stood up to his full six feet two inches from where he had been leaning against the bar. He was wearing his usual mud-spattered overalls. "I don't want blokes ogling her cleavage."

"Just because I've got a very nice cleavage." Betsy smoothed down her T-shirt, riveting every pair of male eyes for a few seconds.

"A wedding is a solemn occasion," Barry said. "You're supposed to dress like for chapel."

"But it's not chapel, is it? It's church and they are more liberal," Betsy said. "And what's more, there's going to be dancing afterwards, isn't there, Evan *bach*?"

"So I gather," Evan said. "Bronwen's really the one to ask. She and her mother have been making all the plans."

"You're doomed, boyo," Evans-the-Meat said. He turned to the other men. "Already he's letting the little lady make all the decisions."

"Only because I don't have time," Evan said. "She's got school holidays, hasn't she? And I'm working hard on this case."

"The missing girl, you mean?" Charlie's face was suddenly solemn. "They never found her?"

Evan shook his head. "That's why I came over here. Some of you helped in the search that day, didn't you?"

"I did," Charlie said. "And so did Barry, and you two, right?"

"Did any of you go right up as far as Glaslyn?"

"I did," Barry said.

"So did I," Fred Roberts, one of the other men, answered.

"You didn't happen to notice a red glove lying close to the water-line, at the bottom of that steep scree slope, did you?"

Barry and Fred exchanged looks. "A red glove?" Barry said. "I remember looking down at the lake and asking myself if she could possibly have fallen in. Then I thought that she'd have had to be bloody stupid to try to climb down that scree—and if she had been on the path above and just stumbled, then she wouldn't have fallen all the way down. There are those rocks that would have stopped her fall."

"So you would definitely have noticed a red glove then?"

"I'm sure I would have," Barry said.

"None of you saw a mobile phone, I suppose? Any vehicle tracks?"

"Vehicle tracks? There were search and rescue vehicles up there. They'd have made tracks, I suppose." Barry looked puzzled.

"We weren't looking for vehicles," Charlie Hopkins said. "We were looking for a missing girl."

"And what about mine shafts? Did any of the searchers check around any of the mine openings?" Evan asked.

"I'm sure they did," Barry said. "Anyway, it wouldn't be easy to fall into one of those mine shafts—they've all got warning signs and they're mostly sealed off. She'd have to be particularly bloody stupid, in fact."

Evan downed the last of his Guinness. "I'd better be going," he said. "Thanks for your help, boys."

"I don't know that we've been any help," Charlie Hopkins said. "What do they think happened to her, then? They can't possibly think she fell down a mine shaft, can they?"

"It's one possibility they are considering," Evan said. "They've also had divers in the lake."

Charlie shook his head. "You'd have thought, with all those people around, someone would have heard a splash, or a cry for help, wouldn't you?"

"You'd have thought so," Evan agreed.

"Well, she can't have vanished into thin air," Charlie said.

But that's just what she had done, Evan thought as he stepped out into the fresh evening air.

He opened his cottage door carefully, half expecting to find his mother lying in wait, but mercifully the place was quiet and empty. He heaved a sigh of relief and bent to pick up his mail. Among the usual number of offers for double-glazed windows or cheap trips to Turkey there was a slim typewritten envelope, addressed to Constable Evan Evans and the future Mrs. Evans. The one that Evans-the-Post had been curious about. When he opened it, he saw why. He found, to his surprise, that it contained music. No words, no heading. Just two lines of musical notation. He stared at it for a while but he couldn't read music and it meant nothing to him.

Bronwen could read music, however. Evan made his way up the hill as quickly as he could. It was a hard slog at the end of a long day and in semi-darkness. That four-wheel drive vehicle was obviously a necessity, he decided.

"In here, *cariad*," Bronwen called as he let himself into their new cottage. Evan followed her voice into the bedroom. Bronwen was on her knees on the bare floor.

"I'm measuring." She looked up. "I was down at the antiques shop today and Mr. Cartwright thinks he knows where he can get us a brass bedstead. So I'm trying to see which way it would fit."

"I hope you're going to polish it," Evan said. "Brass tarnishes awfully quickly."

"Oh, don't be such a spoilsport." Bronwen scrambled to her feet to kiss him. "You know very well that you would hate a house furnished with all that cheap modern stuff. We have to have furniture that belongs, and a brass bed definitely belongs here, doesn't it?"

"As long as it's got a comfortable mattress on it, I really don't care," Evan said. "But stop doing that for a moment, please. I've got something to show you." He handed her the sheet of paper. "Take a look at this."

"It's music." Bronwen examined it. "Where did it come from?"

"Somebody sent it in today's post. No return address. Typewritten envelope. I have no idea why anyone would want to send us music."

"Perhaps some budding composer has written us a special anthem for our wedding," Bronwen said excitedly. "What a pity we don't have a piano anymore. I'll miss having the school piano to play, but I can't see how we'd have room for one up here, or how anyone would be able to carry it up the mountain."

"You have your guitar," Evan said.

"Yes, that will have to do, if I can unearth it. I'm afraid this room is still in total chaos." She rummaged among boxes of clothing, more books, hiking boots, until at last she located the guitar in the far corner, dragged it out, and took it from its case.

"Now let's see." She carried the guitar through to the living room and sat at one of the chairs in the window. "Put the music down on the table here and I'll play it."

She played the series of notes, then looked up. "If it's an anthem for our wedding, it's not very good, is it?" she asked. "It doesn't really go anywhere."

"It's not really a proper tune, is it?" Evan said. "Repetitive."

"It's very strange." She examined the paper. "No title, no hint of whom it's from. I wonder what key it's supposed to be in? It may sound better with the right chords to accompany it, but the person hasn't written in the clef or the key signature. No sharps or flats, I mean, so I don't know what chords to put with it." She continued to stare at it. "Starts on b, ends on d. That really doesn't make sense. I mean why would anyone write music that goes BAD DAD, DAD DEAD—"

She broke off, staring wide-eyed up at Evan.

"What are you talking about? Where does it say that?" Evan asked.

"I was reading the musical notes, and that's what they spell out."

"Bad dad, dad dead?"

Bronwen nodded, still staring at the paper. "And then it goes on to say BAD DEB, DEB DEAD." She dropped the paper as if it burned her. "Oh my God, Evan. Somebody's sending you a message."

Chapter 12

An hour later, Evan stood in the forensics lab at police headquarters in Colwyn Bay, watching impatiently as the technician tested the sheet of paper. The technician had already gone home for the day and had to be called back in. He wasn't too happy about it.

"It's a piece of music," he said in disgust as Evan handed him a manila file containing the page. "What sort of crime are we looking at?"

"Not sure," Evan said. "I'm asking for a rush on this just in case it has anything to do with the missing girl on the mountain and the bunker we found."

"That bunker was pretty clean of prints. Only the one good set, and you've already spoken to that bloke, haven't you?"

Evan nodded. "And ruled him out, I believe. This may be something quite different, but just in case . . ."

"Two sets of prints on it." The technician looked up. "Both pretty clear."

"Those would be mine and Bronwen's," Evan said. "We both handled it. What about the envelope?"

"Multiple sets on that, of course, but if your man has been careful to wear latex gloves when handling the paper, he'll have kept them on when he touched the envelope too."

"Right," Evan said, disappointed. "So we're none the wiser. There's no other way of finding who might have sent it?"

"If he licked the stamp, we can probably extract DNA, but that's no use to us unless we have his DNA on file. And we're not likely to have that unless he's already been arrested for a sex crime." He put the sheet of paper back into a file. "What we need is to have everyone's DNA registered when they're born. It would save us a lot of trouble. They'll get around to it eventually, I suppose."

Evan left the lab, and drove to meet Inspector Watkins in Caernarfon. He had also been on his way home when Evan called him.

"This better be good," he said as Evan came in through the police station door. "I thought I was finally going to get a hot meal on time tonight."

"Me too," Evan said. "And to tell you the truth, I don't know what to make of it."

He handed Watkins the sheet of paper, plus another sheet on which he had written the letters spelled out by the music. "Pretty ingenious," Watkins said. "That's the first time in my career that anyone has sent us a message in music. How did you find out what it said?"

"Pure luck. Bronwen played the tune and thought it was badly written music. So she said the notes out loud." He shrugged. "It may just be some kind of sick joke, of course. It is the summer holidays. Maybe some local kids have got nothing better to do with their time."

"But whoever created this took the trouble to wear latex gloves, right?" Watkins shook his head. "Would you go to all that trouble for a prank? And the bloke who dug the bunker wore latex gloves too. My feeling is that we have to take this seriously until proven otherwise."

"And since it's music, sir, it made me wonder if there was any connection to that other musical thing yesterday."

"What thing?"

"Remember they were laughing about it at the station? Someone requested a piece of music to be played in honor of my upcoming wedding on Bore Da North Wales."

"Right. What was the piece?"

Evan shrugged. "It didn't mean anything to me. Some heavy classical Russian thing. Bronwen will remember what it was."

"You'd better get a copy and see if the notes spell anything out," Watkins said.

"Good idea. And we finally have something to work on, don't we? Someone called Debbie or Deborah has been killed, and maybe it's her dad as well."

"Or maybe it's the sicko's dad. The Deb part will be easier to work on. We can contact the national crime center and see what unsolved cases they have on their files."

"Not necessarily unsolved," Evan said. "Our man could have been released from jail or a facility for the insane. The cases could be decades old."

"True enough," Watkins said. "We'll have Glynis do her flying fingers bit on the computer in the morning."

"If you don't mind, I'd like to do what I can, right away," Evan said. "I keep thinking about the missing girl, you see. I mean, if the divers don't find her in the lake, it means that she could be with him and still be alive."

"I know what you mean," Watkins said. "I've been feeling the same way. This case is really getting to me. I keep thinking what her family must be going through."

"It's so frustrating not knowing what to do next," Evan said.

Watkins nodded in agreement. "Tell me about it. We've searched. We've put her picture in the paper, we've contacted other police regions, but it seems that we should be doing more."

"Now we finally do have something to go on," Evan said. "Someone is leaving me musical clues. That must mean that music is important to him. We can work on that, can't we? I mean, check local music societies and choirs—see who buys classical music at local record shops."

"Yes, we can do all that," Watkins said, "but I'm not optimistic. If you ask local music societies if they have any loner male members who might be a bit odd, I bet they'll name you quite a few."

"We can follow up on them."

"We can. But men who dig bunkers probably are not joiners."

"One of my National Parks workers sings in a choir. I suppose I'd better recheck him, even though he wasn't working on the day in question."

"It wouldn't hurt, I suppose."

Evan sighed. "And I'll go and see what I can dig up on girls called Deborah, Debbie, or Deb."

"Check out the name on the list of missing girls, too," Watkins said. "She might never have been found, like this girl now."

Evan felt sick. He couldn't get the image of those handcuffs in the bunker out of his mind. No girl would be that tall, which meant she'd be hanging there—

"Right," he said, switching his mind back to business.

Watkins went to move away, then suddenly clapped him on the shoulder. "Hold it, Evans. We've neither of us had anything to eat. Let's pop across to the pub first and grab a pint and a meat pie."

"It's a bugger, isn't it?" Watkins commented as he took a long swig from his beer glass in the Ship across the street. "Between you and me, Evan, I don't know about this one. They tell us to go for the facts, and if you examine the facts, we don't have a crime. The girl could have run off with a young man she met at the hostel. She could have dropped her glove. The bunker could have been made for an amateur film. The musical clues could be some of your mates having a laugh . . ."

"And yet you don't think so?"

Watkins shook his head. "If I trust my gut, then my gut gives me a bad feeling about all this. Maybe it's the fact that he's been meticulous in not leaving fingerprints. Nobody goes to that amount of trouble unless it's important."

"We can't give up until we find her body, anyway."

"No, we can't do that." Watkins took another swig of beer. "This is a bloody awful job sometimes. I wish I'd listened to my old mother and gone into accounting."

"You'd have died of boredom." Evan chuckled.

"Maybe I would. Right, then. Let's down the rest of this and get back to work."

It was after ten o'clock when Evan finally arrived home. Their search had produced only one Deborah—Debbie Johnson, age fifteen, who was last seen trying to hitchhike home after missing the last bus from a cinema near Birmingham. It seemed that Deborah was not a popular name among those to be murdered or abducted. Evan let himself into his house and stood in the hallway, savoring the silence. He went through to the living room and discovered Bronwen, fast asleep in his armchair with her coat over her. She looked so young and peaceful, like a princess from a fairy tale, that Evan stood there, gazing down at her. She must have sensed his presence because her eyes fluttered open. "What time is it?" she asked with a sleepy smile.

"Just after ten."

"I must have fallen asleep." She sat up. "I came to make us some dinner. Luckily I arrived about ten minutes before your mother and I'd taken possession of the stove so there wasn't very much she could do, except to look at my mushroom risotto as if I was feeding you monkey brains or cooked dog. Accompanied, of course, by a recitation about how your father always had a proper meal when he came home. I don't know what she'd have done if I'd told her I used to be a total vegetarian." Bronwen chuckled.

"So what did she do?"

"When she saw she wasn't going to be allowed near the stove she stumped back to Mrs. Williams in a huff, muttering that Mrs. W. had made her famous steak and kidney pie and if you still felt peckish you could always visit her later."

"I do feel peckish, come to think of it," Evan said. "D.I. Watkins and I grabbed a meat pie and a pint earlier, but the pie tasted like cardboard."

"I can warm up some of the risotto," Bronwen said. She got up and headed for the kitchen. "So, I'm dying to hear about the piece of music. Did they think it was some kind of clue or threat?"

"We're definitely taking it seriously," Evan said. "There were no fingerprints on the paper. To my mind, that must tie it in with the bunker. Most of the items there had been wiped clean, and the only good prints came from a stockboy at the supermarket."

"The same person, eh?" Bronwen lit the gas and spooned rice into a saucepan. "Why do you think he contacted you particularly?"

"Perhaps he thinks I'm the not too bright one on the team, so he'd rather deal with me."

"Or the other way around. He's read about some of the cases you've solved in the paper and he thinks you are the one worthy of matching wits with him."

"Oh come on, Bron." Evan looked embarrassed.

"No, I mean it." Bronwen looked up from stirring rice. "You've had some publicity about some of the cases you've solved. Why else would he send you clues if he didn't want to match wits with you?"

"It's strange, isn't it? If he's managed to spirit away a girl with no trace, you think he'd be glad to get away with it, not draw attention to himself and risk getting caught."

"They do say criminal types often have big egos, don't they?" Bronwen said. "Perhaps he can't bear the fact that the police seem to have made no progress. He's giving you a little help."

"And if he's the type who clearly enjoys taking risks, which he must do by constructing that bunker almost under the noses of everybody who hikes on the mountain, he might get his kicks from being one jump ahead of the police. Leading us by the nose only to show how clever he is."

Bronwen nodded. "Which presupposes he still has the girl alive, do you think?"

Evan considered this. "There would be no point in leading us on if the girl was already dead. He wants us to come and find her. And if we get too close, then he'll dispose of her." Evan took a deep breath. "God, I feel so angry about this, Bronwen. Watkins feels the same—that we should be doing more, but we aren't sure what to do."

"Can't they extract DNA from evidence these days?"

"They can. The lab tech said they can extract DNA from the saliva if he licked the stamp, but if the bloke's DNA isn't on file anywhere, then how do you match it?"

"Of course." Bronwen stopped stirring and looked up. "And what about that music on the radio yesterday? Do you think it's the same person sending you another message?"

"I suspect it has to be. Two musical clues in two days is more than coincidence, isn't it? And why ask for some classical piece to be played for us? I'm not known for my love of classical music."

"Neither am I, really," Bronwen said. "I like some of it, but I wouldn't call myself a music buff."

"I'm going round to the radio station in the morning to see if they have the request letter on file there, or if it was called in, the number it was called from. What was the piece again? It didn't mean anything to me so I couldn't remember when Watkins asked me. A shipwreck, wasn't it?"

"It was from Rimsky-Korsakov's *Sheherazade* symphonic suite. I've heard it before but it's not anything I know terribly well. I wonder if the title is important? He must have chosen it for a reason."

"What does 'Sheherazade' mean? What's it about?"

"It's Tales from the Arabian Nights."

"Weren't they all tall tales about giant birds and genies in bottles?"

"That kind of thing."

Evan shook his head. "Well, I can't see a connection there—unless we're dealing with an Arab. What about the shipwreck part? Could he be holding the girl on a boat? There are some old wrecks around the shoreline here. I suppose we'd better take a look at them in the morning."

Bronwen put a plate of food in front of Evan. "It seems to me the most obvious clue you've got is that Deb and Dad are dead. Known facts."

"We're working on that. So far I've only been able to come up with one missing girl called Debbie, and she was a fifteen-year-old who vanished hitchhiking on her way home from the pictures in Birmingham. She seems to be a possible runaway. It doesn't seem a likely tie-in."

"No, it doesn't," Bronwen said. "If we believe the music, then the father and Deb were punished because they did something to displease the music writer. I wonder, whose dad? His own?"

"No way of finding that out," Evan said. "We can't look into the sons of every older man killed in the past twenty years."

Bronwen watched him eat. "He expects you to solve it, Evan," she said. "Otherwise he'd never have sent you the clue. It must be solvable. Somewhere around Britain there must be a missing Deborah, unless, of course, he means the other kind of deb—you know, a debutante."

Evan looked up from his food. "A debutante? I thought they stopped doing that years ago, didn't they? When was the last time girls were presented at court? Before I was born, I think."

"I know they're not officially presented anymore, but there are still upper-class girls who have a season and who meet the queen at a royal garden party, so I suppose you could still call them debs. I went to school with a couple of girls like that, so I know they still exist. The Honorable Amanda Fanshaw-Everingham was one."

"You're making that name up." Evan laughed.

"I'm not. She was definitely a real person. And God, was she thick. Penny Mowbray was the other one who moved in royal circles and had a coming-out ball. Awfully well connected. Her father played polo with Prince Charles and her elder sister was dating a minor royal. But she was fun. One of my best friends, in fact." Bronwen grinned at the memory. "She almost got me expelled."

"Doing what?" Evan was intrigued. He knew almost nothing of that stage of Bronwen's life. He knew she'd been to a girls' boarding school while her parents were abroad, but he hadn't realized it was the kind of exclusive school where the girls dated minor royals.

Bronwen was still smiling. "When we were in the sixth form we borrowed the games mistress's car to go and meet some boys from the nearby boys' school. Penny assured me that she'd learned to drive, you see, and that we could borrow the car and nobody would ever catch us. Only she didn't confide until too late that she'd only driven on a disused airfield. She wasn't used to traffic and she'd never driven in the dark. We didn't dare turn on the headlights in case someone noticed us. We actually knocked some poor man off his bike and the police were called. There was an awful fuss."

"I'm sure there would have been."

"Luckily, it wasn't too bad. The chap wasn't badly hurt and his motorbike wasn't damaged and Penny's family was so influential that the school didn't want to lose her, so they let us both stay. But we were terrified for a while. It taught me a lesson. Not Penny, though. She just thought it was a lark."

"Have you stayed in touch? You could invite her to the wedding."

Bronwen shook her head. "You tend to lose touch with schoolfriends when you go to university. And now I've lost touch with most of the uni crowd too."

Evan reached out and took her hand. "Bronwen, I don't want you to feel that you're cut off in a backwater, you know. If you want to go and visit friends, or have friends to stay here—it's fine with me. If there are people you want to have to the wedding . . ."

She leaned over and planted a kiss on his forehead. "You're very sweet, you know," she said. "But strangely enough I'm perfectly content with where I am and who I am. When will you get that into your head?"

Evan gave her a long hard look before he went back to his food.

"But now we're speaking of weddings," Bronwen said cautiously, "now I have you trapped—I would like to find out when you might possibly be free."

"Bron, I leave the choosing of brass bedsteads in your capable hands," Evan said.

"It's not just that, Evan—although I am going into town tomorrow to see if my wonderful antiques dealer has come through on his promise. My parents will be arriving in a couple of days and there are still so many things up in the air. How many people have you invited from the village, for example? Have you just issued a general invitation? How many are likely to show up? I need to know because Mummy would be furious if so many locals showed up that her friends and relatives didn't get enough to eat and drink. And we still haven't told the caterer exactly what we want in the way of food and drink. I know we discussed a possible menu, but . . ."

"Whatever you think is best," Evan said.

"Evan, that's not good enough. It's your wedding too." She stood over him, arms folded defiantly.

"Bronwen, you knew when you agreed to marry me that I'm a policeman, and when I'm on a case, that case has to come first. I don't know when I'll get a day off. Maybe not until the wedding. I'm sorry, but that's just the way it is."

"But at least you can take the time to discuss things with me." Bronwen still sounded aggrieved. "The caterer has to know our menu very soon."

He reached out and drew her to him. "Bron, listen. I know nothing about the kind of food and drink your parents like. You've met my mother. If she was catering the wedding, it would be dainty sandwiches with the crusts cut off, Welsh cakes and wedding cake, and tea. She might allow one glass of champagne each for the toast."

"Which reminds me," Bronwen added. "Your mother did mention that Mrs. Williams was very put out that she hadn't been invited to do the eats. Apparently she always does the eats for local weddings. It's a tradition."

"Oh dear." Evan looked up, half smiling. "You know she really does cook well, and she was very good to me when I first came here."

"Good to you? She tried to fatten you up like a prize turkey—and marry you off to her awful granddaughter."

Evan laughed. "She was good to me, Bron, and I don't like to upset her. Don't you think we could ask her to make some of her fabulous cakes?"

"I suppose we could," Bronwen said.

"And so that we don't tread on any more local toes, why don't we buy a whole lamb from Evans-the-Meat? I'm sure the caterer can arrange for a barbecue spit."

Bronwen's face lit up. "Perfect. See I knew I only had to discuss it with you. We'll order assorted hors d'oeuvres, salads to go with the lamb, and the wedding cake, accompanied by various small delicacies baked by Mrs. Williams. That should satisfy everyone."

"See how easy that was. I knew there was no reason to get in a tizzy about something as simple as a wedding."

Bronwen smiled. "I suppose I'm pushing my luck if I want answers on the music to be played at the ceremony?"

"So long as it's not the Shipwreck from *Sheherazade*," Evans said, "or music that spells out anything, I don't care."

Chapter 13

He sat at his computer and called up Finale, his music composition program. His fingers, poised above the keyboard, trembled in anticipation. He knew exactly what the notes were going to spell out this time and he almost salivated in anticipation. But he mustn't rush things. Give them time—time to search and to fail. And then—then he'd strike. Everything was prepared. Even though the secret room on the mountain had been discovered, he really had to congratulate himself how quickly and smoothly he had made alternative arrangements. More convenient really. And definitely more of a challenge. He loved challenges. But he must stay calm and not be too eager. There would only be one opportunity. He couldn't risk making a mistake.

Evan had risen with the sun, his head buzzing with things that had to be done that day. The moment he'd discovered the musical clue, everything changed. Until then he'd half believed that Shannon Parkinson had met with an unfortunate accident on the mountain and her body would be discovered in a disused mine shaft or deep in the lake. Now he was sure that all the pieces belonged together. The man who left no fingerprints in the bunker was the same man who had sent the strange musical threat. They were dealing with the kind of twisted mind that enjoyed playing games and staying one step ahead of the police. This kind of thing was completely outside Evan's sphere of experience and he felt cold chills every time he remembered that he had been singled out as the recipient of the letter. Why had the man chosen him? There had to be a good reason. Was he the one charged with finding the girl before it was too late?

He made himself a cup of tea, then scrambled into his clothes and drove down the hill. He passed Mrs. Williams's house just in time to see his former landlady bringing in the milk bottles. She waved and called out to him. He waved back. At least he'd been spared breakfast with his mother.

A half hour's drive brought him to the seaside resort of Llandudno, favored by genteel English holidaymakers in the eighteen hundreds. The bygone elegance still lingered in the design of the long promenade and some of the faded seafront hotels. Evan drove past the main shopping center and located the radio station by its transmission tower. He went inside to find a hive of activity. Bore Da North Wales started at seven o'clock and it was seven-ten when Evan walked in.

"Are you our talk show guest?" the receptionist asked as he stood looking around at the bright mural on the reception area walls. It was a stylized rendition of Llandudno with the Snowdon range behind it.

Evan told her his business and was soon shaking hands with Dewi Lewis while the Beatles strummed their way through "I Want to Hold Your Hand."

"Constable Evan Evans?" the small, sprightly man said. He had been a well-known former comedian in his younger days and retained his stage presence and his chirpily bright voice. "I remember playing the request a couple of days ago. Getting married, eh? Rather you than me, mate. Tried it three times. Ended up a pauper."

Evan explained about the musical clue and the sinister coincidence that a strange piece of music had been requested for him.

"I thought it was an odd choice for a wedding," Dewi Lewis said.

"Something about a shipwreck, wasn't it? Frankly I thought someone was having a good laugh at your expense."

"I hope you'll be able to help us catch him," Evan said. "So what I need to know was how the request came in?"

"We get them all ways. Phoned in, postcards, and of course via e-mail these days. Siannaid, our program coordinator, will be able to help you. Down the hall, to the right. Whoops—Beatles ending, gotta run." He darted back to his seat, put on his headphones, and addressed the mike with a bright smile.

"He wants to hold your hand, Noreen. How about that? I'd keep this one. Most of them want something quite different these days, don't they?"

Evan left him to seek out Siannaid. "We log all requests in a big book," she said. "That way we can check if someone is trying to get on the air all the time, or is bugging someone. See, here's this week's. The one for you came by postcard."

"Do you think you still have it?"

"Probably." She got up, rummaged in a file, then waved it triumphantly. "See, here it is."

Evan took it. It was posted in Bangor. The words on both sides were printed, not written. "Signed, 'A well-wisher.' No name," he said. "I'd like to take this with me. We'll need to test it for fingerprints."

"Be my guest," she said.

"Oh, and Siannaid," Evan hesitated at the doorway. "If you get any more requests for me, or for Inspector Watkins or D.C. Glynis Davies, will you call the Caernarfon police station right away and let us know?"

"Be happy to," she said. "I've always wanted to help solve a crime." She scribbled down the request on a notepad and pinned it to the corkboard behind her.

If only all the public was that keen on helping the police, Evan thought, as he swing the ear in the direction of Colwyn Bay and police headquarters. In the forensics lab he had the postcard tested for fingerprints. The problem this time was too many, as opposed to too few. The postcard would have been sorted, handled by a postman, then by various people at the radio station. Evan knew that he could probably track down the various postal and radio employees to match their fingerprints, but his gut told him this was a waste of time. The sender would have left no fingerprints. He would have taken no chances this time, either.

He glanced at his watch and saw that he'd better put his foot down if he wanted to make it back to Caernarfon for the eight o'clock briefing.

As Evan came into the room on the dot of eight, he was startled to see D.C.I. Hughes standing by the white board like an impatient teacher. Two uniform branch sergeants and Glynis Davies sat staring at him in silence.

"Ah, there you are, Evans," Hughes said in a way that always seemed to imply that Evans had been out somewhere enjoying himself when he should have been working.

"Yes, sir," Evan said. "Did you want to see D.I. Watkins? He should be here any minute." '

"I should hope so." Hughes glanced pointedly at the clock on the wall, "since it's one minute past eight. Standards appear to be getting very lax around here."

"No, sir, but we've all been putting in really long days on this case," Evan said. "D.I. Watkins and I didn't go home until ten last night."

"And yet apparently with precious little to show for your efforts," Hughes said in his clipped, annoying voice. Unlike Watkins, who looked like a policeman caricature in his fawn raincoat and well-scuffed shoes, D.C.I. Hughes, who had recently been promoted to the supervisory rank in Caernarfon, would have been taken for an assistant in an upscale gents' clothing store—always immaculately turned out in dark suit, silk handkerchief in his top pocket, starched shirt, highly polished shoes, a slim line of mustache on his upper lip, dark hair graying in a distinguished way at the sides. Fastidious and annoying, Evan thought, as he watched him brush an imaginary speck from his sleeve. He had a way of speaking that always managed to be condescending and hinted that every other member of the force was a bumbling idiot. Since he had little talent for detective work, the feeling was reciprocated.

"Sorry I'm late, everyone," Watkins breezed into the room, then froze when he saw the D.C.I. standing at the front. "Oh, good morning, sir. I didn't expect to see you. Thanks for your help on procuring the profiler. I'm sure he's going to prove most helpful. We expect his report today."

"Take a seat please, Watkins." D.C.I. Hughes motioned to a chair in the front row. "I have some concerns that need to be addressed about this Shannon Parkinson case."

Watkins sat, giving Evan a swift glance of inquiry. Evan shrugged.

"Last night I received a phone call from the chief constable of Merseyside Police," Hughes said. "It seems that Mrs. Parkinson, Shannon's mother, has become frustrated that we haven't managed to find her daughter. She wants the Liverpool police to ascertain what has been done so far and what should have been done. Their chief constable commented that he knew we were a small force and perhaps we lacked adequate manpower to conduct a full-scale search. He offered to lend us some of his top men to make sure the task is carried out properly."

Hughes paused and looked around the faces that stared blankly at him. "Needless to say, I took this as rather insulting. Under the cloak of an offer to help was the insinuation that we were not up to the job. I told him that he could rest assured that every possible lead was being investigated and that outsiders with no experience in the Welsh mountain terrain would be of little use."

Another dramatic pause. Hughes cracked his knuckles, making Evan wince. "But having said that, I find that I have my own concerns about this case. I am wondering if perhaps too much has been left to officers who are well meaning but definitely lacking in experience." His gaze moved from Evan to Glynis. "We may be too late to remedy any harm done through inexperience. If indeed we do have a sex offender involved and he has managed to slip through our grasp with the girl, then we may no longer be able to save her. But I can't sit by and risk the reputation of the North Wales Police. As of now I am taking personal control of this case."

There was a collective intake of breath. If Hughes noticed it, he didn't betray the fact.

Watkins got to his feet. "With all respect, sir, we have been working exhaustively since the girl disappeared. Other than the fact that we thought we were simply looking for a lost hiker when the first search was conducted, before the bunker was found, I can't think of anything that should have been done differently."

Hughes inclined his head slightly. "With all respect to you, Watkins, I see that inquiries in the field, questioning possible witnesses in Llanberis and at the National Parks Service, were left to a very junior member of your team—one only just out of training and still on probation. This kind of thing requires someone with tact and experience. And you should have called in a profiler the minute the bunker was discovered."

"May I state, sir," Watkins glared at him and Evan noticed his clenched fist, "that I have complete confidence in all members of my team. And may I remind you that you were the one who pointed out to me that we didn't actually have a crime? Maybe we still don't, until divers can give us a negative report from Lake Glaslyn and we have teams to check out every accessible mine shaft on the mountain."

A flicker of annoyance crossed Hughes's face. "I made that remark at a time when I fully expected the girl to be found. We all did. I'm going to take a look at that bunker for myself, as soon as I have given out today's assignments, so that I can make my own assessment of the situation. And I want to see reports on the various lines of inquiry so far—Constable Davies?"

"Yes, sir?" Glynis eyed him with a cool stare.

"I understand that you were given the task of compiling a list of possible sex offenders, those on parole, and local mental patients."

Glynis winced. "I have managed to compile a list of those treated in local psychiatric facilities," she said. "I don't think we call them mental patients these days, sir. Not very PC."

Evan glanced at Glynis's composed, confident expression with admiration and decided that none of the men present would have had the balls to give the D.C.I. a public dressing down in front of the troops. He held his breath for the explosion. Instead, Hughes gave an embarrassed half-cough. "Ah yes, Davies, you're right, of course. Psychiatric patients. Would that be PC enough for you?"

If there was sarcasm in the remark, Glynis didn't seem to notice it. She grinned. "Yes, sir. That would be most appropriate. Would you like to see the list?"

"It's not the list I'm interested in, Constable, it's your deductions from the list. A trained eye can pick out those who warrant further investigation."

"I've already checked on those who would have had the right sort of psychological profile, the means to build a bunker, and the time to be on the mountain that afternoon," Glynis said, "and the results have been negative."

"You've double-checked their alibis for that particular afternoon?"

"Yes, sir."

Hughes waited for further explanation. Hearing none he said, "Right. Good work." Hughes cleared his throat. He hated being one-upped.

"And Evans—you were detailed to investigate possible sightings of the girl, both in Llanberis and among National Parks Service employees? Is that correct?"

"Yes, sir." Evan's flat tone matched Glynis Davies's.

"And yet you turned up nobody who recalled seeing her?"

"If you go to Llanberis you'll find the place teeming with holiday-makers," Evan said. "A large portion of them are young hikers who look just like Shannon Parkinson. The shop and café owners are so overworked that there is no way they'd recall anything unless it was completely out of the ordinary. If a man had come down the mountain with an unconscious girl over his shoulder, then maybe they'd have noticed."

Hughes frowned at him. "So you suspect she may still be on the mountain, hidden somewhere?"

"It's hard to say, sir. If she is, she's well hidden. Our dogs didn't manage to sniff her out. But I have reason to think she is still alive."

"Why is that, Constable?"

"Because somebody has been sending me musical clues."

"Musical clues? What musical clues?"

Evan related the facts on the sheet of music and the radio request.

"Why wasn't I informed about these?" Hughes demanded, glaring at Watkins.

"Because I opened the letter yesterday evening after you'd gone home, sir," Evan said. "Then I took it for testing at our forensics lab. It was only when we found no fingerprints on it, apart from mine and my fiancée's, that we knew we must have something relating to our crime scene."

"I see." Hughes was silent, digesting this. "This does put a new complexion on things, doesn't it? The question is, where we go from here?"

"Excuse me, sir," Evan said, glancing across at Watkins, who sat sullen and silent, "but it seems to me that we have something concrete to work with for the first time. We're dealing with someone who wants us to play his game. He wants us to come and find the girl. He's giving us tantalizing hints he wants us to follow up on. We know music is important to him or he'd never have sent musical clues. And we have a name—Deb. Deb somebody has been killed because our man thought she deserved to die."

Evan was conscious of the complete silence in the room.

"Then the first thing to do is to conduct a search on the national crime databases," Hughes said. "Find out if any girls called Deborah are listed as murdered or missing."

"Already been done, sir," Watkins couldn't resist saying. "We only have one name and she doesn't seem to fit the bill. A fifteen-year-old in Birmingham accepted a lift in a strange car and hasn't been seen since. She'd had a drug problem and fought with her parents, so is being considered a runaway."

"Ah." Hughes fell silent again.

"This need not necessarily be a currently open case, need it?" Glynis asked. "This could be something that happened years ago, that is not on anybody's computer list, but resides in a cold case file in someone's basement."

"Good point, Davies." Hughes actually smiled. Glynis had been his protégée at one stage and apparently he had forgiven her former insubordination. "Can we leave the task of calling individual police forces and digging up cold case files in your capable hands, then?"

"Absolutely, sir."

"And Watkins?"

"Sir?"

"You're very quiet. What are your priorities for this morning?"

"I was rather waiting for you to tell me my duties, sir."

Hughes's face gave a twitch of annoyance. "Good God, no. It's not like that at all. Just because I felt that I should add my expertise to this team doesn't mean that your own roles are in any way diminished. Good Lord, no. We're a team here, people. Partners against crime, right? Every one of us should feel free to speak up, make suggestions and express opinions. So please feel free to speak up, Watkins. I hope I'm not an intimidating personality and you don't only see me as an authority figure."

Evan heard the muttered "pompous twit" escape with Watkins's breath.

"Right, sir. I've got to pick up the profile, which should be ready by midday. I also thought I should double-check with the Birmingham police about their missing girl case."

"I find it hard to believe that nobody saw our missing girl," Hughes said. "Apart from sending Constable Evans out to interview people in Llanberis, what has been done to alert the general public to the girl's disappearance?"

"We put up posters, sir," Watkins said. "And we ran the girl's picture in the local newspapers."

"Presumably that was before we had definitely come to the conclusion that we were dealing with an abduction."

"We still haven't come to that conclusion one hundred percent," Watkins said. "We have a missing girl, we've found a bunker, unused, and Constable Evans has received a couple of weird musical messages. But are they all linked or just strange coincidences of timing?"

"I think we have to assume that they are linked, until we find otherwise, don't we?" Hughes said, looking around at the group for general assent. "We have to go forward as if a girl's life is at stake and every second counts. We need more media, Watkins. Get the girl's picture on the television tonight. Suggest that she may have been in the company of an older man."

"We don't know that he's necessarily older," Evan ventured.

"Evans, the girl is seventeen years old. If she was abducted by a seventeen-year-old boy, he certainly wouldn't have gone to all this trouble. What teenage boy do you know who would stock a bunker with classical music? No, if it had been a boy her age, he would have raped her, bashed her over the head, and dumped her down the nearest mine shaft."

Evan couldn't disagree with this assessment. He nodded. "But the words 'older man' make me think of someone"—he was about to say "your age" but stifled it just in time—"someone maybe fifty or more. This bloke doesn't need to be that old."

"Older than she is, Evans. Let's not split hairs." Again the twitch of annoyance on Hughes's face.

"Ted Bundy wasn't an older man. He was young and good-looking," Watkins commented, probably wanting to back up Evan against Hughes.

Hughes looked startled. "We're talking serial killer now, are we? What makes you jump to that conclusion?"

"The musical clues do say that Deb and Dad are dead," Evan said. "That's two to start with."

"I wasn't suggesting we're looking for a serial killer necessarily," Watkins said. "Just that criminals don't always look the part."

"Quite so." Hughes agreed. "But you've brought up an interesting point, Watkins. Has the modus operandi been checked? Have we been in touch with the National Criminal Intelligence Service to find out if they have any similar abductions on the books? This man may have tried it before and enjoyed it enough to want to repeat it."

Evan glanced up at the apparently nonchalant way Hughes said this. It's a girl's life we're talking about, he wanted to shout.

"I did contact them, sir," Glynis said. "They could come up with plenty of abductions, but no bunkers dug underground."

"It need not have been underground last time," Watkins pointed out. "He could have tried a shed or a garage or an abandoned building before and found that was too risky. Or perhaps his fantasies are getting wilder and he liked the extra element of being trapped underground."

"Quite possibly," Hughes said. "I think I'd better get onto NCIS myself right after I've seen the bunker, just to make sure we don't overlook anything this time."

Evan and Glynis exchanged looks.

"And I think we should send some boys in blue out to requestion people in the Llanberis area." He held up his hand as Evan half rose from his seat in protest. "Someone may have noticed a young girl in the company of an older man, especially if she was being coerced into going with him."

"If she was still alive and had her wits about her, I don't see how she could have been coerced," Evan said. "She could hardly have walked down the mountain with a gun in her back."

"So how do you propose finding her, Constable?" Hughes demanded.

Evan flushed. "I think we should follow up on the musical angle. Talk to any local music societies, choirs, and maybe see if we can locate the shop where the CD player and the classical CDs were purchased. If by any chance our man bought that whole stack at once, someone might have remembered."

"The music angle. Yes, that's worth pursuing. In fact, why don't you do that this morning, after you've shown me the bunker."

Evan's face fell. A morning in the company of D.C.I. Hughes was not what he would have chosen. He was itching to follow up on his own leads—the music shops, the societies and choirs. And Roger

Thomas of the National Parks who sang in a choir should have his alibi for last Tuesday double-checked. Then there was Rhodri Llewelyn, whom he had been told to ignore, but couldn't.

"Very good, sir," he said in a resigned voice. "Would you like to go right away?"

They set off in silence. Evan was conscious of D.C.I. Hughes sitting beside him. Even his breathing managed to sound critical. Evan felt annoyed with himself that Hughes always managed to put him on the defensive.

"So tell me, Evans," Hughes said after a long silence. "I'm curious. Why do you think that the bugger chose you to send the musical messages to?"

"I've been asking myself the same thing," Evan said cautiously. He didn't repeat Bronwen's suggestion that he was the brightest of them. "I was wondering if it's because I was born in this area and know it better than anyone else. I'm a local. I speak Welsh."

"Then why wasn't the musical message in Welsh?" Hughes demanded.

"You're not a Welsh speaker yourself, are you, sir?" Evan asked.

"I manage fairly well. I've taken courses."

"You try writing anything in Welsh using only the first eight letters of the alphabet," Evan said.

"Point taken," Hughes said. "So you think he's singling you out because you should know something that happened locally, or you might even know him?"

"It's the only reason I can think of."

"And you can't come up with any suspects?"

"No, sir."

"It's certainly very strange," Hughes said. "This whole case is the strangest thing I've ever encountered in my years on the force. It's almost as if someone has thrust us into a script and is expecting us to play our parts."

Evan looked at Hughes with surprise and respect. Hughes had hit the nail on the head. That's exactly how he had been feeling about the whole thing.

"Do you reckon it might be a setup, sir? That someone is having a good laugh at our expense over this? A group of students trying to fool the police by dropping a series of weird and wonderful clues?"

"It did cross my mind, Evans. Maybe we are being made fools of. When we've run ourselves ragged, they'll come forward and let us know that they've been filming the whole thing, like *Candid Camera*. I don't know." He let out a long sigh.

"Except that Shannon Parkinson really has disappeared," Evan said.

"Except for that," Hughes agreed.

"So we have to keep plugging along until we find her, don't we?" Evan asked.

"Yes, we have to do everything we can to find her."

For once Evan felt a spark of camaraderie between them.

"This place is chaos," Hughes grumbled as they drove through Llanberis, looking for a parking space. "What's the matter with all these people? Why can't they go abroad on holiday like everyone else?"

"I think they're mostly from abroad," Evan replied with a grin.

"Bloody nuisance," Hughes muttered. "Park there. In the handicapped zone. We won't be long."

Evan turned into the handicapped space, glad that he was in an official police vehicle for once and glad that the suggestion to take up a handicapped space had been from Hughes. He retrieved the aluminum stepladder he had brought for the task and led the way past the line waiting for the Snowdon Railway, past the little train itself, puffing as it disgorged its passengers onto the platform. They joined a steady stream of hikers setting off on the Llanberis path up the mountain. Some of them were well equipped, with sturdy boots, sticks, water flasks, and backpacks. Among them were also some families with little children in shorts and sandals, even one young mother in a halter top and flip-flops. How on earth far did they think they would get? Evan wondered. And if the weather changed, drenching them in freezing rain, what did they intend to do then?

They hadn't gone far when Evan noticed Hughes breathing heavily. He also noticed the polished Italian shoes were now covered with the dust of the trail. Hughes was definitely not an outdoorsman. Evan wondered what he was good for—certainly not people skills. Didn't speak good Welsh, didn't do well in the outdoors . . . How did someone rise to the rank of D.C.I. with apparently so little going for him? he asked himself. Another case of the useless being bumped upstairs.

The stand of woodland appeared, nestled into a curve of the mountain's flank over to the left of the path. "This way, sir." Evan struck out across the rough terrain. The whole area was still taped off with white police tape.

"Didn't anyone station an officer on watch up here?" Hughes asked.

"I believe they did to start with," Evan said. "I suppose they've finished taking forensic evidence from the site. I suggested they put a surveillance camera up here, but I don't know if anything was being done about that."

"Expensive and apt to get vandalized," Hughes said, so Evan had a pretty good idea who had shot down that suggestion.

They ducked under the tape and followed the trail of trampled grass and bracken to the site of the bunker. Evan hadn't been there since the first evening and for a moment he couldn't recognize where the bunker was located. Then he saw that an attempt had been made to disguise the site. The sods that concealed the trap door had been put back in place and a blackberry bush trailed across it. Evan lifted back the brambles and removed the sods that had concealed the wooden trap door.

"Well disguised, I must say," Hughes said. "Presumably the profiler was brought up here?"

"Definitely." Evan swung the trap door open with some difficulty. Cold, stale air came up to meet him, accompanied by the sense of dread he had felt the last time he was here.

As Hughes said nothing, Evan lowered the ladder, then climbed down onto it.

"Mind how you go, sir," he couldn't resist saying as Hughes's foot appeared above him. Hughes climbed down with surprising agility, pausing to dust off his jacket at the bottom.

"Now, let's take a look at what we've got here, shall we?" Hughes took the flashlight from Evan and shone it around the walls. "Rather well done," he commented. "Quite cozy, in fact."

"Take a look on the wall up there, sir," Evan said. "You won't find that cozy."

The flashlight arced up to the area Evan had indicated. Evan stared, then grabbed the flashlight without asking. He shone it on the other walls, then back to the first spot he had indicated.

The handcuffs were missing.

Chapter 14

"They can't have gone!" Watkins reacted with an expletive when Evan called him on his mobile at D.C.I. Hughes's instruction. "Was there evidence they'd been torn from the wall? Vandals, do you think?"

"There was no sign that they had ever been there," Evan replied. "If I hadn't seen them myself, I wouldn't have believed they existed."

"So someone took the trouble to take them down carefully," Watkins said. "Either it was a thrill-seeker, or our man is one cool customer."

"He's one cool customer," Evan agreed.

Hughes made impatient fluttering gestures that Evan should hand over the phone to him.

"Hughes here, Watkins. They were there when you brought the profiler yesterday?"

"Of course they were. I pointed them out to him."

"And nobody's been there since?"

"None of our blokes," Watkins said. "Forensics had already finished their sweep of the place, so we didn't leave a guard posted on the site, just taped off the whole area. So theoretically anyone could have found it. Had they broken the police tape across the top of the bunker?"

Hughes repeated the question for Evan.

"There was no tape," he said.

"Then someone removed the tape."

"Watkins, arrange for forensics to send someone up here right away, to check for fresh fingerprints," Hughes barked into the phone.

Evan thought this would be a waste of everyone's time. A man who had been so meticulously careful about fingerprints so far, who had been so daring as to remove handcuffs from under the noses of the police, would not have made so easy a mistake at this juncture. The big question was where he had now taken the handcuffs and whether they were being put to use.

As they arrived back at the police station car park, Evan saw a young man running toward him. It was Paul Upwood.

"Constable Evans. I'm so glad you've shown up."

"You don't have any news on Shannon, do you?" Evan asked.

"I was going to ask you the same thing," Paul replied. "I left the youth hostel yesterday. I couldn't stand being cooped up there, and people giving me strange looks as if I had something to do with it. Well, I did, didn't I? I mean, if I'd taken care of her the way I promised her mum, she'd still be safe."

Evan couldn't deny this last statement. "So where are you staying now?"

"I checked into a B&B near Bangor Station last night," Paul said, "but I really don't know what I should do next. If I can still be of help here, I'll stay, of course, but I'm due back at work on Monday. I've got a summer internship and I don't want to blow that. So do you think it's all right for me to go?"

"We know where to contact you, don't we?" Evan said. "And as you say, you're not doing any good by sticking around here, worrying."

Relief flooded across Paul's face. "Thank you. I can't wait to get home to familiar surroundings. This whole thing is like living a nightmare." He paused and reconsidered. "Of course, if I go home, I'll have to face Shannon's family, and that will be pretty nightmarish too. But at least I'll be home, with my own things."

"Just one thing," Evan said. "Did you and Shannon ever meet an older man at any time you were here?"

"An older man?" Paul frowned. "What kind of older man?"

"I wish we knew," Evan said. "There is some hint that maybe Shannon may have been abducted."

"Oh no." Paul stood there, his mouth gaping open.

"So you don't recall any encounter with an older man?"

Paul screwed up his eyes. "Just in passing, like? You meet people on the trail when you're hiking, don't you? You say a few words and then you forget about it. Now you mention it, I do remember saying hello to several older men. There was one nice old bloke with lots of white hair. He told us he was seventy-four and he still walked five miles every day of his life. He came from the Potteries—Stoke-on-Trent, I think he said. And then there was another man, not so old. Middle-aged, I suppose you'd call him. The type that looks very fit—army type, you know. Short hair, jersey and cords, big boots. Shannon was sitting on a rock and she'd taken off her boots because her feet hurt her. This bloke stopped and said she'd wreck her feet if she didn't get better boots."

"Anyone else?" Evan asked.

Paul screwed up his face in concentration. "There was an older Frenchman at the hostel. He didn't speak much English and Shannon's taking A-level French so she translated for him. He seemed very pleasant." He paused, then sighed. "I can't think of anyone else."

"You have my phone number, don't you?" Evan said. "Call me if you remember any other encounters at all. It could be something quite harmless like sitting next to someone in an ice cream parlor. Any time you noticed an older man looking at Shannon."

"We didn't go to ice cream parlors," Paul said. "We were here on a strict budget. We're both students, you see. We had breakfast at the hostel, packed sandwiches for lunch, and brought along those dried packets of curry for our dinners. Look, can I go now? If I hurry, I can catch the twelve-thirty train from Bangor."

Evan put a big hand on Paul's shoulder. "All right, Paul. Off you go. We'll keep in touch."

"Thanks." He chewed at his lip. "Thanks for trying, Constable Evans. Do you think there's any chance we'll still find her—alive, I mean?"

"There's still a chance. Say your prayers."

"I'm not what you'd call religious," Paul said.

"Say them anyway. It can't hurt."

Paul nodded. "You won't give up on her, will you?"

"Oh, we never do that."

"Right." Paul stuck his hands into his jacket pockets. "I'll be off then."

Evan watched him walk away. Should he have run this decision past Inspector Watkins? Was there any more information to be gleaned from Paul Upwood's subconscious? And was it just coincidence that one of the older men Paul described resembled the National Parks ranger Eddie Richards?

Another visit to the National Parks Headquarters was definitely in order.

Evan was about to follow D.C.I. Hughes into the building, but then decided to seize the chance to take off on his own. After all, he had been given permission to check out links to a musical background. And if there was time, then Rhodri Llewelyn's wary gaze was still nagging at him.

A visit to the local library gave him the addresses of the various choirs and music societies in the area. He called the contact number for each of them and asked them to fax a list of members with names, ages, and addresses, and whether married or single. When this request was met with puzzlement, he went on to explain that the police were trying to track down someone who was sending musical threats. He didn't mention the disappearance of the girl.

None of the people he spoke to thought that any of their members would do such a thing. All upright, law-abiding, chapel-going citizens. And most of them female, except for the male voice choirs. Old Mr. Herbert was unmarried, but he was also a deacon at his church. Mr. Phibbs was unmarried, so to speak, but he did share a house with Mr. Nesbit.

Evan was left with no good leads and a feeling that he hadn't expected any. He didn't need a profiler to tell him that this man was a loner. A tour of record shops in the area brought only blank stares and Evan realized quickly that to the young people serving behind the counter, he counted as old. How would they be expected to remember an older man who came in to buy classical CDs, or a CD player? He would have been dismissed as boring and not worth their attention.

Evan did ascertain from the manager of Virgin Records in Bangor that their computerized inventory system would show which items were sold on a particular day. But if the man paid cash and nobody remembered him, there was little use in pursuing this line of inquiry.

Of course he hadn't expected any major breakthrough. Anyone who was careful not to leave fingerprints would have been equally careful to pay cash and not draw attention to himself. Evan suspected that he wouldn't be the kind of man who drew attention to himself anyway. Inoffensive, quiet, shy—the sort of man who drifts through society unnoticed. Who has to live out life through secret fantasies. There were plenty of those about. But most of them didn't turn those fantasies into reality.

He was anxious to see the profiler's report and was heading back when he noticed Lloyds Bank on his right. Before he knew what he was doing, he had swung off the road and parked outside. As he pushed open the glass door, he suddenly realized he had no idea what he was going to say to Rhodri Llewelyn and that he might well scare him off if he didn't tread carefully. He stepped away from the door, and held it open to let two elderly ladies totter in side by side.

When he finally went in, he saw the line waiting patiently at the one open window. Hillary Jones was working there. Rhodri Llewellyn's window beside her was unoccupied. He was about to leave when the back door opened and Mr. Shorecross came out. He saw Evan, looked momentarily surprised, then smiled as Evan came over to him.

"Back again, Mr. Evans? Can I do something for you today? More loans for antique furniture?" He smiled.

"I just wanted a word with your employee Rhodri Llewelyn," Evan said. "But I see he's not here."

"No, he's taking a few days off this week. Summer holiday." A frown crossed Shorecross's face. "Most inconvenient. I told him so. As you can see, we can't operate efficiently with one teller, and our third person is out on maternity leave until September. It's so hard to find good employees these days. If they are young and female they get married, if they are married they have babies, and if they are like Rhodri Llewelyn, they have no loyalty to their employers. Not like when I was growing up. My father was a bank manager too, you know. It was a respected position in those days. Looked up to. Front pew in church. Now it doesn't mean a thing anymore. A glorified shop assistant, that's what it's come down to."

Evan gave a sympathetic nod. "So could you give me Llewelyn's home address?"

"May I ask what this is about?"

"Nothing to do with the bank, sir. We're still attempting to tie in Miss Jones's prowler with the case of this missing girl."

"Still no sign of her? Dear me, that's bad. You can't really think that Miss Jones's Peeping Tom may have abducted this girl?"

"Probably not," Evan agreed. "We have very little to go on, but we have to follow up on any leads at this stage."

Shorecross leaned closer to Evan. "Surely you don't suspect our Mr. Llewelyn? He's an odd sort of fellow, I grant you that, but I don't think he'd hurt a fly. He's painfully shy around girls. Between you and me, I think he has a soft spot for Miss Jones and he was quite angry when she told us about the Peeping Tom. I think he volunteered to stand guard outside her house."

"She didn't take him up on the offer?"

"She didn't want to encourage him." Neville Shorecross smiled.

"But by all means, question him if you must. I'll write down his address for you."

He printed the name and address neatly on the back of a deposit slip. "There, that should do it. Although I don't think you'll find him home this week. He's off somewhere, leaving us in the lurch. And if he thinks I'll be recommending him for promotion when the assistant manager's job opens up in Conwy, he can think again."

Evan climbed back into his car. He wouldn't want to be Rhodri Llewelyn when he returned! Even though he had been warned that Rhodri was away for the week, Evan was curious to see where he lived. It turned out to be not too far from Hillary Jones—within walking distance, in fact. A plain grimy row house like all the others in a street that backed onto the railway line. The door knocker was well polished, however, and the front step was scrubbed to Mrs. Williams's standard. Evan knocked and the door was opened an inch or so as a suspicious face looked out.

"I'm looking for Rhodri Llewelyn," Evan said. "I'm D.C. Evans, North Wales Police."

The portion of the face that Evan could see through the crack in the door looked horrified. "Police? He's not done anything wrong, has he?"

"This is just a routine inquiry, madam."

The door opened wider and an old woman wearing a pinny over her clothes grabbed Evan by the arm and almost yanked him inside. "You'd better come inside before the neighbors see you," she said.

Evan found himself in a dark, narrow front hall with brown wallpaper. The smell of pine cleaner and furniture polish was so overwhelming that he had to fight back the urge to sneeze.

"Are you his mother?" Evan asked cautiously, because she could equally have been his grandmother.

"That's right. Rhodri's my boy. And a good boy, too. You'd better come in the kitchen."

She led Evan down the hall and into a small kitchen, almost filled with a well-scrubbed pine table and a Welsh dresser along one wall. Bronwen would have her eye on that, Evan thought.

"Sit down. Cup of tea?" She motioned to a chair at the table. Evan squeezed himself in and sat.

"Thanks. *Diolch yn fawr*." He threw out the Welsh, always a sign in Wales that the other person has the chance to continue in either tongue.

"I don't speak Welsh," she said as she got a cup and saucer down from the dresser. "I met Rhodri's father when he was working in London. I came back here with him. Biggest mistake I ever made."

"You don't like Wales, then?"

"Hate it. Unfriendly people. Awful weather."

"So why do you stay?"

"That's a stupid question. I stay because I'm stuck here. He won't leave. Neither him or my boy. They like it here. They like being Welsh."

"What does your husband do, Mrs. Llewelyn?"

"As little as possible," she said, and put the tea down in front of Evan with such a thump that some slopped into the saucer. "He works at the post office, that's what he does. Sorting letters. Then he comes home, flops in his chair, and watches the telly. What kind of life is that? I ask you. A wasted life. That's why I've got such high hopes for our Rhodri. He's a lovely boy, Mr. Evans. Always been so good to me, never a day's trouble. Routine inquiries, you say? Nothing my boy's done wrong?"

"I just need to talk to him, Mrs. Llewelyn. Could you tell me where I can find him?"

"He's away. He packed up his rucksack and he's gone off walking. I don't know where. Could be anywhere in Wales. That's what he likes doing when he can get away—setting off with his rucksack and walking. Doesn't seem like much of a holiday to me. Why don't you go abroad this year? I asked him. You make decent money at the bank. Why don't you take one of those package holidays to Spain? You might meet a nice girl there. But no, he likes Wales, he likes walking and he likes being alone."

"He doesn't have a girlfriend?" Evan asked.

"Not at the moment. He's had his eye on a couple of girls, but neither of them were suitable. There are so few nice girls around these days. Little tramps, most of them. Rhodri's so sensitive. I wouldn't want him to be hurt." The implication was obvious—it was Mother's standards they hadn't lived up to, not Rhodri's.

"Does he like music?" Evan asked casually.

Her fact lit up. "Music? He loves music. He's always been very musical. Well, the Welsh are, aren't they? He plays the piano so nicely and recently he's taken up all kinds of strange instruments—dulcimers and zithers and heaven knows what. I can't say I like that kind of music myself, but he seems to enjoy it. I'm only glad he's got interests outside his work so he won't turn out like his good-for-nothing father. Finished your tea?" She took the cup without waiting for his answer, washed and dried it, and hung it back in its place.

Evan got to his feet. "Thanks for the tea, Mrs. Llewelyn. When do you expect Rhodri back?"

"Sunday evening, ready to go back to work on Monday."

"And you don't know where I can find him until then?"

"No idea. He'll send his mum a postcard, I expect, but the way the post office is these days, I won't get it until after he's back. What can you expect with lazy louts like my husband sorting the letters?"

She led Evan back along the hallway. Through the open sitting room door Evan glimpsed a highly polished upright piano, the top almost covered in china dogs, photos, and various other ornaments. No wonder Rhodri needed to get away for a few days, Evan thought.

Chapter 15

Evan put his foot down and drove as fast as the traffic would allow. Surely Watkins could no longer deny his hunch about Rhodri Llewelyn. A loner with a dominating mother, shy around girls, a music lover who was at home tramping the hills—what more could they want, for God's sake? Was the holiday leave taken at the last minute like this because he had the girl hidden away somewhere?

A car pulling a large caravan swung out into the traffic from an adjacent field, causing Evan to brake hard and slowing everything to a snail's pace. Good God, but these holidaymakers were clueless! For a second he wished he were a traffic cop. He gripped the wheel, fuming with impatience, but there was no chance to overtake until he turned off at the roundabout and into the police station car park. He hurried into the building and was about to enter D.I. Watkins's office when Glynis Davies's head came around the adjacent door.

"No use looking in there. He's not in," she said.

"Where is he?"

"Gone to fetch the profiler. Chief Inspector Hughes decided he wanted to talk to the man in person rather than just read a report."

"Lucky profiler," Evan said. "And where is the great man himself?" He dropped his voice.

Glynis grinned. "Nowhere to be seen for the moment. And I've got a bone to pick with you."

"What have I done?"

"Not kept him away long enough. You could have made that tour of the bunker last at least a couple of hours and given us a chance to get on with our work. As it was, he was back here before I'd even had a chance to get going. He stood breathing down the back of my neck as I searched the various databases. And when I was actually in the process of e-mailing the NCIS, he picked up the phone behind me and was calling them at the same time with exactly the same questions. I felt like an idiot!"

"Sorry," Evan said. "The moment we saw that wall with the handcuffs gone, we came rushing back here."

"And then you conveniently managed to disappear." She frowned at him.

"I did have instructions to follow up on the music issue."

"And you found something? You came down the hall like a man with a purpose."

"I have come up with one lead that may be worthwhile," Evan said. He glanced up and down the empty hallway.

"I was about to pop across the street to that Greek place for a coffee," Glynis said. "Do you want to come with me?"

"Coffee? My stomach feels as if it's lunchtime."

"It is." Glynis glanced at her watch. "Maybe they'll make us a gyro to go. Quick, before the big guns return and catch us."

They made for the front door and had crossed the street before Glynis asked, "So what did you find out?"

"You remember the girl at the bank and the Peeping Tom incident?"

Glynis nodded. "And you were suspicious of the young man who worked with her at the bank?"

"He was distinctly uncomfortable, all the time I was there. Why would anyone feel uneasy in the presence of a policeman, unless they've got something to hide?"

"But I thought he'd been checked out and cleared of the Peeping Tom incidents?"

"The report says so, but I went to have a word with him on my way back and I find that he's taken time off from work. So I went to visit his home and he lives with a very domineering mother and he likes music and walking in the hills by himself."

"Sounds like the type, all right," Glynis said, "but I imagine that description fits a lot of young men who are perfectly harmless. You should go and talk to the officer who checked him out last time—in Bangor, was it?"

Evan nodded. "That's right. D.I. Jenkins, I believe. Do you know him?"

"I've met him. Not the brightest button in the box, I would say. But I expect he'd do a thorough job. So did you turn up anything else, during your music search?"

"Nothing. Frankly I didn't expect to." Evan pushed open the café door and held it as she passed through. For once she let him do so without comment. "We're dealing with a meticulous loner. He probably had all this planned out in minute detail."

They ordered their coffees and gyros and once they were outside again, Glynis asked in a low voice, "What do you make of the handcuffs vanishing like that?"

"That's pretty alarming, wouldn't you say?"

Glynis shrugged. "He may just be showing us that he can come and go as he pleases under our noses. In fact, I rather think that whoever is doing this is enjoying baiting us. It's his idea of sport."

"So what about you? Did you get anywhere this morning with Hughes breathing down your neck?" Evan asked.

"Not really. We looked into a couple of abductions, but they didn't seem to have much in common with this one. And Inspector Watkins talked to the Birmingham police about the girl called Debbie who disappeared. They have an idea who might have been involved from the description of a van, but they haven't been able to pin anything on him."

They stood together outside the front door, sipping their coffees.

"That's what's so strange about this case," Evan said. "Usually somebody sees something. In Birmingham they spotted a van. This time we're on a well-trafficked mountain and nobody sees a thing."

"I know. It's so frustrating."

"Perhaps we'll find out more when Rhodri Llewelyn comes back on Sunday," Evan said.

Glynis looked up at him, squinting in bright sunlight. "I hope you haven't jumped to a conclusion too quickly and based on too little. Make sure you leave your mind open to other possible suspects, okay?"

"Yes, Mother," Evan said.

Glynis smiled. "And speaking of mothers, how are you surviving with yours here?"

"Luckily I've been away most of the time. It's poor Bronwen who is stuck with her. She keeps trying to take over my kitchen and cook for me, and tells Bron that she's not feeding me properly."

"I expect Bronwen can handle her. She seems like the kind of person who can handle most things."

"She's amazing. She's virtually had this whole wedding dumped on her. We were planning a quiet little ceremony and drinks for a few friends and then her parents jumped into the act and now it's a major production, but Bron seems completely unfazed."

"I hope we get this case solved before the ceremony, or the church may be lacking a bridegroom."

"Don't say that." Evan grimaced. "Bron would kill me."

"Eat your gyro," Glynis said, "I can see a squad car approaching. We'll be back to work in a second."

Evan unwrapped the wax paper and took a big bite of warm pita and spicy lamb.

"I'm glad you suggested grabbing take-out food," he said. "I would have probably settled for a warmed-over sausage roll in the canteen."

"I never eat in there as a matter of principle," Glynis said. "There are certain levels to which one should not be expected to sink."

Evan examined her. She was indeed a most unlikely police detective—well bred, well educated, smooth, elegant, stunning-looking . . .

"What?" she asked. "Do I have food on my face?"

"No, you look just fine." Evan smiled. "I was just wondering whatever made you decide to go into the police force?"

"To annoy my family, mainly." She took another bite of pita bread. "They're rather like Bronwen's folks—county set, manor-house, hunting, all that kind of outdated stuff. My mother was even presented at court, if you can imagine it."

"Interesting you should say that." Evan took the final bite and tossed the crumpled wrapper into a nearby bin. "Bronwen suggested that the Deb in the message could have been a debutante and not somebody called Debbie."

"But there haven't been any debutantes in my lifetime, so it would have had to be a long-ago crime. Which would make our man at least sixty. Do men of sixty-plus go around abducting young girls?"

"I don't see why not," Evan said. "And even if there haven't been any official debutante presentations, girls are still introduced at royal garden parties, aren't they? And some parents still give balls and that kind of thing?"

"I suppose they do," Glynis agreed. "I can't think of anything worse, personally."

"So do you think it would be possible to get a list of that type of girl?"

"Are you giving me more work?" She looked at him with a half-smile.

Evan shrugged. "Just a thought. I'm sure you're right about this man wanting to play games with us. Since he's giving us a clue, he obviously expects we can solve it. We haven't come up with any girls called Deborah who've been abducted or murdered in recent history. Do you think it's possible that we're looking at a really old crime? In which case, why has he been inactive for so long?"

"Perhaps he hasn't, but nobody's caught him. Perhaps he's abducted or killed other girls, only their names don't fit into the first eight letters of the alphabet," Glynis suggested.

They broke off as Inspector Watkins came toward them accompanied by an elderly man with a trim white beard.

"Ah there you are, Evans, Davies," Watkins called out. "Is the D.C.I. back yet?"

"I don't know, sir. We just popped across the street to get a coffee," Glynis said.

"Well, this is Dr. Hirsch, our profiler. The D.C.I. particularly wanted to meet him in person."

Dr. Hirsch inclined his head in an old-fashioned gesture, then stepped through the door that Watkins had opened for him.

"Tell the D.C.I. we're waiting for him in my office, will you?" Watkins called as he went inside.

As Evan and Glynis watched them go, Glynis turned back to him. "I'll see what I can do about the debs," she said. "The Lord Chamberlain must have a list."

"A most interesting profile challenge," Dr. Hirsch said, looking with satisfaction around the little group that had assembled in Watkins's office. Hughes had commandeered the best chair. Watkins perched on the corner of his desk, Sergeant Jones sat on the stackable metal chair, and Evan and Glynis were left to stand by the door. The tension was almost palpable.

"You must understand," he continued, "that I created this document before I was informed of the latest facts, but I think you'll be interested in the conclusions I came to. Right. To proceed." He paused and pushed his spectacles up his nose. "He has presented us with a most interesting scenario in that bunker. In a way it struck me as too perfect—almost as if he was creating a stage set, designed to elicit certain responses."

Evan looked at him with interest and nodded. He realized that he had felt something of the same all along.

"But based on what I observed, this is what I have come up with. Middle-aged white male, middle class or above. Well educated. Good brain, but may be unappreciated at work or stuck in a dreary job he considers beneath him. Appearance is important to him. Definitely obsessive/compulsive. Represses emotions, appears well controlled. Neatness and order are paramount to him. He is fit and probably has some experience in the outdoors. He may like to build things as a hobby."

He glanced up and smiled. "My next conclusion may interest you in the light of yesterday's communications. Music is an important part of his life."

The silence in the room was complete. Outside, a thrush was singing in a tree.

"Fascinating," Hughes said at last. "Most interesting."

Watkins turned to Dr. Hirsch. "Do you mind if we ask questions?"

"Of course not."

"I was just wondering how you came to some of those assumptions. Middle class, middle-aged, white male?"

"His choice of supplies and his choice of music. The tins of food represent basic supplies to him—baked beans, tinned spaghetti, beef stew. All English childhood comfort foods, aren't they, but maybe not for the current generation, indicating that he may be a little older. But he has also added some freeze-dried meals that you can only buy at upscale camping stores."

"Is that what made you think he has experience in the outdoors?" Evan asked.

Hirsh shook his head. "The camp bed," he said. "It's an expensive, lightweight model for serious campers, but it's also a model that was discontinued about ten years ago. I presume he's owned it for some time and used it, since it shows signs of wear. Unlike the bed linen, which was brand-new, as was the mattress. No chance of picking up skin particles for DNA samples, I'm afraid."

"Obsessive/compulsive?" Watkins asked.

"The CDs were arranged in logical order. The very choice of so much Bach indicates that order is important to him, but he's arranged the Bach in order of composition date, showing he knows and values his music."

He looked around the group. "You'll note also that he has stocked an ample supply of music but no reading material. In his mind one has to have music to survive. Not books, however."

"It could also be that one can listen to music in the dark but one needs good light to read," Glynis suggested. "A prisoner left in that bunker may not have wished to risk using up the last of the batteries."

"Good point, Davies," Chief Inspector Hughes couldn't resist saying.

"Absolutely," Hirsch said. "And of course the perfectionist, obsessive/compulsive behavior is exhibited in the precision in the construction of the bunker—it is extremely well constructed, you know—and the way the bed was made. Perfectly folded hospital corners—"

"Could that mean that he has some kind of hospital training?" Watkins asked.

"Possible." Dr. Hirsch considered this. "I feel it's more likely that he is obsessively neat. And Inspector Watkins has told me about the musical clue received yesterday. Most gratifying, as it verifies my conclusions—the importance of music, his belief in his own intellectual powers, his own cleverness. He's throwing out a challenge because you are not solving things quickly enough for him. He is confident that he can give you clues and yet he'll always manage to stay one step ahead of you. This is fun for him."

"Why the bunker? Is that part of his fantasy and fun?" Watkins asked.

"He may not live alone."

"Surely this kind of man would be a loner?" Hughes said.

"He may live with a relative—his parents, perhaps?"

"And the handcuffs?" Watkins asked. "Are they his idea of fun?"

"More probably his fantasy. They do elicit a gut response, don't they? A psychological torture. If he brought a girl there as a prisoner and he didn't use them, she'd be conscious of them on the wall and wonder when and how he was planning to use them."

Evan swallowed. "Excuse me, sir," he ventured, "But you said before that your feeling was that the man had created something like a stage set, to elicit certain responses. I have to confess I felt the same way. So now I'm wondering whether this whole scenario was designed as a smoke screen and he has the girl somewhere quite different."

Hirsch looked at him and nodded slowly. "That is possible. If he captured the girl the afternoon before you discovered the bunker, it makes one wonder why he didn't take her there right away. Unless, as you suggest, he never intended to."

"Why go to all the trouble of building the bunker, which would have taken a lot of effort, if he never intended to use it? And the lack of fingerprints?"

"Again it could be amusing to him to watch you chaps responding."

"This is all most interesting," Hughes interjected, "but if he's taken the girl somewhere else, where do we start looking?"

"I wish I could tell you that," Hirsch said.

Chapter 16

He finished typing the letter, printed it out, folded it carefully, and put it into the envelope. Then he affixed the stamp and smiled at the address on the envelope. " 'Will you walk into my parlor?' said the spider to the fly," he whispered to himself.

"A lot of bloody good that was," Watkins muttered as he returned from escorting the profiler and met Evan still sitting with Glynis and Sergeant Jones. "Short of going door to door and seeing who turns down his sheets with hospital corners and eats baked beans, I don't see how we'll ever manage to track him down."

"Excuse me, sir." Glynis Davies touched his arm. "I've been thinking."

"The little lady has been thinking," Sergeant Jones said and got a warning frown from Watkins and Evan as well as a stony stare from Glynis herself.

"As I was saying," she went on, "everything we've done presupposes that our man has a history here, in this area. He's been seen by a psychiatrist, joined a music society, bought those CDs locally. What if he is just a summer visitor, like all the other tourists? What if he's living in a caravan, maybe? What easier way to transport tools and supplies? He could have parked close to the mountain and carried up supplies at will."

There was silence in the room.

Caravan—the word sparked a reaction in Evan's gut. It hadn't been long ago that he had been called upon to search a caravan park for a missing child. He saw how easy it would have been to bring a girl down the mountain and into a waiting caravan.

Watkins cleared his throat. "And is it your opinion that he and his caravan are still in the area?"

"I hope you're not going to ask my boys to search every bloody caravan park in North Wales again," Sergeant Jones said. "We've already done that once this year."

Glynis shrugged. "If he saw that the bunker had been discovered, maybe he's taken off in a hurry. I've just had another thought—" she frowned at Sergeant Jones before he could open his mouth. "Maybe he removed the handcuffs because they could have identified him. After all, how many suppliers of handcuffs are there in the country? We could probably have tracked them down, given the chance."

"Damn," Watkins muttered. "Why didn't we think of that before?"

"We were working through all the other angles," Glynis said. "We still have the photos taken in the bunker, don't we? I think we could blow up those photos and possibly track down the supplier on the Web. I'll give it a try."

"I've just had another thought, sir," Evan said.

"The little gray cells are positively buzzing this afternoon, aren't they?" Watkins commented, but with a smile.

"We could put out a call for videos," Evan continued. "Some of those tourists will have taken videos and photos of their trip up Snowdon on the day that Shannon disappeared. It's possible that they would show a caravan or camper van parked at the start of the path up the mountain. Who knows, maybe we could even pick out a license plate number."

"That's a good point, Evans. Call the local papers and TV, will you? And let's at least get a list of names of addresses from all the caravan parks in the area. Any vans with single males in them, especially those who checked out last Tuesday. That would at least be a start. Your boys can do that, can't they, Bill?"

"I suppose so," Sergeant Jones said grudgingly.

"And ask them to be on the lookout for any camper or caravan parked alone in remote areas," Evan added. "On the offchance that he is holding the girl captive somewhere in the area still."

Sergeant Jones shot Evan a look that clearly indicated he wasn't going to be bossed around by a mere detective constable, went to say something, then changed his mind. "Can't do any harm, I suppose," he muttered, and left the room, letting the door bang shut behind him.

Watkins looked up at Evan. "I take it that your investigations into the music angle didn't come up with anything productive?"

"Nothing, sir. But I did look into that young chap at the bank I told you about and I don't think we should dismiss him completely. Apart from not being middle-aged, he really fits the profile. He lives with a very dominating mother, he's shy and withdrawn, he loves music, and he's a great outdoorsman."

"But presumably he can account for himself last Tuesday. Wasn't he at work?"

"Yes, he was," Evan had to admit. "That's right. I was in the bank with Bronwen around four o'clock. I remember seeing him there. But couldn't he have made it up to Llanberis and back in his lunch hour?"

"A long lunch," Watkins said. "And he'd have needed time to stalk a girl on the mountain and hide her away somewhere." He grinned. "I think you're getting a fixation with this bloke, Evans. Apart from the fact that he looked uneasy when you saw him, you've got nothing to go on. Perhaps you saw him parking on a double yellow line once and he's been feeling guilty ever since, who knows?"

"But listen to this, sir. He's taken leave, unexpectedly. The bank manager is angry with him for leaving them in the lurch. He's off somewhere walking in the hills, according to his mother."

"He's still a long shot, Evans. Any other bright ideas?"

Evan frowned. "I thought that maybe I should take another look at a couple of National Parks employees. According to Paul Upwood, Shannon spoke to a man on the mountain resembling Eddie Richards, one of the park rangers. Eddie says he was nowhere near Snowdon that day. And the other ranger, Roger Thomas, is a shy sort of chap who's a music buff. He had the day off on Tuesday and says he was practicing with his choir in Bala."

"Easy enough to check," Watkins said. "You'll do those this afternoon, then?"

"Right you are, sir." Evan nodded. "But what about the Dead Deb? Is Glynis going to keep working on that angle?"

"What about her?" Watkins said. "We've checked around the UK and drawn a blank. No unaccounted girls called Deb show up."

"So why give us that clue if we can't solve it?"

"Warning us that he has killed other girls before?" Watkins suggested. "Raising the stakes for us?"

Evan shook his head. "We are supposed to know what he's talking about," he said. "I'm sure of it."

Shortly afterward Evan was in a police car, driving south to the National Parks Headquarters again. It was slow going, clogged with tour buses, cars piled with children, beach balls, luggage—and then there were the caravans. Lots of them. Caravans wherever he looked, in fields, on the road, stopped in lay-bys. How on earth could anyone check all of them? It was truly a hopeless task. If the kidnapper really had brought the girl down to a caravan, they could be anywhere by now. He could have killed her and waited for the ideal opportunity to drop her into a lake, down a mine, or even to bury her.

But the letter was mailed from Bangor, he reminded himself. And the postcard requesting the music was mailed locally too. The man had stayed around the area after the girl was kidnapped, at least long enough to mail letters. Recalling the postcard at the radio station reminded him that the musical request on the show was one aspect he hadn't yet looked into. What if the first notes of that music also spelled out a warning? On impulse he turned off toward Porthmadog. He seemed to remember there was a music shop in the High Street. There was, but they didn't have a score of *Sheherazade*.

"You wouldn't happen to know what the opening notes of the Shipwreck theme of it would you?" Evan asked.

The young girl behind the counter looked blank, as if he was speaking Chinese. "Come again?" she asked.

Evan repeated the question.

"Just a second," she said. "I'll get Mr. Cuthbert."

A few minutes later an elderly man came from a back room, hastily wiping what looked like cream and jam from his mouth.

"Sorry about that," he said. "My neighbor bakes wonderful Welsh cakes and she always brings me some when they're hot."

"I wouldn't pass up hot Welsh cakes either," Evan agreed, and explained his request.

"There are various passages in the suite in which the ship and wave motif occurs," Mr. Cuthbert said slowly. "You wish to know the notes that open the Shipwreck sequence?"

"I'm not quite sure," Evan said. "I know the part they played on the radio was called something like the Ship and the Sea, or the Shipwreck. It was quite strong, with lots of brass and cymbals clashing, but I'm not a musician."

"It's the motif you're probably looking for," Cuthbert said. "The musical phrase that is repeated. I'm not sure what key it's in, but I can probably make a stab at it." He went over and opened a piano lid. Then he tried some tentative notes. "Yes, that's about it."

He looked up at Evan and Evan nodded. "That sounds right."

He played it again.

"And those notes are?" Evan asked. "The actual notes you are playing."

Mr. Cuthbert called them out. They spelled nothing.

"Of course it probably wasn't in that key," Mr. Cuthbert said. "I've got pretty good pitch, but not perfect."

"If it was in another key, what notes would it be then?" Evan asked.

Nothing meaningful was spelled after several more attempts.

"Right. Thanks. Sorry to trouble you," Evan said.

"What exactly were you looking for?" Cuthbert asked.

Evan explained and the man shook his head. "What a strange business. So you've no idea why he chose this particular piece of music?"

"None at all," Evan said. "I can't see what a piece of music about a shipwreck has to do with a missing girl in North Wales. But thank you for your time. You can get back to those Welsh cakes before they're completely cold."

He left the town of Porthmadog and headed back to the main road. None at all, he repeated to himself. Storm at sea. Shipwreck. There were wrecks around the coast. Was it possible that the girl was hidden away in a boat somewhere? Were they being led on one wild goose chase after another and was the man watching them, enjoying their helplessness?

His hands gripped the steering wheel in frustration. Something was just not right about the whole thing. He had felt it right away and he still felt it. He tried to picture a man lurking on the mountain, taking his chance to grab Shannon Parkinson. Was she a random grab or had he seen and stalked her before? In which case, how did he know she'd part company with her boyfriend? No, it must have been random. In which case, was he looking for a particular type of girl? Might it be worth obtaining a picture of the missing Debbie in Birmingham to see if they looked at all alike? He took this one step farther—what about other girls who were missing, presumed abducted? Did any of them resemble Shannon Parkinson?

And when the man had grabbed Shannon, how did he keep her quiet? How did he get her down from the mountain without being observed?

And what had any of this to do with some old piece of music about a shipwreck? Who was Deb and how did she die? Was it all really an elaborate hoax? Was someone getting a good laugh at the North Wales Police force's expense?

He looked up in surprise as he found himself approaching the turn off for the Parks Headquarters. He had been so lost in thought that he had no recollection of driving there. Today, he was in luck. Eddie Richards was actually in the office. He seemed surprised to see Evan again but answered his questions with polite resignation. No, like he said, he hadn't been on the mountain that day. If Evan wanted to check, he was delivering brochures to the Parks office in Betws-y-coed that afternoon. And he didn't remember stopping to help a girl with boots that were hurting her.

"Right. Thanks, Mr. Richards," Evan said. "I've been told to question everybody again, so I'm doing it. Do you like music, by the way?" He cursed himself for asking the question in such a clumsy and obvious way. If Eddie Richards were the man he was looking for, he would be well and truly warned by now.

"Music?" Eddie Richards shrugged. "I suppose I like it as much as the next bloke. I used to enjoy the singing in chapel when I was a kid, but I can't hold a tune myself, as my wife will tell you when I try to sing in the bath." He chuckled at that. Then his face grew serious. "I suppose there's a good reason for all these questions. Now, do you mind telling me what all this is about?"

Evan explained as much as he could.

"Someone has been able to build a complete bunker in the woods not far from the Llanberis path," he said. "That means that someone has been able to carry tools and supplies up without being noticed."

Eddie Richards nodded. "Ah, so it makes sense that a Parks vehicle could do that. But where does the music come in?"

Evan told him that too and he shook his head. "You're dealing with a real nutter, aren't you? Someone who's gone off the deep end. I only wish one of us had spotted him digging his bunker or abducting the girl. Poor little thing, I wonder if she's still alive?"

"I wonder, too," Evan said. "It seems to me that we're running around in circles, getting nowhere." He glanced across the room at the receptionist who was busy on a phone call. He lowered his voice. "What about Roger Thomas? He likes music, doesn't he?"

"Roger? He lives for that choir of his. Always singing. Drives some of the other employees round the bend to hear him But as far as being the man you want—no, Roger's a good bloke. Always ready to lend a hand, is Roger. Quiet, like. Withdrawn, but a good bloke. I'd depend on him in a jam."

Evan left the building feeling secure about Eddie Richards's innocence but still uneasy about Roger Thomas. He had summed up Eddie as a reliable sort and one whose judgment was sound. And Eddie had thought that Roger Thomas was a good bloke. But Evan had been on the force long enough to know that good and evil were not always what they seemed. As a police detective, it was his job to double-check everything, including the alibi of a man who reputedly lived for his music.

Chapter 17

As soon as Evan was back at his car, he took out his mobile phone and called the number listed for the Cor Meibion y Moelwyn in Blaenau Ffestiniog. He found he was talking to a Mr. Howard Rhys-Davies, who revealed himself instantly as a pompous and self-important individual. Evan suspected he was probably on the small and mousy side to look at.

Yes, indeed, he was correct. The choir had practiced last Tuesday at the hall in Bala, in order to get a feel for the acoustics. And yes, Roger Thomas was one of their longtime and loyal choir members, who definitely would not have missed a practice unless he'd been on his deathbed.

This was what Evan had suspected he'd hear. He thanked the man, but just before hanging up he remembered to ask, "What time was the practice last Tuesday afternoon?"

"It wasn't in the afternoon, young man, it was Tuesday evening, at six o'clock," Howard Rhys-Davies said. "We have too many members who work for a living and can't get away during working hours, so we have to have evening rehearsals these days."

"Six o'clock," Evan repeated. "And Roger Thomas showed up on time?"

Evan heard the man suck in air through his teeth. "Now that you mention it, he came in a few minutes late, which isn't like him. But we were only just getting our music in order, so he didn't miss anything. May I ask what this is about? Mr. Thomas hasn't done anything wrong, has he?"

"We're just checking statements at this stage, Mr. Rhys-Davies. Nothing to worry about." Evan hung up and flipped his phone shut. Roger Thomas had lied then, and he didn't seem like the kind of man who would lie without a compelling reason. And he would have had a whole afternoon free before he got to his choir practice in Bala a little late . . .

Evan checked on Thomas's home address and drove straight there. He was surprised to find it was a semi-detached council house on an estate at the edge of Harlech. He didn't know why he should be so surprised, except that he had a mental impression of park rangers living in remote cottages like his own. As he checked off street numbers and realized which house belonged to Roger Thomas, his pulse quickened. A caravan was parked in the front garden. Evan almost broke into a run as he pushed open the front gate and went straight to the caravan. He tried the door, which was locked, but he found that by climbing onto the hitch, he could see into the back window. It was a good-sized van, immaculately neat, with a table and bench at one end and a bed across the other. Down one wall were sink, fridge, and cooking surface, all gleaming. But no sign that the van had ever been occupied. No closet in which a girl could be imprisoned.

Of course she wouldn't still be in there, Evan told himself. Thomas would only have used the van to transport her to the place he had prepared for her—another bunker, or even a room in his house.

"Hey, you. What do you think you're doing? Get down from there—you'll scratch the paint."

The voice behind Evan startled him and he stepped down awkwardly, almost twisting his ankle. Roger Thomas stood at his open front door, glaring at him.

"Oh, it's you—Constable Evans," he said, the bluster going out of him like a deflated balloon. "May I ask what you're doing with my caravan?"

"We've been asked to check all caravans in the area, Mr. Thomas. And since I was on my way to visit you, I thought I'd better take a look at yours too."

"Check them for what?"

"A young girl has been abducted, Mr. Thomas. A caravan would be one way of transporting her out of the area."

"And you think I might have done something like that?" Roger Thomas demanded, his face flushing scarlet. "You think I might have abducted a girl?"

"We have to check everybody who could have been in the area, Mr. Thomas. And National Parks workers could obviously transport a girl down a mountain without drawing attention to themselves."

Roger Thomas glanced up and down the street and noticed a woman had come out of the house opposite, ostensibly to put out milk bottles. "You'd better come inside," he said.

He led Evan into an immaculately neat front room, dominated by a grand piano. On the mantelpiece were several trophies and a framed photograph of Roger's choir.

"Take a seat." He indicated a sofa, slip-covered in chintz. "Look, Constable, I'm as anxious as the next bloke to help you find this girl, but I already told you I wasn't working that day. I was nowhere near Snowdon. I did shopping in the morning and I've got the Tesco receipt to prove it, and that afternoon I was singing with my choir in Bala—which you have to admit is a good, long drive in the other direction." He stared at Evan defiantly. "And you can check with my choir director if you want to."

"I already have, Mr. Thomas," Evan said.

"There you are, then."

"And a couple of interesting facts came out. He told me that the practice was not in the afternoon at all. It was in the evening."

Roger Thomas frowned, as if considering this. "Well, I suppose it was early evening by the time we started," he said. "At this time of year it's light so late that you don't really think it's evening until around eight, do you?" He paused, waiting for Evan to say something. "It was certainly afternoon when I left the house to drive there," he added defiantly.

"Went by the scenic route, did you?" Evan asked.

"What's that supposed to mean?"

"Your choir secretary, Mr. Howard Rhys-Davies, remembered that you were a little late. You came running in, looking flustered and out of breath, after the practice had started."

Thomas flushed bright red again. "That's ridiculous. I was two minutes late, at the most. They hadn't even started singing. Fancy bringing that up. Really, that man is insufferable sometimes."

"Just why were you late, Mr. Thomas, if you had all afternoon to drive there?"

"If you really must know," Roger Thomas said, "I took an afternoon nap and I forgot to set an alarm. I don't normally sleep during the day, but I'd had a rough week. I was horrified when I woke and found it was already four-thirty."

"I see," Evan said, not taking his eyes of Roger Thomas for a second. The man was clearly uncomfortable in his presence, but that could be his embarrassment at being caught out. If he came from a good old working-class Welsh background, admitting to taking an afternoon nap would be the same as confessing to a major sin. Daylight hours were for honest labor. Only slovenly, idle, non-chapelgoing, English people would think of resting in the afternoon.

"Well, thank you for your time, Mr. Thomas," he said, rising from the sofa. "Sorry to have bothered you again."

He noticed the look of relief that flooded across Thomas's face as he escorted Evan to his front door. "That's all right. I suppose you have to do your duty and question a lot of innocent people before you find the guilty one."

"I just hope we do find the guilty one and that poor girl is still alive when we find her," Evan said. He stepped out into a wet wind, blowing off the ocean. Any minute now it would rain.

"Looks like we're in for a change in the weather," Thomas said, staring out at the dark shape of Harlech Castle, looming between them and the Irish Sea.

"I hope the bad weather's not planning to stick around," Evan said. "I'm getting married a week on Saturday. Marquee, champagne on the lawn—all that kind of thing. It could turn out rather soggy in the rain. The ladies won't want to get their hats wet."

"Not much you can do about it either way, is there?" Thomas said. "Sounds like a rather grand affair, isn't it?"

Evan grimaced. "My fiancée's mother's idea, not mine."

"It always is," Thomas said and they exchanged a grin.

The first raindrops spattered onto the concrete area where the caravan was parked.

"Nice caravan you've got there, Mr. Thomas," Evan said. "Do you take it on many trips?"

"Actually, I only just bought it," Roger Thomas said.

"Really?"

"I came into a small inheritance and I thought how nice it would be to be able to go around the country, attending music festivals. She's a beauty, isn't she?"

"Very nice, yes," Evan said. "So you haven't even had a chance to try it out yet?"

"Not apart from cooking on the stove the first evening I brought it home, just to make sure it worked properly. But I have leave in September and then I'll be off to Ireland with her. There's a Gaelic Festival in Cork I'd like to attend. Would you like to have a look inside? It's very well designed."

"All right." Evan allowed Thomas to show him around, although he had seen almost everything there was to see from the window. He left Roger Thomas's house feeling confused and uneasy. Roger Thomas certainly fit the profile in many ways—he lived for his music, as Eddie Richards had said. He lived alone. He had just acquired a caravan. And yet Evan suspected that the person they were looking would not have made his musical connections so obvious. Also Thomas was a faithful choir member—a joiner, therefore.

Evan had to admit that his answers made perfect sense. Everyone overslept once in a while. He was certainly proud of his newly acquired caravan. The caravan didn't appear to have been used before. And yet he had definitely been nervous and uncomfortable in Evan's presence. Why? The normal response from a park ranger should have been to ask what he could do to help. Thomas had seemed strangely disinterested in the missing girl. Could that be because he knew where she was and any further searches would be wasting their time? Evan wished he knew more about psychology. In no case more than this one did he feel that he was stumbling blindly in the dark, grasping at straws. Why hadn't anyone come up with a good, easy truth drug yet? He wondered. As he approached the bridge across the estuary that would take him back to the police station, Evan thought about Eddie Richards. Eddie seemed like a level-headed sort of bloke. Would it be a good idea to ask Eddie to keep his eyes open and report back on Roger Thomas? Probably not exactly ethical. Besides, they were dealing with a person of intellect. If he'd managed to outwit the police so far, if he'd managed to kidnap a girl on a crowded mountain and dig a bunker a few yards from a path, he wasn't going to slip up now. For the moment they'd just have to play his game at his pace.

Chapter 18

The wind had increased as the storm came ashore, whipping the usually calm estuary into waves that slapped against the low bridge. The way back seemed to take forever. The rain was coming down fiercely now, peppering the windscreen and making the wipers work furiously. Evan was conscious again of the number of caravans he passed, parked in lay-bys or moving at snail's pace up the hills. How could anyone hope to stop and search them all? He certainly wasn't going to try in this weather and at this late hour. He decided to report to the D.I. by phone and perhaps find that he wasn't needed anymore tonight. That way he could branch off to Beddgelert and save himself a twenty-mile round trip.

The D.I.'s phone was picked up and a muffled voice growled, "Watkins."

"Where are you, sir?"

"In the middle of a shepherd's pie. Is that Evans?"

"It is. On my way back from interviewing the National Parks employees again. Would you like my report now, or will the morning do?"

"Have you uncovered anything that requires immediate action?"

"Not really, sir, just a hunch about Roger Thomas, one of the park rangers, who has just bought a new caravan and . . ."

"Then let me get back to my dinner, Evans. There's a good chap. The wife has been complaining that I haven't had dinner once with the rest of the family all week. She's glaring at me even as we speak. Meeting at eight in the morning, okay?"

"I've still got the squad car I checked out."

"Drive it in tomorrow morning, then. It's not likely to get stolen from outside your place, is it?"

With that Watkins hung up. So that was that. Released from duty for the night. Evan felt exhilaration until he reminded himself that somewhere a young girl might still be imprisoned and wishing herself dead. Another day gone and none of them a step closer to solving any aspect of this baffling case. Still, Bronwen would be pleased. He'd be able to give her a whole evening of undivided attention and they could discuss seating plans and music and all the hundred and one details that weddings seemed to require.

By the time he had driven up the Nant Gwynant Pass, he had conjured up a vivid picture of dinner waiting for him. Bronwen would have a meal on the stove, they'd open a bottle of wine and have time to enjoy each other's company, which certainly hadn't happened for a good while.

Evan opened his front door cautiously, sniffing the air to see if there were any good cooking smells, and if those smells involved either Bronwen or his mother. The house was silent.

"Bron?" he called and his voice echoed down the dark hallway. "Mam?"

No answering voice. That had to mean that Bronwen was up at the cottage and she'd got everything working up there. Smart girl, he thought. There would be no chance of mothers-in-law dropping in unexpectedly up there, especially not in weather like this. Evan took off his jacket and put on his rain gear before he tackled the hill. He could hardly take a squad car up that track, even if it would make it. The ground was already slippery and squelchy as he climbed the track and rivulets of water cascaded past his feet. They would have to get that four-wheel drive before the winter or the walk home would be a nightmare. The wind whipped at his clothes and the rain stung

155

his face and bare hands. Lovely August day, he said to himself with black humor, and pictured all those tourists huddled in their caravans or at their hotels.

The high peaks on either side of the valley had been swallowed into cloud. Wisps of cloud had come down almost to the cottage itself and several sheep huddled miserably beside his wall, trying to escape the worst of the wind. They glanced up in alarm as he approached and moved away reluctantly as he opened the gate.

"Bronwen? Where are you?" Evan called as he opened the door and stepped onto the flagstoned floor of the entry. No answer. No good aromas coming from the kitchen, either. He looked around and saw that Bronwen had indeed been busy in his absence. Apart from a couple of boxes of books and an air mattress on the bedroom floor where the brass bed would eventually go, all the furniture was now in its rightful place—plates and cups neatly arranged on the new Welsh dresser, foodstuffs on the pantry shelves, and the copper pots hanging above the stove. It looked just like a home, and an inviting, comfortable home at that. Evan was truly impressed and felt a stab of guilt that she had had to do all this alone. She must have worked like a dog—Evan smiled to himself as he realized something. Of course, her parents were due to arrive sometime over the weekend and she wanted to make sure everything looked perfect for them. She was probably still out hunting down that damned brass bedstead.

It was frustrating not to be able to contact her. If only she'd move into the twenty-first century and get a mobile phone like everyone else in the world. He made up his mind to go ahead and buy her one, whether she liked it or not. A policeman needed to stay in contact with his wife. Now he hesitated, looking around the kitchen and wondering if he should try to cook something for their evening meal. He opened the fridge, then the pantry. There were lamb chops and fresh beans. He could manage both of those, but he shouldn't start the chops until Bronwen came back. He took down a saucepan and sliced the beans, leaving them in water, ready to cook. He put the chops on the grill and peeled some potatoes.

The wind howled around the cottage and drummed on the roof. She was going to be soaked to the skin, out in weather like this. There was little point in going looking for her when he had no idea where she had gone, but he didn't like to think of her standing at a bus stop, waiting. Then it occurred to him that his mother might possibly know where she had gone. He was about to leave when he noticed the basket of logs beside the big stone fireplace. Bronwen would probably like to come home to a fire on a night like this, he decided, and he got one going. Then he put his hood back on and slithered his way down the hill.

"*Escob annwyl!* Would you take a look at the boy!" Evan's mother exclaimed as he was ushered into Mrs. Williams's kitchen, dripping, sodden, and caked in mud where he had sat down unexpectedly. "Don't tell me you've been up on mountains in weather like this?"

"Just up to our cottage to see if Bronwen was there—but she's not. I wondered if she might have told you where she was going."

Evan's mother gave him a cold stare. "Miss Price and I are not on the friendliest of terms, as you may have noticed. Why would you think she'd stop to confide her business to me?"

"And whose fault is that?" Evan demanded, feeling tired, wet, and now frustrated. "You haven't exactly welcomed her as a daughter-in-law with open arms, have you?"

"I've been nice enough."

"You still call her Miss Price, Mam. You told her to her face that her cooking wasn't good enough . . ."

"Just trying to help." Mrs. Evans sounded grieved. "Most young women would want to learn how to feed their future husbands and keep them happy."

"Bronwen already knows how to keep me happy. She doesn't want you hinting that you're the only one who can look after me properly."

"Well, that's true enough, isn't it? I cooked for you and your father all those years. Who would know better than I?"

"I'm a grown man now," Evan said, more softly. "My tastes have changed. And anything Bronwen does suits me just fine."

"I came here early especially to help you with the wedding plans," Mrs. Evans said. "But both of you are ignoring me and turning down my offers of help."

"Mother, I'm on a very difficult case. I've been putting in twelve-hour days. I feel badly that I've had to leave everything to Bronwen so far, and frankly I've no idea what stage the wedding plans have reached. I'm sure we'll want you to help when it comes closer to the actual event."

"And Mrs. Williams here is waiting to hear the details, too. She doesn't know how many little cakes to bake until you tell her how many guests you're expecting. It's not fair, Evan, to keep us all in the dark."

"Mam, I told you I've hardly had a chance to speak to Bronwen, much less to find out how many people are coming. I'll ask her to come and talk to you, all right?"

Evan's mother looked across at Mrs. Williams. "It will have to do, won't it? And I could always make some of my sausage rolls for the party. I've always been a dab hand at sausage rolls, haven't I? Your father used to say I had the lightest touch with pastry he'd ever met—but of course he'd never tried your pastry, Mrs. Williams," she conceded.

Mrs. Williams had been bustling around the kitchen, tactfully staying clear of this family feud. Now she stepped between them. "I tell you what, Evan *bach*. Why don't you and your intended come and have dinner with us tonight? I've made a lovely lamb *cawl*, just the way you like it, and there's plenty for all of us. And we'll have a moment to discuss exactly what you need from us."

"That's very kind of you, Mrs. Williams," Evan said. "I think we'd like to take you up on that. Bronwen will be wet through by the time she gets home and she'd probably be delighted to have dinner waiting for her. I don't know where she went, but I'm going to drive down to Caernarfon to look for her. She's probably out chasing that brass bed again."

"Chasing a brass bed?" Both women looked startled.

Evan smiled. "She wants the cottage furnished with antiques. She's set her heart on a brass bed."

"Pity I didn't know that a few years ago when my auntie died," Mrs. Williams said. "We gave several of them to the rag and bone man."

"It was a pity you didn't hang onto them," Evan agreed. "You should see what price they're fetching now."

"So I heard. Ridiculous, isn't it?" The two women exchanged glances again.

"Still, I must say that I think the old furniture is better than this modern stuff," Mrs. Evans said. "You can't go wrong with a good, strong Welsh dresser in the kitchen."

"You must come up to the cottage and see the one that Bronwen found for us," Evan said, offering an olive branch.

"Up that hill? You seem to have forgotten that I'm an old woman now."

"Mother, Mrs. Owens-the-Sheep goes up and down that hill every day and she's older than you."

"Maybe she hasn't had such a hard life." Evan's mother stared out of the window with a pained expression on her face.

Evan decided he wasn't going to win any discussion right now. "I'll be right back then," he said brightly. "The shops will have closed at five-thirty, so Bronwen should be home any minute. I'll probably pass her coming up the hill on the bus when I'm driving down."

"Take your time, and drive carefully," Mrs. Williams called after him. "All those foreign tourists out there, driving like maniacs. The stew will stay hot for you."

Evan went back to his home, just in case Bronwen had left a message on his answering machine rather than call his mobile. As he shut the door behind him, he noticed a letter, caught in the mail slot. He pulled it free and felt his heart rate rise. Another typed envelope, just like yesterday's.

He tore it open and found himself looking at two lines of music. Dammit, he muttered. Who could read music in the village? Why hadn't he paid more attention when Bronwen interpreted those notes yesterday? Various men who sang in the local men's choir or at chapel came to mind and he knew where he'd find some of them at this time of day. He stuffed the letter under his parka and braved the storm again.

The bar at the Red Dragon was particularly noisy as Evan pushed open the heavy oak door. He noticed instantly that a good sprinkling of holidaymakers, caught in the storm, had joined the usual inhabitants. Several families sat around the tables in the ladies' lounge, and as he made his way to the main bar, Betsy came out of the kitchen with plates balanced on her hands and arms.

"I'll be with you as soon as I can, Evan *bach*," she called out to him in Welsh, "but the place is full of bloody foreigners tonight, all wanting their dinner. We've run out of shepherd's pie and toad in the hole. It will be beans on toast soon."

"No rush, *cariad*," Evan called after her. "You take your time."

She turned and gave him a dazzling smile, instantly making him remember why there had been speculation among the villagers at one time as to whether he'd choose Betsy or Bronwen.

As he approached the bar, he noticed Barry-the-Bucket staring at him with a look that was none too friendly.

"She's a good girl, your Betsy," Evan said rapidly. "Hardworking. You could do worse."

"Just because you're about to enter a life of slavery, don't wish it on the rest of us, boyo," Barry said, but he was grinning now. "What are you drinking—the usual?"

"I don't think I've got time for a drink, thanks all the same," Evan said.

"No time for a drink?" Charlie Hopkins spun around, almost spilling his own pint of Robinson's. "What kind of talk is that? And what would you be doing in a pub if it wasn't seeking liquid refreshment?"

"I need some help translating a letter," Evan said.

"Foreign, is it?" Charlie asked.

"No, it's music, actually." He suddenly remembered that Barry played guitar in a band. "You read music, don't you, Barry?"

"*Tippen bach*—just a little bit," Barry replied.

"This is very simple," Evan said. "Can you come over here with me for a second? I'll buy your next pint by way of a bribe."

"All right." Barry followed him to an area that was somewhat less crowded.

Evan produced the letter. "I just need to know what notes these are."

"Oh, I can do that. I thought you meant real music." Barry glanced down at the sheet of paper. "It's B A D E E on the first line and B A D B E B B on the second line. Is that what you wanted?"

Evan tried to keep calm as he reached for the piece of paper. "Right. Thanks, Barry."

BADEE. It didn't take a genius to figure that much out, given that the last note had repeated the word bad.

"Is that all you wanted? You going to take up piano then?" Barry asked him with a grin. "Or are you planning to sing at the wedding?"

"What? No. No it's something else entirely."

"Are you all right, boyo?" Barry asked.

"Yes, yes, I'm fine," Evan attempted a smile. "Look, can I buy you that pint later, if you don't mind? I have to get back to work right now. This is pretty important."

He didn't wait for an answer, but ran back out into the wind and rain. He found it hard to breathe and not just because the storm was hitting him full in the face. Suddenly everything was different. It had now become personal. The letters in the first line of music, BADEE. That was clear enough. Evan Evans had to be EE. But the second line, BADBEBB. That made not sense at all. Who was Bebb? Or was it a misprint for Deb again? He had to risk D.I. Watkins's wrath and call him right away.

He went back to his house to take his mobile phone from his jacket pocket and noticed that the light was blinking on his answering machine. So Bronwen had called home after all. He felt relief flooding through him as he pressed the PLAY button.

"Constable Evans?" a man's voice said. "This is Mr. Cuthbert from the music store. You came in this afternoon asking about the *Sheherazade* suite. I've been giving it some more thought. I believe you mentioned a missing girl who might have been imprisoned? Well, it just struck me that Sheherazade is the tale of the Thousand and One Nights. The Emperor, or Sultan, I believe he's called, takes a different wife every night and has her killed in the morning. Sheherazade becomes his wife and tells him such good stories that he keeps her alive night after night, wanting to hear the next episode. But she knows he'll only keep her alive as long as she keeps him amused. I hope this helps a little." The message clicked off.

The world stopped.

"Only keep her alive as long as she keeps him amused." That was why the music had been chosen for him. And suddenly he knew what the musical notes spelled out.

"Oh my God," he gasped. "He's got Bronwen."

Chapter 19

Panic made it impossible to breathe. He stumbled around the room like a drunken man, knocking into a chair that clattered to the ground behind him. It was lucky that Watkins's number was on his speed dial because he couldn't have forced his fingers to punch in numbers. The phone at the other end rang, then a crisp female voice said, "The party you require is not available to answer your call at this moment, please leave your name and number and . . ."

Evan hung up. He doubted that Watkins would ever switch off his mobile. The storm must have interrupted communications somewhere down the line. He punched the next number on his speed dial.

"Caernarfon police station. How can I help you?" a male voice said.

"Who is this?" Evan demanded.

"Constable Pritchard here," the voice remained calm. "More to the point, who are you?"

"Evans. Who else is on duty?"

"Only me and Sergeant Howells at the moment."

"No C.I.D.?"

"I don't think so. Just a minute, I'll go and look."

Evan waited impatiently until Pritchard said cheerfully, "It looks like D.C. Davies is still in the computer center. Do you want to talk to her?"

"Of course I bloody want to talk to her," Evan exploded, then regretted it instantly. "Sorry, mate, it's a real emergency."

"Right-oh. I'll put her on."

And Evan heard Glynis's calm, well-bred voice saying, "This is D.C. Davies."

"Glynis," he shouted into the phone, "he's got Bronwen. What are we going to do?"

"Evan? Is that you?"

"Sorry. Yes. I couldn't find her anywhere and then there was more music and I know why he played that piece on the radio and I don't know what to do . . ." The words spilled out in a torrent.

"Calm down. Take a deep breath," Glynis Davies said. "Now, are you sure that Bronwen has been kidnapped?"

"He has to have her, doesn't he?" Evan could hear himself still shouting. "She's not anywhere to be seen, and the music is about a sultan who keeps young women alive only as long as they please him. And there was another letter. It says Bad EE, and then Bad BE-to-be."

"Oh God. Any sign of a struggle? Any sign at all that she was kidnapped?"

"No. Nothing. There was food in the fridge at the cottage ready for dinner, so she was intending to cook up there. No sign at all that she was at my place. I can ask around to see if anyone noticed her, but I just don't think I can do that right now."

"Of course you can't. Come on down to the station and I'll round up everyone else. And Evan, drive carefully. We don't want you going off the road, do we?"

"All right."

"Don't worry, Evan. We'll find her. Bronwen's a resourceful woman. She can take care of herself."

He wanted to believe that. Bronwen wouldn't give in without a fight. But against a captor who was bigger and stronger, who might have a weapon—who had handcuffs waiting for her? He tried to put the image from his mind, but he couldn't. Only one thing was absolutely clear: When he found the man, he'd kill him.

Fields and rocks and the occasional house flew past as he drove down the pass. Llanberis was deserted. All of the tourists had retreated to the few cafés and pubs that were still open, or gone back to their B&Bs. The terminus of the Snowdon Railway loomed like a ghostly shadow above the road. A sudden, chilling thought shot through Evan. The bunker, now unguarded, to which the kidnapper apparently could come and go as he pleased. What if he knew the police were no longer guarding it? What if he had taken Bronwen there?

Evan couldn't drive on. He had to check for himself, just in case. He parked outside the station and started up the path. Usually, the sun would still be setting at this hour, but cloud had come down to swallow the mountain in darkness. Rain and wind battered him as he ran up the steep ascent. He had left his torch in the glove compartment of his car and cursed himself for his lack of forethought. What if his quarry was there too, and had a weapon? A voice in Evan's head reminded him that he should wait for backup, like any well-trained cop. He kept going, however, until he reached the point where he had to leave the path. That same voice went on to remind him that his father hadn't waited either, when he had burst into the middle of a gang of kids in Swansea, and it had cost him his life. But Bronwen's life was at stake now and that was all that mattered.

He blundered into the woods, stumbling and tripping as he refused to slow down. At first he couldn't even find the bunker, but then a wisp of white tape, flapping wildly in the wind, helped him locate it. His cold wet fingers fumbled to remove the turf and brambles that concealed it and to open the hatch. At last he had it open and stared down into darkness.

"Bronwen?" he yelled. "Are you there? It's me—Evan."

She might well be gagged, of course. He strained his ears for any muffled sound, but it was impossible to hear over the shriek of the wind and the drumming of rain on leaves. What if she were lying unconscious? He knew he'd have to go down to check, but he didn't know how he'd get out again. The biggest, strongest piece of furniture down there wasn't tall enough to enable him to hoist himself back up, even if everything were not slippery with rain.

He should call for backup.

He knelt down and leaned into the darkness. It wasn't quite dark outside yet. Surely he'd be able to make out the light shape of a body. Suddenly he was struck with great force in the middle of his back and he toppled forward into the hole. Blackness rushed up to meet him.

When Evan opened his eyes, he wondered if he'd gone blind. The world around him was completely, utterly dark. He waved his hand in front of his face and saw nothing. Then his nostrils took in the damp, earthy smell and he realized where he was: in the bunker with the hatch closed above him. His heart raced as he fought back the panic that threatened to overwhelm him. Of all the nightmares of his life, being buried alive was the worst of them. He got to his knees and began to crawl around the damp earth floor. The bunker had not been as well designed as its builder had hoped—there were already puddles where the rain was seeping in. How long had he lain there? A few minutes? An hour? Every bone in his body hurt and he realized how lucky he had been not to have broken his neck when he pitched in headfirst. But one shoulder sent out stabbing pains of fire as he put weight on his hand. He ran the other hand over it. Probably not dislocated as he couldn't feel a bone protruding. Separated, then? He'd done both during his rugby-playing career and both were equally painful.

He continued his patient crawl until he bumped into one wall, then he moved along the wall to the first corner. At least Bronwen wasn't hanging from those handcuffs. This brought a small measure of relief. Along the next wall, he located the toilet bucket, then the bed, which was also untouched and empty, although damp now. The bedside table with the lamp on it should be beside it. He felt around, trying to locate it. Had it been taken away for testing and not returned? At last he found it, lying on its side. He must have knocked it over during his fall. He felt around until he located the lamp and prayed that the fall hadn't shattered the bulb. He flipped the switch. Nothing happened. Then he remembered that it was battery-operated, gave the battery compartment a good thump, and was rewarded with flickering light. The dim glow confirmed that the hatch was indeed shut tight.

He fought against the panic that threatened to overwhelm him. He'd been claustrophobic all his life, made worse when a primary school teacher shut him in the cupboard as punishment. Beads of sweat appeared on his forehead and he realized he was breathing rapidly.

Think calm, he told himself. Nothing to worry about. I'm safe. They'll find my car and come looking for me. Everything will be all right.

He tried to keep other thoughts at bay, but they started creeping in. He realized that the kidnapper must have known his mind rather well. He'd known that Evan would have to stop and check out the bunker as he drove past, and he had been waiting for him. This was probably just an extra point scored. I can get the better of you any time I want to—was that what he was saying? Evan realized that they were playing a game of egos, a mental chess game. Why me? he thought. Why is he directing his hate at me? Why not my boss?

He yawned loudly. Sleepy. He couldn't be sleepy. It wasn't even late yet. Unless—unless the air supply had been blocked up. He held the lamp close to the ceiling where there had been a fresh-air vent. And he noticed that there were no raindrops beneath it. Blocked, then. Not as safe as he had believed. He looked around the bunker. How long before the air he was breathing was replaced by the carbon dioxide he was breathing out? Surely an hour or two—time enough to be rescued. But what if they didn't notice his car in the car park? It was off the main road, after all. What if his adversary had taken his keys while he was unconscious and driven the car somewhere else? Panic returned as he fumbled in his pockets. He sighed with relief as his fingers closed around the cold metal of his key ring.

Still safe, then. All he had to do was sit and wait . . . unless. His mind now played another script. His adversary returning with a canister of gas—any kind of chemical poison in an aerosol can would do—removing the plug and spraying it calmly into the small space.

That was enough for Evan. He had to make an attempt to escape. He righted the bedside table and stood on it. His fingers just touched the wood of the hatch. He dragged over the bucket and stood it on top of the table. Then he used the wall to balance himself as he climbed up. Pain shot through his shoulder as he tried to raise his left arm, but he placed both palms firmly on the hatch and pushed. There was an ominous cracking sound and the flimsy table collapsed under his weight, sending him sprawling to the floor.

This time he thought he might vomit with the pain. His head felt dizzy and he had to lean against the cold firmness of the wall to steady himself. His eyes searched the bunker again. *Escape.* He must get out while he could. Most of the tins and other supplies had been taken away for testing. The bed was too flimsy to stand on. But there must be some way of getting out. There were supplies here and he was a resourceful man. The bedsheets had also been taken for testing but Evan peeled back the mattress and examined the aluminum frame. If he could take it apart, he might be able to make something to push the hatch open. He could lash parts of it together to make a ladder.

Full of enthusiasm now he got out his key ring, which had a small penknife attached to it, and attempted to dismantle the bed frame. It was extraordinarily well made and there seemed to be no way to unscrew the folding legs. He tried brute strength, but his damaged left shoulder wouldn't give him enough power. He tried leaning it against the wall and attempting to climb up the springs, but he couldn't get high enough. And he realized something else. All this exertion was using up his supply of oxygen too fast. He could hear his head singing and his thoughts were becoming more confused. Sleep. That was a good idea. Just lie down and sleep. Everything would be all right in the morning . . .

Chapter 20

"Leave me alone," Evan shouted as something cold and wet slapped against his face. For a moment he thought his mother was waking him up to go to school. Then he opened his eyes and squinted in bright light. Someone was shining a torch on him and rain was dripping onto his face.

"Thank God," said a voice, and Inspector Watkins's face appeared above him. "Come on, lads. Let's get him out of here."

Paramedics arrived and Evan was hoisted up into the rainy night and hurried toward a waiting ambulance.

"Don't take me to hospital," Evan protested, fully conscious now and trying to sit up. "I'm fine. I have to help find her. We'll need every man on the job."

"Shut up and lie down," Watkins said, walking beside him. "You're not doing anything until they've given you the once-over at the hospital. You should thank your lucky stars you're still alive. What did you bloody well think you were doing, going up to that bunker alone?"

"I know it was stupid," Evan said, "but I was driving past and I got this overwhelming feeling that Bron was in there. I had to stop and look. I was peering inside when he must have pushed me and I fell. I tried every way I could to get out, but he must have stopped up the air vents because I passed out." He looked around at the worried faces, following him down the track. "How did you find me?"

"You can thank Glynis for that," Watkins said. "She became concerned when you hadn't shown up and said someone ought to go looking for you in case you'd driven your car off the road. Lucky you were in the squad car. That was easier to spot. Easy there," he added as the paramedics hoisted the stretcher into the ambulance. Then he scrambled up beside Evan.

"You're not allowed to ride in the back, sir," one of the paramedics said. "Why don't you follow in your vehicle, if you want to accompany him?"

"Don't talk such bloody rubbish," Watkins snapped, perching beside Evan. "There's a young woman been kidnapped and I'm not wasting any precious second. We need to talk on the way, so start driving, and the quicker the better."

The young man gulped, went to say something, then thought better of it. He closed the back doors and went around to the driver's seat.

Evan glanced at Watkins. "You can be bloody domineering when you've a mind to," he said.

"You bet I can. Are you going to be all right? You haven't broken anything?"

"I did something to my shoulder when I fell. Apart from that I'm okay."

"So fill me in on what we've got so far," Watkins said. "What made you first think she'd been kidnapped? Glynis said something about music and a new letter?"

"I got home and there was no sign of her," Evan said, frowning as he relived the event. "I thought she must have gone shopping. She's been spending half her life shopping recently, what with the wedding and furnishing the cottage. Then there was a message on my answering machine." Evan told the inspector about the Sheherazade story, and then fumbled in his jacket pocket to produce the letter.

"What does Bad Bebb mean?" Watkins asked.

"I couldn't figure that one out to start with," Evan said, "but as soon as I suspected that Bronwen was missing, I realized. It must be Bronwen Evans-to-be."

"Ah. Yes. Could be." Watkins sighed.

"You shouldn't be wasting this time with me, sir," Evan said. "We have to get onto this straightaway. We might not have much time."

"I think we have some time, son," Watkins said. He'd called Evan a lot of things before, but never son. "If he'd been planning to kill her straightaway, he wouldn't have bothered to send you notes. He wants you try to find her. It's part of his game. I'll wager there's another note in the post right now with more tantalizing instructions on it."

Watkins pulled out his mobile phone. "Davies? Watkins here. He's on his way to hospital. Yes. Seems to be fine, thank God. Is the D.C.I. there yet? Right. I'll be coming as soon as I drop off this lad. In the meantime let's get some things in motion, shall we? I want someone up in Llanfair, questioning everyone who might have seen Bronwen. What time they saw her last. Did she leave by bus or in a car? What kind of car? You know the drill. And I want someone at the sorting office to see if we can intercept another letter. Oh, and I need to talk to D.I. Fuller in Bangor. I'd like a video camera on the postboxes at the main post office there—just in case our suspect chooses to post his letters where there is complete anonymity. Got it?"

"Yes, sir," Glynis's voice came down the line. "And I've already . . ."

"Good thinking," Watkins's voice said. "Be with you as quickly as possible."

He hung up.

"What has she done?" Evan asked.

"She's getting a list of phone calls made to Bronwen's number."

"She's a really bright girl," Evan said.

"She certainly is. She'll probably wind up as chief constable before you and I retire. If she doesn't go daft and marry some local yokel first."

Evan went to smile, then grimaced in pain as the ambulance went over a bump in the road. The pain instantly switched his thoughts back to Bronwen. Had he hurt her? Was he intending to? Those handcuffs, high on the wall, flashed across his mind and he fought to turn off the image. If he'd so much as touched her . . . Evan gritted his teeth. "Can't they make this bloody ambulance go any faster?"

Then it was all action as he was wheeled into the bright lights of casualty at Ysbety Gwyneth.

"There will be a wait, because he's not critical," the nurse at the admitting desk said.

"He's North Wales Police and he's needed instantly on a kidnapping case and there will be no wait," Watkins said.

"We'll do our best," the nurse said frostily. "He'll have to go to triage to be assessed. And if he's not critical, I'm afraid we do have to prioritize."

"Look—It's his fiancée who has been kidnapped." Watkins leaned toward her half confidential, half threatening. "Every moment he is here is one less officer for us on the case. Two while I'm here. And we're wasting time arguing."

The nurse looked flustered and rose to her feet. She disappeared behind a curtain and almost instantly Evan was wheeled in.

"There's nothing much wrong with me," he said to the doctor, who looked like a sixth former in a white jacket. "I've done something to my shoulder, that's all."

"And he was almost suffocated and buried alive in a bunker," Watkins added. "Give him a thorough checkover, but as quick as you can, okay?" He took out his phone again. "I'm going outside to call for transport and I'm off to the station. I'll have a second car waiting for you. Don't let them mess you around. If you have any trouble, call me."

Then he was gone.

"Bit of a bastard, your supervisor, is he?" the young doctor asked Evan with a grin.

"He's a good bloke. Gets things done," Evan said.

"X-rays first then," the doctor said.

"Do I really need X-rays? That will take time. You can feel what's wrong with my shoulder, can't you?"

"I won't be able to tell if you've cracked a collar bone."

"I've played rugby before with a cracked collar bone. Let's just strap me up and get me out of here."

"All right, but I can't be responsible then if a bone sets crookedly."

"I'll come back and get X-rays as soon as I've got a moment," Evan said, "but I've just found out my fiancée has been kidnapped by a madman who tried to kill me. You wouldn't want to be lying around in some hospital if that was you, would you?"

"No, I wouldn't." The doctor took out his stethoscope.

Fifteen minutes later Evan was on his feet, feeling somewhat woozy, but determined as he made his way out to the squad car.

"So have you been given a clean bill of health?" D.C.I. Hughes asked as Evan walked into the police station and a roomful of people.

"Not exactly, sir. I didn't want to waste time on X-rays so I've my arm immobilized and a shot of painkiller. That should carry me through for now. Is there any news?"

A uniformed constable got up and motioned for Evan to take his seat. Evan sat, gratefully.

"Would you like to fill in Evans on what we've been doing so far, Watkins," Hughes said, indicating to Evans that he had probably only just got there himself.

"We've got a couple of men asking questions in the village," Watkins said. "They haven't called in anything so far. Hopefully we have someone going through the mail at the main sorting office to catch any more letters to you, and Glynis has been onto British Telecom to come up with a list of phone calls."

As if on cue the door opened and Glynis Davies came in, waving a piece of paper. "Got it, sir. She had a phone call from her mother at ten-thirty, another from her mother at one, and then a call from a local number at two. The local number turns out to be an antiques dealer in Caernarfon."

"That antiques bloke. Why didn't I think of him before!" Evan jumped to his feet. "He fits the profile. Loner. Just moved here. Played classical music in his shop, and I could tell he fancied Bron by the way he looked at her."

"What's the address?" Watkins was already heading for the door.

"It's Past Times Remembered, on Church Street in Caernarfon. Owner is Andrew Cartwright," Glynis said.

"That's right. Mr. Cartwright." An image of the tall, slim, slightly effeminate man came to Evan. "And I believe he said he was renting the premises over the shop."

"Right, lads," Hughes said. "I want Cartwright brought in for questioning immediately and while he's gone I want his premises searched, top to bottom, inside out. Jones—I'll leave you to assign men to the job. Make sure they check anywhere a body could be hidden—trunks, wardrobes."

"Right you are, sir." For once Jones seemed as keen as any of them. "You heard the D.C.I., boys. I'll bring him in, and Pritchard and Roberts, you conduct the search."

"What about me, sir?" Evan asked. "I want to do something. I'd rather be doing something."

"You'll be in on the interview, Evans. As long as you can keep cool," Hughes said. "We can't risk your losing your temper and jeopardizing everything."

"I'll behave myself, sir," Evan said. He glanced across at Watkins and knew exactly what the other man was thinking. If they could just get Cartwright alone, they'd make him talk all right . . . Evan wished that they could have conveniently forgotten to call in D.C.I. Hughes until the morning.

Chapter 21

Andrew Cartwright looked pale and drawn as he entered the interview room, flanked by two uniformed officers. They went through the formality of introductions. Evan noted that Cartwright started when he recognized him.

"You've read Mr. Cartwright his rights, Jones?" D.C.I. Hughes asked.

"Yes, sir."

"And you understand the implications? You have the right to have a lawyer present."

"I don't understand anything," Cartwright said. "One minute I was sitting in front of the telly, watching the ten o'clock news. The next I was being dragged away like some common criminal. I don't even know what I'm supposed to have done. Does this have anything to do with not declaring VAT on every item I've sold?"

"More serious than VAT violations, I'm afraid," Hughes said, in his clipped voice. "You made a phone call today to a Miss Bronwen Price."

Cartwright's face registered surprise. "Bronwen Price? Yes, I did phone her around two o'clock. She'd been looking for a brass bed and I was able to locate a fine specimen for her. I called her to tell her

I had it in the shop, if she'd like to take a look at it. She said she'd come as soon as she could."

"And?" Watkins asked. "What time did she arrive at your shop?"

"She didn't." Cartwright said. "I waited for her all afternoon. I even kept the shop open extra late, in case she hadn't managed to get a ride down from her village earlier, but she didn't come."

"So you haven't seen Miss Price at all today?" Watkins asked.

"I just told you." Cartwright looked around at the policemen.

"And she didn't phone to say why she was detained?"

"No. I heard nothing more from her after that one phone call. Now, will somebody tell me what this is about?"

"Miss Price is missing," Hughes said. "Presumed kidnapped."

"Good God." Cartwright's pale face turned one shade whiter. "But you can't suspect that I . . . ?"

"The last known contact she had with anybody today was your phone call at two o'clock."

"This is absurd." Cartwright gave a hysterical laugh. "It's Kafkaesque. You can't just haul somebody in because he made a phone call. I was helping Miss Price find a brass bedstead. That's all. Why would I want to kidnap her? What am I supposed to have done with her? You're very welcome to search my premises."

"Our men are doing that very thing right now," Hughes said.

Evan had kept silent so far, not trusting himself to speak, but he leaned forward in his seat now. "Did you go out at all this evening, Mr. Cartwright?"

"This evening? Yes, I went to the fish and chips shop to buy some dinner and to post a letter."

"To whom?" Watkins asked.

"To my mother. I write to her every week. She likes to know I'm all right and she won't use the telephone."

Until now Evan had remained silent, trying to phrase the right questions in a way that would catch Cartwright off guard.

"Do you have a computer, sir?" Evan asked.

Cartwright turned to him. "Yes. Of course. One needs a computer these days. I find it most useful to do Internet searches for items."

"What about other programs? Do you use your computer for entertainment purposes also?"

Cartwright flushed. "Are you hinting about visiting porn sites? Stuff like that?"

"Oh, good lord, no. Nothing like that," Evan said. "No, I meant more like music programs." As he said it he wished back the words. Talk about unsubtle. That wasn't going to catch anybody off guard.

"Music programs?" Cartwright sounded surprised. "You mean for downloading songs—that kind of thing?"

"For writing music."

"I'm afraid I don't understand what you're getting at. I don't write music. I have no musical training."

"But you like listening to it. You play it in your shop." Evan had risen to his feet.

"Well, yes. I was advised to have suitable background music playing in the shop. It sets up the right ambiance."

"What about hiking?" Evan switched tactics. "Do you get out into the outdoors much?"

"I like the outdoors," Cartwright said, "but I haven't done much real hiking recently. I—I haven't been too well."

"You've just moved to the area, I believe." Watkins glanced at Evan, standing poised and ready to spring, and took over. "What did you do before you came here?"

"I lived in Greater London and I worked for a big company. An advertising company, actually."

"And why did you leave?"

"I wasn't well."

"Cancer or heart?"

Cartwright flushed. "Actually, I—had a nervous breakdown. I was diagnosed with bipolar disease. Obviously I had to move to a less stressful lifestyle. I received some severance pay and used it to open my little shop here. Now, could I please go home? My doctor says I'm not supposed to be upset. It's very bad for me."

"Constable Davies will take you to the cafeteria and get you a cup of tea," Hughes said. "And then we'll see."

"Wait." Evan barred his way. "You can't let him go yet. He must know something."

"That's enough, Evans." Watkins quietly took his arm. "Sit down."

Evan sat, breathing heavily and in truth rather ashamed of himself as Cartwright was led out.

"If you can't control your anger, Evans, we'll have to remove you from the case," Hughes said.

"Sorry, sir. It's just that—"

"We understand perfectly," Watkins said. "But it's not going to get us anywhere."

"Well, what do you think?" Hughes asked as the door closed behind them.

"He doesn't seem to be our man," Watkins said slowly. "No musical background. Probably not the strength to dig that bunker."

"I'll have our lads bring in that computer, just in case," Hughes said. "It should be easy enough to see if it has a music composition program and if the letters were written on it. And we'll run a background check. You obviously think he was lying, don't you, Evans?"

Evan had wanted so badly to believe that they had found their man. "He admits to a history of mental disease," Evan said, almost forcing the words out as he tried to stay detached. "but he did seem quite bewildered to be here. I rather think that the man we're dealing with would act with indignant righteousness."

"Yes, I agree with that," Watkins said. "But he could be putting on a good act—poor little me."

"Interesting about the VAT." Hughes smiled. "It's amazing how often they confess to petty sins for us, isn't it?"

"We're not going to just let him go, are we, sir?" Evan asked.

"I think we should keep him for a while," Watkins said. "Just in case a stint in a dark cell makes him decide to tell us anything else."

"At least until we've given his premises the once-over," Hughes said. "Why don't you go and take a look for yourself, Watkins, just to make sure they're not missing anything."

"And I'm having Evans driven home," Watkins said.

"Absolutely not," Evan said. "I'm staying here, ready to do what it takes."

"Did nobody at detective training ever mention obedience to superiors?" Watkins said. "Look, boyo, you're probably in shock, you're dosed up with pain pills. You're about to lose it and you're better off in bed tonight."

"I'll be fine. I can't just go and—"

"I'll tell you another good reason for being home: What if she hasn't been kidnapped? What if she's off on some strange errand, or she met her bridesmaid and they decided to go for a drink together and she shows up, perky and smiling, asking you to look at the delightful table centers she's found?"

"She would have called if she was going to be late," Evan said flatly, trying to will himself to accept this scenario. "Besides, someone was damned serious about killing me."

"Granted. But if she was kidnapped and manages to escape? If she's allowed to put through one phone call to you—you'll want to be there, won't you?"

D.C.I. Hughes put his hand on Evan's shoulder. "Go on, lad. Do what he says. You'll be more use to us after a good night's sleep."

Evan stood up, trying not to let them notice that he had to put a hand on the back of his chair to steady himself. "You don't need to spare a man to drive me home," he said. "I can drive myself."

"You're not allowed to drive legally with one arm," Watkins said. "One of the boys will drive you home and bring you back tomorrow, and no arguing. Don't worry, we'll keep you up to date if we find out anything at all."

"Before I go, don't you want a picture of her?" Evan asked. "We need to get her picture out everywhere as quickly as possible. I'm sure I've got one in my wallet. I've a better one at home, of course.

We need it to make tomorrow's papers, and put out flyers and the early TV news . . ."

"Strictly speaking, we can't regard her as a missing person yet," Hughes said.

"Of course she's bloody missing!" Evan yelled, not stopping to consider that he was shouting at a superior officer. "What about the letter? What about someone kicking me into a bunker?"

"I agree there are signs that we should take very seriously," Hughes said, "but I don't know that we have a mandate to announce her as missing to the media. What if she went off on a last-minute whim? What if she decided she needed to take more time to think about her marriage? We'd look like fools."

Watkins stepped between Hughes and Evan. "On this occasion I'd rather look like a fool than do anything to risk the life of that young woman. Give me the photo, Evans. I'll get Glynis to send it to the media immediately."

"Watkins, may I remind you—" Hughes began.

But Watkins cut him off. "God God, man, we're talking about Evan's fiancée, here. Would you sit back and wait if it was your family member that had been kidnapped?"

The two men stared at each other for a long moment before Hughes said, "Do what you have to."

Watkins took Evan's arm. "Come on, boyo. I'll walk you out to the car. You look as white as a sheet. Don't keel over on me now."

Evan stared out of the window all the way up the hill to Llanfair. They passed the parking area beside the Snowdon Railway, now rain-lashed and deserted. If the man had been lurking by the bunker, had he got Bronwen hidden somewhere close by? Was there another bunker as yet undiscovered?

"Tell Inspector Watkins to check out the area around the bunker with dogs. I'll give you an item of Bronwen's for the scent," he said to the constable who was driving him. "And I'll get you a better photo of her to give to the media when you drop me off. I wonder if they've finished interviewing people in the village yet and whether anyone saw her leaving?"

As he said this, another thought came to him. The kidnapper was an outdoor type, one who hiked up a mountain to dig and furnish a bunker. He was fit and at home in the outdoors. What if he had approached their cottage from the mountain and dragged Bronwen away unseen from the village?

Why had they ever thought that a remote shepherd's cottage was such a charming idea? He saw now that its very location had probably exposed Bronwen to danger.

"Oh, and suggest that forensics go over the cottage to see if they pick up any trace of an intruder. She could have been kidnapped from the cottage."

The young constable looked at him with interest. "You're only a D.C., right?"

"Yes."

"And you go around telling your inspector what to do? If we tried that, we'd be crucified."

"It's my fiancée, mate," Evan said. "I'll do whatever it takes and I don't care what toes I step on. Look, if you don't feel comfortable talking to Inspector Watkins, or the D.C.I., then I'll call them myself."

"No, it's okay. I expect I can do it. You're supposed to be taking it easy."

"I don't know how I can take it easy, knowing that some bastard has got Bronwen," Evan snapped. "I want to be out there, helping to find her."

The car came to a halt outside Evan's front door. The world spun around as he stood up and he had to lean against the car for a moment. Then he noticed something—light shining out between the closed curtains. Someone was in his cottage. Hope leaped through him. The inspector had been right. She'd been delayed somewhere. Some stupid errand. And now she had come home. He grunted in pain as he pushed open the front door and charged inside.

"Bronwen?" he shouted.

"She hasn't come home yet. I thought you went to pick her up." Evan's mother rose from the armchair where she had been sitting, watching television. "Didn't you find her?" She stopped short when she saw him. "Nothing's wrong, is it? You look dreadful. Come here and take off your jacket—you look all in."

"Ow, leave me alone!" Evan yelled as she tried to yank off the jacket. "I've hurt my shoulder, Ma. I got—we've had a spot of trouble."

"A spot of trouble?" She helped him ease off his jacket. "You're all strapped up. What happened?"

He looked at her worried face and found that he couldn't tell her about the bunker. He couldn't tell her about Bronwen either.

"I fell," he said.

"Just like when you were a little boy, always falling down, you were. I spent half my life taking you to the casualty department." She smiled at him.

"And I don't suppose you've had anything to eat yet, either?"

"No, I haven't."

"Well, Mrs. Williams sent you a pot of her lamb *cawl*. I've been keeping it warm on the stove. Now sit down and I'll serve you."

Evan allowed himself to be waited on. He tried to eat the soup but it was almost impossible to swallow.

"Come on, now. Eat up. It's not like you to be off your food." Mrs. Evans sat beside him and watched each mouthful into his mouth. Evan got the feeling that she would have spoon-fed him if he'd stopped. He managed to get a few mouthfuls down before he shook his head. "I really can't, Ma. They gave me a shot of pain medicine at the hospital and it's made me feel queasy."

"Then the best thing you can do is go to bed. I'll bring you up a cup of tea, or would you rather I made you Ovaltine, like I did when you were a little boy?"

"Tea would be fine, thanks."

"Do you need help getting undressed?" she called after him as he ascended the stairs.

"Ma, I'm a grown man."

"Sometimes even grown men need looking after by their mothers," she said.

Evan managed to get into his pajamas and into bed before the tea arrived. Mrs. Evans placed it on the bedside table, stroked back his hair, and smiled down at him. "Now, isn't this nice. Just like old times. Soon you won't be my boy anymore and it will be up to Miss—up to Bronwen to look after you."

Evan squeezed his eyes shut to try and shut out the pain. He was supposed to be looking after Bronwen. That's what husbands promised to do—love and cherish and take care of her for the rest of her life. He had let her down.

Chapter 22

Bronwen opened her eyes to total darkness. She had no idea where she was. When she tried to move, she found that she couldn't. Her wrists and ankles were somehow bound together. She felt tape sticking to her, pulling at the hairs on her skin. She tried to open her mouth and found that it too was taped shut. Her head felt heavy and confused and she realized that she must have been drugged. The cup of coffee. He had offered her a cup of coffee and had watched her as it clattered from her lap, as her speech slurred and she lost consciousness. He must have kidnapped her, got her out somehow and brought her here—wherever here was. Am I in another bunker? she wondered. She rolled onto her side.

She was lying on what appeared to be a mattress. When she extended her arms, she touched cold concrete. It took her a long while to stand up, and when she finally achieved an upright position, her head swam around and she fought back nausea. She stood there in complete blackness, afraid to move, afraid what she might find, afraid of falling over and bumping into God knows what. She took a deep breath, then she started moving forward in tiny hops, taped wrists extended in front of her, until she bumped into walls. Bigger than the bunker Evan had described. But cold and dark. And musty-smelling. She completed a tour of the walls without finding a door. Then another fit of nausea swept over her and she had to retreat back to the mattress on the floor. At first she couldn't locate it and panic threatened to overwhelm her.

Calm, she told herself. Stay calm. You are alone in a small room and it's only a matter of time before you find the mattress again. She inched her way along the wall and around the corner until her feet kicked at it. There she huddled, shaking, with her knees drawn up, until the nausea receded. This couldn't be happening. It wasn't real.

A deep rumble made her lift her head. She felt the floor shaking. An earthquake? The rumble subsided. When the second rumble came, she identified it. A train. A railway line passed close by. Her first thought was the Snowdon Railway and that this was another bunker dug on the mountainside. Then came a third, more violent rumble, this time accompanied by a distant mournful shriek that changed pitch as it faded. An express train siren. I'm near the main line, she thought, and somehow that made her feel more hopeful. Along the main line were cities and towns and people. Someone would come and find her and she would be rescued.

Evan dosed fitfully and uncomfortably. Every time he drifted into sleep, it was into nightmares. He couldn't wait for dawn. When the first light appeared over the eastern mountains, he got up and dressed awkwardly. If anything he ached more than the night before. The painkiller had worn off and his shoulder hurt every time he moved. Added to that were bruises and muscle pulls from the various falls he had taken.

He came downstairs and was relieved to find that his mother had gone back to Mrs. Williams's house. With any luck he'd be gone before she showed up wanting to cook his breakfast and asking more questions. He called the police station and asked to be picked up, then he cooked himself an egg while he was waiting.

When he arrived at the station, just before seven, he found

Watkins and Hughes sitting together in the cafeteria. He suspected that they hadn't been to bed all night.

"Here's Sleeping Beauty, looking fresh and lovely," Watkins commented in an obvious attempt to keep things light.

"I didn't get much sleep," Evan said, pulling up a chair beside them. "Any news?"

"Not much," Hughes said, staring into his empty teacup. "Several people in your village saw her getting on a bus just after two. The bus driver thinks he remembers her but he can't remember where she disembarked. He says the bus was crowded and a lot of people got off at every stop. Fair enough, I suppose. But we've intercepted the next letter."

"Can I see it?" Evan asked.

Hughes looked up now. "I think perhaps you'd rather not see it. It will only distress you. It's just . . . rather spiteful threats."

"Written in musical notes?" Evan asked.

"In musical notes, as you say."

"Then at least we know he has got her."

Hughes nodded. "Yes, I suppose we can conclude that."

"What about the antiques dealer? We let him go?"

"Yes, we let him go. The search turned up nothing."

"Pity," Evan said. "So what do we do now? What do we have to go on? He must have slipped up somewhere. There must be one fingerprint on something . . ."

"And if there is?" Watkins said quietly. "Unless he has a record, we won't be able to identify him. We can hardly fingerprint the whole of North Wales."

"What about a footprint?" Evan asked. "It was wet up there. He must have left a footprint in the mud by the bunker."

"And we've had half a dozen men tramping over it since," Watkins said. "Not to mention that it's been raining steadily all night. But it's worth a try, I suppose."

Glynis Davies came into the cafeteria. "Ah, there you all are," she said. "They've just been running a piece on the early morning radio show. If everyone in North Wales knows that she's missing, at least that will put more pressure on her kidnapper."

"Let's hope it's not too much pressure and he decides she's a liability," Hughes said. Evan wished he hadn't.

"What we should be doing," Glynis said, pulling up a chair beside Evan, "is working out why he singled Evan out. This is obviously designed to punish Evan specifically—the musical request and the letters, all directed to him. And he calls him Bad EE. Why?"

"Any ideas, Evans?" Hughes asked.

Evan frowned and shook his head.

"It could be a payback," Watkins suggested.

"Payback?" Evan asked.

"For a case you've worked on," Watkins said. "Someone you sent to prison who is now out? Someone with a major grudge."

"Then the first step is to go through all the cases you've been involved in, Evans," Hughes said. "Not necessarily just the big ones. A deranged man could carry a grudge from a traffic fine."

"The obvious one is that choir director we arrested for murder," Evan said, "but he's still in prison. Apart from that, I really can't think. I'll go through the records."

"And if it's not someone that Evan has previously arrested," Glynis said thoughtfully, "it could be something to do with this case we're working on right now. The first kidnapped girl. Maybe Evan was getting too close and this was to warn him off."

Hughes looked sharply at Evan. "What aspects of the investigation were unique to you, Evans?"

"The National Parks people," Evan said. "I was the only one who interviewed them."

"Any likely candidates?"

"I would have said Roger Thomas," Evan said slowly. "He's passionate about music. He's just bought a new caravan. He lied about where he was the day that Shannon Parkinson disappeared. The only thing against that is that I interviewed him yesterday afternoon, around five o'clock. Bronwen wouldn't have reached Caernarfon much before three if she caught that bus. Would he have had time to kidnap her, hide her, and get all the way back to his house in Harlech by the time I showed up?"

"It's doable," Watkins said. "A bit of a rush, depending on where he hid her. He could have brought her home with him."

Evan closed his eyes. Surely it wasn't possible that he had sat on a sofa in a living room while Bronwen was in another room in the same house?

"He wouldn't have invited me in if that was the case," he said, finding it hard to get the words out.

"It depends on his personality type," Hughes replied as easily as if he was discussing the weather. "I rather get the feeling that this chap enjoys the thrill and the challenge. Maybe having you in the house gave him extra kicks."

"Anyway, we'll bring him in for questioning and give his house a thorough going over," Watkins said. "What was the address?"

Evan gave it to him.

"Any other park rangers we should consider? Any other lines of inquiry you've been taking—you and nobody else?" Hughes asked.

"There is Rhodri Llewelyn," Evan said. "Inspector Watkins was inclined to dismiss him as a suspect, but I always had a gut feeling about him."

"Rhodri Llewelyn?" Hughes said. "I don't think his name has come up before."

"Young chap who works at the bank," Watkins said. "Evans became suspicious about him after a Peeping Tom incident involving a young female bank employee. But he was working at the bank on the day that Shannon disappeared and I felt we had nothing on him other than Evan's gut reaction."

"Gut reactions are not to be scoffed at," Hughes said. "Bring him in as well."

"He may be hard to find," Evan said. "He decided to take spur-of-the-moment leave and he's gone off hiking."

"Let's get the details on his vehicle and have him tracked down,"

Hughes said. "Any other gut reactions we should follow up, Evans?"

"Not that I can think of, sir," Evan said.

"Right. We all have work to do then, don't we? Let's get on with it." He stood up, brushed away imaginary crumbs, and strode from the canteen.

"Are you all right?" Glynis asked Evan quietly. "You look terrible."

"There's nothing wrong with me apart from an aching shoulder and a few bruises," Evan said. "As you can imagine, I didn't sleep well."

Glynis looked at him with sympathy, started to say something, then shook her head. "Back to work then."

Evan left the canteen and headed for the computer. He wasn't too comfortable with computers, but looking up the list of cases he'd helped to solve shouldn't be too difficult. He wondered how quickly they'd find Rhodri Llewelyn. He should have mentioned that Rhodri had a motorbike. He changed course and poked his head around Inspector Watkins's door. The room was deserted and he was about to leave when he saw the letter lying on Watkins's desk. Again two lines of musical notation. He couldn't help himself. He knew it was going to cause more pain, but he had to see it. He walked across and picked it up. The letters had been written in pencil under each of the notes. And at the bottom of the page was something new. A row of symbols that looked like circles and crescent moons, then an arrow pointing toward them and the letter U.

Evan read the letters, fighting the bile and rage that rose in his throat.

CAGE CAGE CAGE
GAG FEED BED CEDE

Then a row of suns and moons. Not just for decoration, surely. He counted three pairs and realized what they were saying. U have three days.

189

Chapter 23

Two hours later, Evan was staring at a complete list of his case history and was still none the wiser. In none of the cases had he been the lead officer. Until recently he'd only been a uniformed constable. He'd had a few lucky breaks and helped to crack some big cases, but why should anyone's wrath be directed so exclusively at him? Besides, those men in the high-profile cases should still be in prison. He glanced over the list in front of him. The next thing to do was to check that there had been no early releases. After that, someone should talk to family members of the persons he had arrested, to get a sense whether a brother or a son might be the kind who harbored a grudge. But it all seemed so nebulous and so hopeless.

Evan sank his head into his hands.

"Here, I brought you a cup of coffee." He hadn't heard Glynis come into the room. She put a hand on his shoulder. "Only if you tell Inspector Watkins, I'll deny it." She smiled at him. "Any luck?"

"None at all. I've been over and over this list and I still can't think how anyone would bear such a personal grudge against me. Why me and not Inspector Hughes? He was in charge of all the cases."

Glynis nodded. "It does seem strange. In fact, nothing has made sense to me from the moment this case started. It's as though we've got isolated facts and each of them raises a red flag—girl missing on mountain, bunker found, threatening notes, and now Bronwen missing and you shoved into that bunker—but we don't exactly know that they tie together. It's just possible that the first missing girl has nothing to do with the bunker, that the musical clues have nothing to do with the bunker, that Bronwen vanishing has nothing to do with it either."

"Oh, come on," Evan said. "Someone tried to kill me at that bloody bunker."

"Right. I admit that. But what if the chap who dug the bunker simply was guarding it and didn't want anybody snooping around it? What if he didn't build it to kidnap anybody?" She looked at him. "You see what I'm saying, don't you? We need the common thread, the thing that links all of this together."

"All I know is that my fiancée is missing," Evan said.

"You know what was interesting in that last note." Glynis held his gaze. "That he also appeared to have a personal grudge against Bronwen as well. Bad EE, Bad BE. Is it possible that the grudge is against both of you? Something you've done together?'

"Such as what? Who could possibly have a grudge against anyone as sweet as Bronwen?"

"For example," Glynis said, "you are getting married in a week's time. Someone might not want that to happen."

Evan frowned. "You're suggesting someone who might secretly be in love with Bronwen and resent the fact that she's marrying me?"

"Just a thought." Glynis shrugged. "It could be the other way around, but I can't see a spurned woman doing the kidnapping, or digging the bunker."

"I don't have any spurned women in my past." Evan had to laugh. "Only Betsy, the local barmaid, and she's happily hooked up with the local bulldozer driver. Mostly it was the girls who did the spurning."

"Surely not—good-looking, healthy chap like you?" Glynis smiled back at him.

Evan shrugged. "But Bronwen—what kind of secret admirer could she have recently? She doesn't exactly meet a lot of men up there at the schoolhouse. And before she came here, she was married to someone else."

"Maybe her ex-husband doesn't want to let her go."

"No, it wasn't like that at all. I know her ex-husband. He left her for someone else." Evan wisely left it at that, since Bronwen's ex had left her to live with another man.

"How would you ever know if someone was yearning for her secretly?" Glynis asked. "It could be someone she only meets on the most superficial level."

"The antiques chap," Evan said, bitterly. "I could see that he fancied her."

"But it seems he was in the clear."

Evan merely grunted.

"They're still keeping an eye open. Inspector Watkins has put a tail on him."

Evan sank his head into his hands. "This is hopeless, isn't it, Glynis? What are the statistics on someone being recovered alive if you don't find them in the first twenty-four hours? Not very good, are they?"

"We'll find her," Glynis said. "In fact, I have a hunch that this man wants you to find her."

"So that he can kill both of us at once?"

"You can handle him, Evan. He wants you to match wits with him. So, match them. He's given you clues that he expects you to solve. Take your time and solve them."

She closed the door behind her, leaving him staring at a screen. A few minutes later the dispatcher poked her head around the door. "Phone call for you, Constable Evans."

Evan looked up.

"It's a woman," she whispered. "Says her name is Price."

Evan almost mowed her down in his rush to get to the phone. "Bronwen?" he shouted into the receiver.

"No, it's Emmaline, dear. Your future mother-in-law. Where are you both? We've just arrived and not a sign of you. Don't tell me you're working on a Saturday, and I expect that daughter of mine is out arranging last-minute details, if I know her."

"Something like that." Evan could not bring himself to tell her the truth over the phone. It would have to be broken gently at the right moment.

"Well, then, I think we'll go and find our room at the Everest Inn and maybe you'll both be able to join us for lunch in the bar there. Shall we say one o'clock? Lovely. Looking forward to it."

She hung up and Evan gave a sigh of relief. At least he'd given himself some time to work out what he was going to tell them. They'd blame him, of course. He was the one who had put their daughter in danger. That didn't even matter. He blamed himself. He went back to the notes he had scribbled and realized that Bronwen's parents might be able to help him. They'd know if she'd had an annoying boyfriend, a stalker, someone who wasn't quite stable in her past.

Evan slipped out of the building and went to his car. He knew he shouldn't be driving himself with one arm in a harness, but he didn't want to tie up another officer who could be doing something useful. He freed his left hand enough to balance it against the wheel, shifted into gear, and drove off.

Last night's storm had finally passed over, leaving the day crystal clear and sparkling. Dewdrops made leaves and grass appear to be dotted with diamonds. All the colors were enhanced—white sheep against a background of emerald grass and rich blue sky. For once Evan hardly took in the scenery. He stared straight ahead of him, going over and over in his mind what he was going to say to Bronwen's parents.

The Everest Inn was a recent addition to the landscape. A luxury hotel in a decidedly unluxurious setting, it seemed to be flourishing nevertheless, judging by the number of Jags, Mercs, and BMWs in the car park. Evan turned off the road above Llanfair and drove in through the massive stone gateway. He parked his old bone-shaker next to a Jag and wondered if it belonged to the Prices. Bronwen's mother drove a Jag, he knew. He had no idea what her father drove. Evan felt his pulse rate quicken as he pictured facing that formidable man. He took a deep breath and pushed open the etched glass doors that led into the Everest Inn.

The cavernous foyer was deserted. Harp music was playing softly in the background and a fire burned in the river-rock fireplace, even though it was August. The receptionist looked up as Evan crossed the tiled floor. Evan didn't think it necessary to explain himself. He strode through to the bar beyond the fireplace. Bronwen's father's distinctive upper-class voice came through even before Evan spotted them.

"That's the problem with the blighters these days. You should have seen India when I was a child. Trains ran on time." He looked up and noticed Evan. "Ah, here's the wandering bridegroom now. Good to see you, young Evan. So what have you done with my daughter?"

He held out a big, meaty hand.

Evan shook it.

Mrs. Price looked up from her barstool. "Evan, darling. How lovely to see you." A look of concern crossed her face. "Oh no. Don't tell me you've been injured. Not before your wedding. What have you done? You won't have to wear that sling for the ceremony, will you? It will ruin the photos." As usual Mrs. Price conducted a monologue that didn't often require an answer. She looked around behind Evan. "So where's Bronny? She must be run off her feet, poor thing. We mustn't let her get too tired or she'll look pasty-faced and it won't go with white."

She paused and Evan realized that they finally wanted him to speak. He swallowed hard. "Mrs. Price. Mr. Price. I'm afraid I've got . . . I'm not quite sure how to tell you this."

"She hasn't decided not to marry you? Oh, don't tell me the wedding's off." Mrs. Price groaned.

"No, nothing like that. Look, she can't be here, but we're doing our best and I'm sure—" He babbled on until he noticed that the television was on above their heads at the bar. Mrs. Price's gaze was suddenly fixed on the screen.

"If you've seen this woman, if you saw her yesterday, the number to call is—"

"Bronny?" Mrs. Price whispered. "That's our daughter they're talking about, isn't it?"

Evan nodded. "We've been on the case of a missing woman all this week and last night I—I couldn't find Bronwen. So we have to assume the worst—that he's kidnapped Bronwen too."

"Surely not," Mr. Price said. "You say she's disappeared? There must be other explanations. She may have needed time to think about the wedding. Not kidnapped. Not our daughter."

"I'm afraid so," Evan said. "You can see my arm. Someone tried to kill me last night. And there have been threatening messages. We have to assume that this person has got it in for me particularly, or for me and Bronwen."

"Oh my God." Mrs. Price pressed her hand up to her mouth. "What are we going to do?"

"This calls for a stiff drink," Mr. Price said. He snapped his fingers at the barman. "Three large cognacs, please." Then he spun round to Evan. "So exactly what is being done to find my daughter?"

"Everything possible, sir," Evan said. "We're pursuing any angle we can think of. I've been through a list of all the cases I've worked on, just in case someone is still harboring a grudge from a prior arrest. But my fellow officer, D.C. Davies, suggested that this person's anger might be directed against both of us. Someone might want to stop our wedding."

"Who could that possibly be?" Mrs. Price demanded.

"I've no idea. I wouldn't say that Bronwen had an enemy in the world. You can't meet a sweeter person. I just wondered—you wouldn't have any suggestions, would you? Any unsuitable boyfriends in her past, young men who frightened her?"

"The young man she married turned out not to be very suitable," Mrs. Price said shortly.

"I know," Evan said. "But he left her, didn't he? Anyway, I plan on speaking to him today."

"I can't see him kidnapping her," Bronwen's father said. "Not Edward. Not the type."

"This is someone to whom music is important," Evan said. "All the letters were written in code, using musical notes. Was Bronwen ever involved with anyone who was obsessed with music?"

"Of course she didn't exactly confide in us about what she was doing at Cambridge," her father said. "She could have had any number of unsuitable young men there and we wouldn't have heard about it."

"We haven't always been close." Mrs. Price stared at him with wide, hopeless eyes. "Not as close as I would have wished. Our fault partly, I suppose. We left her with her grandmother while Alan was working in the Middle East and then we sent her to boarding school. But she always was independent—didn't take kindly to our trying to run her life."

Bronwen's father cleared his throat. "So do they have any idea— any idea at all—what this chap might have done with her?"

His question was loaded with unspoken fear. Is she likely to be alive or dead? Has he taken her for sexual reasons? That's what he was asking.

"We discovered a fully equipped bunker on the lower slopes of Mount Snowdon," Evan said slowly. "It was unoccupied and apparently had never been used. He may have prepared more than one."

"Oh God." Mrs. Price gasped again.

The barman had placed three brandy snifters on the counter.

"Here, drink this, old girl. Do you good." Mr. Price handed the glass to his wife. She took it mechanically, sipped, and then coughed. Evan received the glass that was handed to him but couldn't force the fiery liquid down his throat. In fact, every second that he stood there, doing nothing, was pure torture to him. He had to be out, rushing around, trying to find her.

He put the glass back on the counter. "Thank you, sir, but I'd better not on duty. And if you'll excuse me, I shouldn't be wasting any more time."

"No, of course not," Mr. Price said gruffly. "If there's anything we could do to help?"

"I don't think so at the moment," Evan said.

"You will call us as soon as you know anything—anything at all?" Mrs. Price's voice was scarcely more than a whisper.

"Of course I will."

He couldn't think of anything else to say. He started to walk out of the bar. At the doorway he turned back. "I will find her," he said.

Chapter 24

It took Evan a while to locate Bronwen's ex-husband, Edward Ferrers. He had moved away from his former London address, for obvious reasons, Evan decided. Too many bad memories. It was lucky that Edward was of the old school brigade. Evan seemed to remember Bronwen mentioning something about Harrow, and the old boys' association was able to furnish a current address and place of business. Public schools never let their alumni slip through their clutches.

"Ferrers here," Edward's slightly breathy voice came on the phone line.

Evan was able to keep his voice calm and even as he explained the situation. Edward had shown himself once to be emotionally unstable and now he almost yelled into the phone, "Bronwen? You're saying that some bastard has kidnapped Bronwen? How could you let that happen?"

At least this outburst verified that Edward himself had nothing to do with it.

"Yelling won't solve anything, Edward," Evan said. "I need your help. We're trying to come up with a motive. We have a profile of the person who is likely to have abducted her. Loner, outdoorsman, passionately fond of music, probably slightly older than we are. So

I'm asking you to rack your brains and try to remember if there was anyone at Cambridge, or anyone who Bronwen ever mentioned, who annoyed her, or followed her around, or even stalked her. Someone with a musical connection."

Edward was silent for a long while, then he said, "There was one bloke at Cambridge who was in a history class with Bron. Odd sort of chap. I suppose you'd call him the typical nerd, horn-rimmed glasses and always had his nose in a book—socially inept. And I seem to remember that he played some instrument—cello, maybe? Well, he did follow Bronwen around for a while, but then he attempted to assault another girl who was in Bronwen's dorm. I think he was arrested for it."

"Her name wasn't Debbie, by any chance?"

"No." Edward sounded puzzled. "I think it was Alexandra. Why?"

"Because the name Deb, or Debbie or Deborah, is apparently important in a clue he left for us."

Another long pause. "I'm afraid I can't think of anyone called Deborah at the moment. Certainly not in our crowd at Cambridge."

"But the man's name—you can remember that?"

"Let me see. I think it was something strange, that suited him. Erwin—that was it. Erwin Gouge."

"Thank you, Edward. That's really helpful." Evan scribbled it down. "If he was arrested, that will give us something to go on, and he'll have been fingerprinted. I'll get onto the Cambridge police straightaway."

"If there's anything more I can do—" Edward let the rest of the sentence hang in the air.

"I'll keep you posted," Evan said. "And if you do happen to remember a Deborah, or anything else that might be important, I'll give you my mobile number."

"Yes, right." Edward attempted to match Evan's brisk detachment. "It will—I mean—you do have some chance of finding her, don't you? You'll do your best. You and she were . . . close, at one stage."

"Close?" Evan's calm snapped. "I'm bloody well getting married to her next Saturday."

. . .

After he hung up, Evan went outside and stood in the fresh breeze, taking deep breaths. He had never liked Edward Ferrers, despised him actually. Ferrers seemed to bring out the worst in him at the best of times, and this was not the best of times. When he had calmed himself sufficiently, he put a call in to the switchboard and was given the number for East Anglia Police. It didn't take long to locate Erwin Gouge on their records.

"That's right. Arrested for attempted assault on a young woman."

"What happened to him?" Evan asked. "Is he in prison?"

"No, he's not—"

Evan's heart lurched. "Then you don't know where he is?"

"Oh yes, I know that." The voice sounded weary. "He hung himself in a holding cell before his trial."

Evan snapped shut his phone in bitter disappointment. So hopeful and now back to square one. He had no alternative but to drive down to HQ and see what Watkins and Hughes wanted him to do next. He got in the car and winced in pain as he adjusted the strapping around his shoulder to allow him to grip the wheel. Then he drove down the pass faster than he should. His brain was whirring in overdrive as the adrenaline continued to flood through his body. Every second counted and they were getting nowhere. They didn't even know where to start. Glynis had been right. What they needed was the link, the one thing that bound all these strange elements together. The key must be somewhere—in one of those messages he had been sent. Someone hated him, or hated Bronwen, or hated the idea of their being together. The clues were pitifully few. A dead father. Someone called Deb also dead. Classical music. A bunker. A girl missing from a mountain path.

Then it was almost as if he heard Bronwen's voice. "I went to school with a couple of girls like that." Debs! A tenuous link at best, but the only one that connected Bronwen to any of the clues. He stopped the car and pulled out his phone again, trying to force his brain to remember everything Bronwen had told him about her school. He didn't know one posh girls' school from another. It was

200

on the Welsh border, he remembered, in the Malvern Hills, and the name had been similar—something to do with monks. Malvern Priory. That was it. He called Directory Inquiries and was given the number for the school. After a couple of rings, a plummy female voice came on the line. "You have reached Malvern Priory School for Girls. The school office is currently closed for the summer holidays. Michaelmas Term begins on September 15. Please leave your name, number, and nature of your inquiry and . . ."

Evan threw down the phone in disgust. Someone had to be at the school. The premises had to be kept running, even in the summer holidays. He had no alternative but to drive there. The thought of driving that distance made him grimace with pain, but he wasn't going to waste time talking it over with Watkins and Hughes, getting permission or not. He put his foot down and at the roundabout he turned onto the A55 in the direction of Chester instead of Caernarfon.

After a weary hour and a half's drive southward through the border hills that have long separated Wales from England, he found himself passing between impressive brick gateposts and then along a driveway lined with rhododendron bushes. At the end of the drive an elegant yellow stone house could be seen, surrounded by manicured lawns. The only indication that this was a school and no longer a stately home was the lacrosse goal posts on the field to one side and the discreet sign stating. PLEASE DRIVE SLOWLY AND WATCH OUT FOR SCHOOLGIRLS. VISITORS MUST REPORT TO THE SCHOOL OFFICE. An arrow directed Evan round the main building to what was obviously a former stable block. The office, however, was locked.

Evan made his way back to the main building, but that too appeared to be locked and deserted. Just as he was walking back to the car, not sure what to do next, he heard the *putt-putt* of an engine, and a tractor, equipped with mowing blades, came into view between buildings, dropping snippets of newly mown grass as it approached. Evan ran to intercept it. An elderly man with a ruddy, weatherbeaten face, wearing the traditional Welsh farmer's woolen flat cap, was driving the tractor and looked up in surprise as Evan hailed him.

"Hello, sir. Sorry, the school's closed for the holidays," he called.

"I'm with the North Wales Police," Evan shouted back over the loud popping of the tractor. "Is there anyone here I can speak to?"

The man leaned forward to switch off the motor. "What's this about then?" he asked.

"A matter of great urgency. Can you tell me where I can contact someone in authority?"

The old man frowned. "The headmistress just left yesterday for her cottage in France and the school secretary's on holiday with her family."

"Is there nobody who could answer some questions about girls who attended the school? Someone must have contact numbers for somebody."

"Hold your horses, young man." The tractor driver held up his hand in a calming gesture. "There's the assistant secretary comes in during the week, but today's Saturday, isn't it? I suppose you could call her at home and see if she'd come in for you to open up the records."

"That would be very helpful," Evan said. "Where would I find her number?"

"The name is Jones," the man said. "Husband's Richard. They'll be in the phone book."

"Jones? Won't that be like looking for a needle in a haystack?"

The old man grinned. "We're on the English side of the border here. Not so many Joneses as where you come from." He looked at Evan curiously. "What exactly is it you need?"

"I need to find out about girls who attended this school about twelve to fourteen years ago. It's essential I get the information right now. A—a woman has been kidnapped." He fought to keep the description impersonal.

"Well, now." The old man stroked his chin. "You could always ask Miss Posey. I expect she'd be at home."

"Miss Posey?"

"Latin mistress. She lives on grounds in one of the staff cottages. Over beyond the kitchen garden there."

"She's been here longer than twelve years, has she?"

The old man smiled. "They all have. They come here as soon as it's clear that they're never going to get hitched and then they stay on until they die. Miss Posey's pushing seventy, but her mind's still sharp enough."

"And she's in a cottage—" Evan had already started to walk in the direction the old man had indicated.

"Honeysuckle Cottage. The third one along. It's quicker to walk than to drive. You can cut across the kitchen garden."

Evan did as he suggested, hurrying between neat rows of runner beans and fat vegetable marrows. Then, on the other side of a tall yew hedge, he came upon a pretty circle of cottages. They must formerly have been occupied by estate workers. Now they were surrounded by well-tended gardens. Honeysuckle was growing profusely over the porch of its namesake cottage and the front garden was a riot of peonies and roses. Evan was about to raise the brass lion's-head knocker on the front door when a woman's voice called, "Can I help you?"

He spun around and spotted the small white-haired woman on her knees, weeding a side bed in the shade of the hedge.

"Are you Miss Posey?" Evan asked. "I'm Constable Evans from the North Wales Police and I need to ask some questions about girls who attended this school."

"Oh dear." The woman got to her feet a little stiffly. Although she was petite, there was nothing frail about her. Her face was set in the sort of expression a teacher needs when dealing with a classroom of difficult pupils. "You'd better come inside, then. Wait a minute while I make myself respectable."

She proceeded to take off a large gardening apron and to wash her hands in the water barrel beside the house, drying them on a faded cotton skirt.

"Come in, then," she said, kicking off muddy gardening clogs at the door and proceeding into the house in stockinged feet. "I expect you'd like a cup of tea."

"Only if it's not too much trouble."

She looked up at him and a smile creased her severe face. "No. It's teatime. I always take a cup myself at four. You can talk to me in the kitchen while I boil the water." She led Evan along a dark, narrow hallway lined with bookcases into a simple but immaculate small kitchen. In contrast to the hallway, this room was bathed in afternoon sunlight. The window was wide open and the sound of a thrush floated in, along with the heady smell of roses.

"Sit." She pointed at a white ladder-backed chair at the table. Evan sat.

"Now. How can I help you?" she asked.

Evan told her. The old woman's face showed alarm. "Bronwen Price? I remember her well. Bright girl. Went to Cambridge. You suspect she's been abducted?"

Evan nodded. He couldn't bring himself to speak.

"How simply terrible. Was this just a random kidnapping or do you know the motive behind it? I don't recall that her family was particularly wealthy, not like some of the girls we have here."

"That's why I'm here," Evan said. "I'm trying to discover the motive. The kidnapper has sent some cryptic clues and one of them mentions Deb. This could be a girl's name, of course, but we can't seem to come up with anyone called Deborah. My colleague suggested that it might apply to a debutante. I know there aren't any official debs anymore, but Bronwen said that there were several girls at school with her who fit that description."

"There certainly were, in her day," Miss Posey said as the kettle whistled and she turned it off. "Not anymore, of course. We were most selective once. Only the girls of the best families. Now we take anyone who can pay the fees. We've even got two girls from Saudi Arabia who insist on walking around in those ridiculous headscarves. I find it most unfair when the rest of our girls have to adhere strictly to the uniform code, but the Head won't risk offending the father, who is some prince or other and ridiculously wealthy."

Evan waited, trying to conceal his impatience, while she rambled on.

"So which debs can you think of who were at school with Bronwen? She told me, but my mind was on other things at the time and the names escaped me. One of them was a quite ridiculous hyphenated name—"

"Amanda Fanshaw-Everingham, I believe." Miss Posey looked up from pouring the water into the teapot. "She's now the Viscountess Montague, of course."

"And the other was Penny somebody?" Evan grasped at a fleeting wisp of memory.

"Ah yes. Penny Mowbray. She certainly qualified as a debutante in the old sense. The family was very thick with the royals. Her mother was the daughter of an earl. The father played polo with Prince Philip." She paused and a smile crossed her face. "Such a naughty girl, but fun."

"There was some incident in which she and Bronwen stole a car?"

"Oh dear, yes. That dreadful incident with the motorbike. They were so lucky that the man wasn't hurt more seriously or the police would have had to press charges. Fortunately he walked away with just some bruises and some damage to his hand, I believe, although Penny's father had to pay for the motorbike."

"Do you happen to remember the man's name?"

Miss Posey shook her head. "I don't think I ever knew it. It was just some tourist who was passing through the area."

"Do you know what Penny is doing now?"

"She died, poor girl. In her early twenties. Tragic accident. She was passionate about riding, like all her family. Her horse took a tumble and she broke her neck. Such a waste."

So the deb had died. But in an accident.

"Any other debs you can think of?" Evan asked. "Any unpleasant incidents while Bronwen was at school—stalkers or a man threatening the girls?"

"Good heavens, no," she said, then her expression changed. "Strange you should ask that. Penny Mowbray played the violin. One day she came into her room and found her violin smashed to pieces. An extensive inquiry was carried out but the guilty party was never found. Some of us suspected it was a certain girl who was jealous of Penny, but we could never prove anything."

She put a cup of tea in front of Evan and placed the sugar bowl and milk jug beside him.

"I always believe in letting people help themselves," she said. "Although I don't take sugar myself."

Evan forced himself to drink the tea while Miss Posey prattled on to him. As soon as he had drained the cup, he stood up. "If you'll excuse me, I have to be going. I've got to try and find out more about that motor accident."

"You don't think it has anything to do with Bronwen being kidnapped, do you?"

"Right now I'm just clutching at straws," Evan said, "but this is a straw and it's the only connection between Bronwen and a deb that I can find."

He left the cottage, hurried back across the kitchen garden, and was soon driving out through the forbidding gateway. He hadn't been driving for five minutes when his mobile phone rang.

"Evans, where the hell are you?" Watkins voice echoed through the car.

"On my way in, sir. Be with you shortly," Evan said.

"I thought you weren't supposed to be driving."

"I didn't want to tie up another officer in waiting on me, sir. I'm doing okay. I had to meet with Bronwen's parents."

"I bet that wasn't a piece of cake."

"Bloody awful. Any news?"

"Nothing big. But we've had Roger Thomas here and your presence would have been useful."

"Roger Thomas? Did you get anything out of him?"

"Strangely enough, yes. We now know why he lied about where he was that afternoon. He was having it off with the lady park ranger. Diana somebody. Rather ashamed of himself and didn't want it to get back to his choir."

In spite of everything, Evan laughed. "Roger and Diana? Good

God. That's something I never would have guessed in a million years."

"We're still looking for Rhodri Llewelyn. Get down here if you're feeling up to it."

"I'll be in as soon as I can, sir," Evan said and hung up, glad that he hadn't had to reveal where he actually was and what he was actually doing.

There was an elderly sergeant on duty at the closest police station in Leominster.

"An accident twelve or fourteen years ago, you say?" he said in response to Evan's request. "Was someone killed?"

"No. It wasn't serious. Some girls, joyriding in a car, hit a man on a motorbike, but he was okay."

The sergeant's face showed scorn. "I expect there's a report on it filed somewhere in the bowels of HQ in Shrewsbury, but we don't have nothing like that here."

"I see." Evan turned to go.

"You probably won't find anyone in records at the weekend," the sergeant called after him, seeming to delight in being the bearer of bad news. "They've been cutting back on support staff. They've cut us down to one officer in the station and one on the beat at weekends too, which is bloody stupid because that's when people have time for crime. Why don't you write down the details and I'll call the request in for you on Monday."

"Monday?" Evan spun back to him. "This is damn important. A matter of life and death."

A smile twitched on the sergeant's lips. "Bit dramatic, wouldn't you say? But then you Welsh like your drama."

Evan's fist curled, longing to hit him. He took a couple of steps toward him, leaning a little too close to be comfortable. "Look you. We have a madman who has kidnapped a young woman—the second woman to disappear in a week. He'd built a bunker with handcuffs in it. He tried to kill me last night, so no, I don't think that life and death is at all an exaggeration!" The words came spitting out.

The sergeant recoiled. "Sorry, mate. No offense meant. But I seriously think you'll have little luck in records on a Saturday, even if they've kept anything as trivial as a minor accident that long. Your best bet would be the local paper. They publish a weekly police blotter and your accident is likely to have made that, especially if it involved girls from the school."

"And where's the local paper?"

"Ludlow. Not quite ten miles from here."

"Thanks." Evan ran back to his car. Frustration and tension were building to snapping point. It was like being in one of those board games in which he was constantly drawing the card that sent him back to Start.

Ludlow was busy with Saturday commerce. He had to ask several times before he found the newspaper office, just off the High Street. The girl at the front desk listened with sympathetic ear and pretty soon Evan found himself going through back issues on microfilm.

"It's all on CD these days." A buck-toothed cub reporter, who'd been stuck with weekend duty, perched on the edge of the desk, ready to chat. "And we write our columns with one of these publishing programs. Ever so advanced we are, for a small paper."

Evan just wished he'd go away. Week after week flashed past on the screen. Burglaries, drunk and disorderly, some weeks with nothing at all. A very law-abiding community, it would seem. Then finally he was staring at it.

JOYRIDE ENDS IN NEAR TRAGEDY

Two students from Malvern Priory were involved in a traffic accident on the Wigmore to Knighton road, late on Sunday, the 18th. Their car, which was borrowed without the owner's permission, struck the motorbike driven by Shrewsbury resident Neville Shorecross, who was passing through the area on a camping trip. Mr. Shorecross was brought to Ludlow Infirmary, kept overnight for observation and then released.

Chapter 25

She woke to light, unbearably bright after hours of darkness. Instinctively, she squeezed her eyes shut and turned away. Her heart jolted in fear as something touched her face. Then she cried out in pain as the tape was ripped away from her mouth. She tried to put her hands up to her burning skin.

Gradually, her eyes were adjusting to the light. She saw now that it came from a trap door above her head. A ladder extended down from it and the hazy form of a person was leaning over her.

"I don't know why I'm bothering to do this," said a well-bred voice. "It's really a waste of time to feed you, when you won't be around much longer, but I suppose I'm a humane person at heart."

Bronwen flexed her stiff jaw and felt her lips stinging as she moved them. "Humane? You're a monster."

"Here. Drink this." He held a glass of water up to her lips.

"The last thing you offered me to drink was drugged," she said.

"This one isn't."

She sipped, relishing the water flowing down through her parched mouth.

"Why are you doing this?" she demanded.

He looked surprised. "You must know why you're here."

"I have no idea, unless I'm fulfilling some kinky kidnap fantasy."

"You didn't notice my reaction when I first heard your name, when you walked into my bank?"

"I noticed nothing."

"You mean you don't remember? The accident?"

"Accident?"

"You stole a car. You and that Mowbray girl. You crashed into my motorbike."

"That was you?"

"It was indeed. You destroyed my life that day."

"Destroyed your life? They said you weren't seriously hurt." Bronwen blinked as she tried to look up at him. Make eye contact. Establish a human connection with the captor. Those were the things one was supposed to do. "You were released from hospital the next morning. Penny's father paid for your bike."

"Paid for my bike?" he shouted, his face distorted now and eyes bulging with rage. "Paid for my bike? What about my life? Who paid for my life?" He raised his left hand and waved it in her face. "Look at this!"

She noticed that the hand was missing the top of a finger. The ring finger.

"It was severed when your car ran over it."

"I'm very sorry, but I hardly see that—I mean, I've watched you write. You're right-handed."

He knelt on the floor, close enough that his breath blew into her face. It was a surprisingly sweet breath as if he'd just cleaned his teeth. "Do you know how many fingers it takes to play the piano? Ten. It takes ten fingers to play the piano. I wanted to be a pianist. I was studying and hoping to get into the Royal Academy of Music."

"Weren't you a little old?" she asked, realizing too late that this was probably unwise. "You looked quite grown-up to us, so you must have already been at least in your mid-twenties."

His face distorted even further. "Yes, I was a little old, but I didn't grow up with moneyed parents like you. My father worked in a bank. In a stupid bank. They were always poor. Terribly genteel, but always scrimping and saving. They paid for my music lessons while I was growing up, but when I finished school they expected me to go out and earn my living. He got me a job in his bank—expected me to be grateful, to be pleased, to be bloody proud. To go to the Royal Academy, to pursue my piano studies would be frivolous. 'A waste of time,' my father called it. He never appreciated my talent."

"And so you killed him."

"How astute of you. Yes, I did. I made it look like an accident, of course. Nobody ever suspected. After that I put every second and every penny into my piano studies. One day I would have been good enough to sit the Royal Academy exam and they would have appreciated my talent instantly. Only you spoiled that for me."

"Penny Mowbray—" She heard her voice waver. "Did you kill her too? Was she the deb?"

"Another unfortunate accident. Nobody ever suspected otherwise. Really, people are very dense. I hunted for you after that, but I couldn't find you."

"No, I was married and living in London."

"Married? But I thought—"

"My wedding next week will be my second marriage."

"Would have been. Unfortunately, you won't have the chance to compare."

Bronwen looked him squarely in the eye. "They'll find me, you know. It's only a matter of time."

He smiled then. "As you say, a matter of time. I gave them three days, but I don't think I'm prepared to wait that long. We'll see. I must say it rather amuses me to watch their pathetic attempts. But I rather think I'll enjoy watching you die."

"How do you plan to kill me?" she asked.

"I haven't quite made up my mind. Too many changes of plan." He looked at the half-full glass of water in his hand. "I must read up on how many days a human can live without water." Deliberately he turned the glass over and watched the rest of the liquid splash onto the stone floor.

"And you really think you'll be able to get on with your life and live with your conscience afterward?" Bronwen asked him.

"Oh yes," he said. "You forget, I've done it before. Third time's a charm, as they say."

"It's Neville Shorecross," Evan yelled into his mobile phone as soon as D.I. Watkins was put on the line. "He was injured in an accident when Bronwen and another girl stole a car when they were at school."

"Neville Shorecross? Who the hell is he?"

"The bank manager at Lloyds."

"The bank manager? Surely not. I bank there too. He's an inoffensive, well-bred kind of bloke."

"It has to be him. The other girl who stole the car was connected with royalty—a deb. And she's dead now. Bronwen might have stopped at the bank yesterday if she was intending to buy that brass bed."

"How the hell did you find this out?"

"I went to the school."

"Where are you?"

"North of Oswestry, just about to join up with the A55."

"Does the word 'permission' feature at all in your vocabulary or are you going to be the rogue officer all your career?"

"Sorry, sir, but I had to act in a hurry. I couldn't risk you saying no on account of my shoulder."

"Too bloody right. I would have done."

"Come on, guv, you'd have done the same thing if someone had taken Tiffany or your wife."

"Maybe I would."

"And I couldn't just sit there and do nothing. I was going crazy."

"Well, get back here as quick as you can. I'll assemble a team and bring back that psychologist chappy. If you're right in what you say, we'll only have one chance and no margin for error, so we're not rushing things."

"I'll be there, sir."

Evan put down the phone and pressed the pedal to the floor. He arrived forty-five minutes later, having exceeded the speed limit all the way. His shoulder now ached alarmingly and he swallowed a couple of painkillers and retied the harness before going into the police station. The team was assembled and paying attention to the profiler.

"—carries a grudge," Evan heard him saying before they all looked up at his entry.

"This is the plan, Evans," D.C.I. Hughes said as Evan returned Glynis's smile. "You will go with Watkins to confront Shorecross at his home. You will do or say nothing to alarm him. We will ask him to come with us and open up the bank, which we will search. We will then thank him for his cooperation and take him home. If what our profiler suggests is true, he will think he has outsmarted us yet again. We will then have the house under surveillance and wait for him to lead us to the girl."

Evan noted he didn't use her name. It was so much easier to be removed from the victim.

"I'd like to have you along, Evans," Watkins said, "but I'm not taking you if you don't think you can keep your cool. He mustn't suspect for an instant that we're onto him. So let me know now. We can bring him in. We can maybe get him to confess, but if we can't get him to reveal where he's hidden her, then there's no point."

Evan did see the sense in this. He nodded. "Don't worry," he said.

"Let's do it." Hughes clapped his hands. "Surveillance team in place?"

Watkins nodded. "Yes, sir."

"Let's go."

Ten minutes later they parked outside a Victorian terraced house in Bangor. An unprepossessing address, not unlike the house in which bank clerk Hillary Jones lived. And not too far from it, either. More thoughts rushed through Evan's already whirling brain.

Neville Shorecross opened the door with a surprised smile on his face.

"Mr. Evans—what a surprise. You must have a very urgent banking need to seek me out on a Saturday."

He was wearing well-pressed slacks and a cardigan over a checked shirt. The typical British gentleman on his day off.

"Nothing to do with banking, Mr. Shorecross," Evan said. "Something more important than that. My fiancée, Bronwen Price, is missing. The second missing woman in a week."

Shorecross's face grew grave. "How alarming. And you suspect foul play? You don't just think she's gone off somewhere and forgotten to tell you?"

"It's our wedding in one week," Evan said. "Her parents have just arrived. Where do you think she'd possibly go?"

"I see. So you're taking me up on my offer."

"Your offer?" Evan asked.

"My Scout search and rescue team. We've been ready and available all week, you know. My boys have a rucksack packed and can be out on the mountain at a moment's notice. They're well trained."

Watkins stepped forward. "It's not your Scouts we're interested in at the moment, sir. We'd like to ask you some questions about yesterday afternoon, if we could possibly come in."

"Come in? Yes, by all means." Shorecross opened his front door wide and ushered them into a narrow hallway. "This way, please, gentlemen. I don't actually have a front parlor anymore, because my piano takes up so much damned space." He pushed open a door to reveal a gleaming polished grand piano, occupying most of the small front room. "Still, I wasn't about to give it up when I moved here. I'll get around to looking for more spacious quarters when I have time. In here, then, gentlemen. I'm afraid it's rather cramped, but it's just me, so I manage."

The back room contained a dining set, armchairs, a large stereo on one wall, and neat racks of CDs. Shorecross motioned Evan and Watkins to the two armchairs situated on either side of a fake log fire. Evan perched uneasily at the edge of his chair. The man seemed so at ease. Was it possible he'd got it wrong and Shorecross wasn't the one?

"Mr. Shorecross," Watkins said, "when did you last see Bronwen Price?"

Shorecross frowned. "You know, I'm really not sure."

"Did she come into your bank yesterday?"

"She may have done. Fridays are always busy for us."

"So you don't remember seeing her? She didn't have a specific interview with you in your office?"

Shorecross frowned. "What exactly are you asking me, Inspector? Are you somehow insinuating that I might be responsible for her disappearance?"

"Oh Good Lord, no, sir." Watkins sounded if anything a trifle too hearty, Evan thought. "We're trying to piece together her movements yesterday afternoon, so that we can work out who was the last person to see her before she disappeared. We know she took the bus down from Llanfair. We know she didn't show up at an antiques store to look at a brass bedstead she intended to purchase. It's possible she stopped in at the bank first, if she was intending a large purchase."

The frown left Shorecross's face. "Come to think of it, I think I did hear her name mentioned. I think I recall Hillary saying something about 'Only one week to go, Miss Price.' But I didn't actually see her, so I couldn't tell you what she was wearing."

"I wonder if you'd be good enough to accompany us down to the bank now, sir," Watkins said.

"Now? What for?" For the first time there was a sharpness to Shorecross's voice.

"We're leaving no stone unturned right now. We'd like to search the bank and have you unlock the vault."

"Unlock the vault? This is preposterous."

Watkins held up a conciliatory hand. "I assure you that we're putting every other business she could have visited through the same degree of security. A bank vault would be a good place to hide someone, wouldn't it?"

"If you wanted to kill them quickly," Shorecross said. "I doubt there would be enough air to keep someone alive overnight." Evan thought that the bank manager shot him a look, to check out how he had fared when deprived of air in a bunker.

215

"If you object to coming with us, you can always just give us the keys," Watkins said.

"Give you the keys? Good Lord, man, I'm responsible for the money at that bank. My head would be on the chopping block if I let you wander around with the keys to my vault."

"I assure you, Mr. Shorecross, that money is the last thing on our minds right now," Evan said.

Shorecross sighed and rose to his feet. "Very well. One must do one's civic duty, although how you think that anyone could stuff a young woman into a vault under our noses is beyond me."

The policemen didn't reply.

"Oh dear, I can't say it looks too good, letting my neighbors witness my being bundled into a police car," Shorecross said jovially as they came out into the street.

"You have nosy neighbors then, do you, sir?" Watkins asked.

"Not particularly. I hardly ever see them as my garage is behind the house." He glanced back at the deserted street. "So, do you have any theories, any suspects yet in the case of these missing women?" he asked, as Watkins steered the car out into traffic. "I could tell you were interested in our Mr. Llewellyn and I must say that his hasty departure has made me a little curious also. I should try to contact him, if I were you. I always felt he was a little—on the strange side, shall we say."

"Good suggestion, sir. Our men are out looking for him as we speak," Watkins said.

"Excellent. Although whether he would have returned to kidnap Miss Price is questionable. And in broad daylight, from what you are insinuating."

"I expect whoever did it will give himself away before too long," Watkins said calmly. "They always do, you know. One little slip. That's all it takes."

"Really?"

Evan felt as if his head would explode, sitting in a cramped car with the man who was holding Bronwen sitting a few feet away from him. Why couldn't they just pull into a secluded byway and

216

knock him silly until he talked? Apart from ethical reasons, he knew why. Because men in similar situations had refused to reveal where they were holding their victims, even under the worst of threats.

He tried to breathe deeply until they pulled up at the bank. After Shorecross had disarmed the alarm system, the tour didn't take long. There wasn't much to see, although Evan noted with interest that there was a security camera over the front entrance. Shorecross opened the door to his office. The two detectives made the motions of looking under the desk and in the coat cupboard, much to Shorecross's amusement.

"All just what we would have expected," Watkins said cheerily. "Now the vault, if you don't mind."

Shorecross led the way. Watkins followed. Evan started to follow then returned to the bank manager's office, giving it another quick inspection. There seemed to be no camera in here. There was a velvet curtain on the back wall. Behind it was not another window, but a back entrance. When he opened the door he found it led into walled parking area, containing rubbish bins. A way out without being seen, he thought, and closed the door silently behind him. On the floor he noticed the hint of a stain on the carpet. When he touched it, it still seemed slightly damp. Cleaning fluid had evidently been used on it, judging by the smell, but he suspected that the lab boys would manage to find out what the original stain was made of. He scraped up as much as he could with his penknife into one of the paper cups from the water cooler and sprinted out to join the other two, who were just emerging from the vault.

"Satisfied, gentlemen?" There was something close to a smirk on Shorecross's face.

"Perfectly, thank you, and sorry to have troubled you," Watkins said.

"Now, if you don't mind, I'd like to get home as quickly as possible. BBC Concert Hall on Radio Four. I listen to it every Saturday."

"You must be quite a musician, sir," Watkins said.

"Yes, music has always been an important part of my life," Shorecross said. "I had hoped to reach the concert stage myself one day,

Chapter 26

The moment he left her, Bronwen started working hard. Now that it was clear she was to be killed, she was determined not to give in without a fight. And that needed the removal of the tape around her wrists and ankles. Her brief chance to look at the space in which she was kept while he had the trap door open revealed a room with walls and ceiling covered in polystyrene tiles. A perfect soundproofed room. Apart from that, nothing. Smooth walls, smooth ceiling. Nothing in the room but the inflated camping mattress and the bucket in the corner. How he expected her to use it when her hands were taped in front of her and her ankles taped together, she didn't know. Men always were pretty clueless about women's bodily functions. She had positioned it in her mind while there was light in the room. She hopped over to it and found, to her disgust, that it was made of light plastic. No use as a potential weapon, but she brought it back with her to the air mattress.

The first thing to do was free either her wrists or ankles. She explored the tape around her ankles and tried to locate an end piece she might be able to pull, but it was impossible at the angle her hands were bound together. She tried digging her nails into it, but that was useless, too. He had done too thorough a job.

Her hands went up to her neck and she located the cross she always wore under her turtleneck. At least he hadn't explored her body while she'd been unconscious. That gave her a small feeling of relief. Her fingers touched the cool gold of the cross. It had been given to her by her grandmother on her confirmation. It was probably too delicate to be much good, but it was better than nothing. She pressed her fingers together around it and yanked hard. The chain cut into her throat but finally snapped, leaving the cross between her fingers.

Then she started digging patiently at the ankle tape. At last she was rewarded with a satisfying pop as the gold cross penetrated the tape. Then she worked like a terrier at enlarging the tear. She dug and scratched with her nails until finally she could stick a finger through the hole and pull and tug. She had no idea how long it took her but at last she had pulled the tape off and her legs were free. Elated with this accomplishment, she got up and moved about the room, getting the circulation back into her feet, ready for possible flight.

The tape around her wrists wasn't going to be so easy, but she'd need her hands free to defend herself, or to escape up that ladder. Now she was sitting back on the mattress, she examined the bucket again. It was cheaply made and the end surface of the metal handle, where it was bent up through the plastic side, was unfinished metal. Slightly rough to the touch. She sat down and clamped the handle between her knees, rubbing her wrists back and forth over this rough piece of metal. She felt tired and weak, conscious that she had had nothing to eat for at least twenty-four hours and only a couple of sips of water in that time before he had tipped the rest away.

They will find me, she told herself, knowing that time might be running out.

And if they don't? The thought hovered at the fringe of her conscious mind.

Then I'll have to help myself.

. . .

"We can't just let him go," Evan said, looking back at the closed front door as they drove away.

"We have no choice," Watkins said flatly. "If we bring him in now, we might never find out where he's hidden her." He glanced across at Evan, who was staring out into the night with an expression of utter bleakness on his face.

"Don't worry, boyo," Watkins said softly. "We've got the place staked out. When he goes to her, we'll follow him. That's the safest way."

"I hope to God you're right," Evan said. "He was so damned composed, wasn't he? So cocky."

"If he's really the one who wrote the notes, he thinks his intelligence is superior to ours."

"If he's really the one?" Evan demanded. "If? If? Are you trying to tell me you're not quite sure he's got Bronwen?"

"I agree he's the best lead we've got so far," Watkins said. "We've no proof, though, have we? Just a moment, boyo." He put out a hand as Evan squirmed uncomfortably in his seat. "We had a couple of our men search Shorecross's house while we took him to the bank, so we'll know more in a minute."

"Did you?" Evan looked impressed. "That was pretty slick."

"Not just a pretty face, am I?" Watkins actually grinned.

"I might have some evidence of my own," Evan said. "While you went into the vault, I stayed behind in his office. Some kind of liquid had been spilled on his floor. The cleaners have obviously tried to clear it up, but I scooped some into a paper cup, just in case."

"Well done."

"Oh, and there's a way out behind the curtain. He could have taken Bronwen out that way without being noticed."

"So, the next thing to do is to establish whether the young lady at the bank—Hillary Jones, is it?—saw Bronwen come in yesterday afternoon, and whether she saw her leave. I'll get someone onto that right away." He glanced at Evan again as they drove into the car park. "Only hopefully none of this will be necessary and he'll

221

lead us to her himself soon. My bet is that we have rattled him and he'll want to make sure she's well hidden and safe or—" He stopped abruptly. As Evan read the rest of the sentence, "or he'll want to finish her off quickly," the words played through his brain.

They got out of the car. Watkins strode out toward the police station entrance. Evan lingered outside, taking deep breaths and trying to calm his racing mind. Something hadn't been right. Something was lurking, just out of reach, in his head. Somewhere in those dealings with Shorecross he had spotted a clue. He went through the whole encounter again, sighed, and followed Watkins into the building.

Roberts, the forensic tech, was sitting in D.C.I. Hughes's office.

"No luck so far, then?" Hughes asked as Watkins came in, followed by Evan.

"Nothing concrete yet," Watkins replied, "although Evans managed to scrape up traces of liquid spilled on the floor at the bank. We can get that analyzed. What about you, Roberts? Did you manage to get into the house?"

"Oh yes. No problem." Roberts grinned.

"I always thought you had criminal tendencies," Watkins said. "Did you find anything?"

"A blond hair on the hall carpet. Of course, we won't be able to identify it for a while and he could have picked it up from a customer at the bank. But apart from that, nothing."

"No attic or cellar?"

"The trap door to the attic has been painted over and not disturbed for years. Those houses don't have cellars. Just an old coal hole in most of them, but this one has been bricked over. Oh, and there was a separate garage behind the house, off a back alley. Nothing in that either apart from his car. The rest of the house was all neat and tidy. Bloody great piano he had, didn't he?"

Watkins nodded. "He claimed he was studying to be a concert pianist at one stage."

"So what now?" Hughes asked.

"We have two men on surveillance," Watkins said. "They'll follow the minute he leaves the house. And we need to get that liquid tested and to establish that Miss Price was seen at the bank yesterday. Evan, why don't you go to interview Hillary Jones?"

Evan nodded. "All right. I'd rather be doing something than sitting around and waiting."

"Oh, and Evans—" Watkins called after him. "Don't give anything away. She might be loyal to her boss and tip him off. I can trust you, can't I?"

"Don't worry. I won't do anything that might put Bronwen in more danger." Evan called over his shoulder as he left the room.

"You shouldn't really keep him on this case," he heard Hughes saying as he reached the front doors. "No good can come from an officer being personally involved."

Evan lingered.

"Have a heart, sir," Watkins said. "He'd go crazy if you made him sit at home and wait. He needs to think he's doing something."

Evan nodded to himself and pushed open the door. His shoulder, forgotten during the tension of the last events, reminded him painfully that he shouldn't be driving. Immediately, he thought of Bronwen. Was she in pain at this moment? He'd kill the bastard if he'd hurt her. His mind pictured knocking Shorecross to the floor with one mighty blow, then kneeling on his chest while he throttled the life out of him. Instantly he was ashamed that he had such violence in him. Wasn't that why he'd joined the police force in the first place—to make society a civilized place where thugs and violence didn't rule? But monsters shouldn't be allowed to exist, he argued with himself. Men who seemed civilized on the outside, who played the piano and wore tweed jackets. . . .

He broke off in mid-thought. He had been trying to picture Shorecross playing the piano and he now knew what was wrong. The piano had been oddly placed in the room. If it was the only piece of furniture, why not in the middle, instead of over to one corner with the keyboard facing out into the room? Surely it would be awkward to play from that position? If he tried to play the highest or lowest notes, he'd hit his elbow on the walls.

Evan's heart started beating faster. The piano had to be in that position for a reason. And there had been a vacuum cleaner in the room. Was that to get rid of the marks when a piano was moved?

He swung off the A55 at the last moment.

Neville Shorecross stood with his forehead resting against the smooth cool surface of the front door until he heard the police car drive away. Then he went through into the dining room and poured himself a sherry. His hand was trembling so much that the crystal stopper clinked musically against the carafe. Music. He needed music to calm him. He switched on the radio and the strains of Tchaikovsky's Seventh Symphony filled the room. Not what he would have chosen. The finality and overwhelming melancholy hit him like a stab in the chest. He would have to do it now. No turning back. On the long roller coaster ride to destruction.

But they didn't suspect, he told himself. They had no clue what they were looking for. Idiots, all of them. He had thought that he might just leave her there, forget about her until it was too late. Now he realized he couldn't risk the house being searched. He would do the deed before they came back and then he could bury the body at his leisure under the cellar floor. Then he'd seal off the room forever and nobody would ever know. His hand shook violently as he contemplated this. It was one thing stringing a wire across a path where a young woman would be riding. It was one thing tampering with the brakes on a car so that his father lost control on a dangerous hill. But it was another to be physically involved in taking a life. Could he do it? Could he actually put his hands around her neck and squeeze until there was no more life left in her? Or smother her? He had no choice. He couldn't let her go, so he had no choice.

Another drugged drink, then. That would make it easier on both of them. He'd offer her a cup of cocoa and when she was asleep, he'd smother her. Thus satisfied, he went through into the kitchen to put some milk on the stove.

. . .

224

Bronwen lay on her mattress, staring into darkness. She had no idea if it was day or night or how long she had been there. Hallucinations floated in front of her eyes. Tiredness overcame her and she drifted in and out of sleep. It was hard to tell the sleep from the waking, except that in the sleep Evan was there. "Don't worry, *cariad*. It's all a bad dream," he was saying, but then she woke and knew that it wasn't a bad dream. It was reality.

She reached out and touched the bucket beside her. She was ready for him when he came. But he might not come for hours, or days. He might never come. Just leave her there to die slowly. That was the biggest fear of all.

She must have dozed off again when she was woken by a sound. Slowly, a square of light appeared above her head. Bronwen sprang to her feet, grabbed the bucket, and stood in the shadows in one corner as the square of light became bigger and the ladder was lowered. She watched him come down, step by step.

"Here, my dear," he said. "My conscience got the better of me. I've brought you a drink. You see, I am a humane man, after all."

She waited. He lowered himself down the last step, the cup in one hand. "Miss Price?" he asked, looking around and surprised not to see her on the mattress.

She stepped from the shadows and swung the bucket at him with all her force. She aimed directly at the cup in his hands. Shorecross let out a shriek as the hot cocoa splashed over him. The cup clattered to the floor.

Bronwen raced for the ladder and started to scramble up. She had reached the top rung and was attempting to haul herself out of the hole when his hand grabbed at her foot. She kicked out but he held on ferociously. Then he grabbed the other ankle and pulled with all his weight.

Gradually she felt her hands losing their grip until she let go and fell to the floor. The fall knocked the breath out of her. Shorecross loomed over her. "You stupid female," he said. "You've ruined a good jacket. I thought I was going to regret killing you, but I have to tell you that now it will be a pleasure."

Bronwen tried to scramble to her feet, but his shoe came to meet her in a violent kick, sending her reeling backward. She put her hands over her face to defend herself as he loomed over her.

At that moment the front door bell rang. Then someone knocked loudly.

"Mr. Shorecross. Police. Open up," a voice shouted.

Shorecross looked around wildly, then started to scramble up the ladder. Bronwen returned the favor and grabbed onto his ankle. He tried to kick her off.

"Don't come in. I've got the girl," Shorecross screamed. "I'll kill her!"

"Evan. It's me. I'm here. Come and get me!" Bronwen shouted.

"I'm warning you, I'll kill her!" Shorecross yelled.

The next moment, the front door shuddered as an attempt was made to break it down. Evan grunted as his body was jolted against the front door and pain shot through his injured shoulder. He pulled out his mobile. "Backup right now. Shorecross's house. He's got her here. I can hear her. He's going to kill her!" he shouted.

Then he pushed past bushes to the front window. The light was on behind the curtains in the front room. Evan wrestled a large stone free from the rockery in the front garden and hurled it at the window, smashing the pane. Then he kicked out an opening big enough to crawl through and climbed into the room. The piano had been pushed forward and the carpet folded back to reveal a trap door cut into the floorboards. He ran to it and yanked it open.

"Don't come any closer. I have a knife at the girl's throat," a voice said from the darkness.

Evan froze.

Suddenly there was a yelp and Bronwen's voice shouted, "He hasn't got a knife, Evan. Come and get him."

"I want my solicitor present," a calm voice said. "I'm not going anywhere until my solicitor is here. I've heard about police brutality. I haven't been well. I need a doctor."

"Let Miss Price come up to me," Evan said. "Nobody's going to hurt you. Let her up now."

He waited and soon Bronwen's head emerged from the hole. Evan hauled her up.

"I knew you'd find me. I knew you'd come," she said, and fell into his arms, laughing and sobbing at the same time.

Chapter 27

It was almost midnight before Evan returned from the hospital to which Bronwen had been taken. Apart from dehydration and some bruises and scrapes, she had weathered her ordeal well, but the doctor insisted they keep her overnight for observation.

He felt utter elation as he drove back from the hospital to the police station. She was safe. Nothing else mattered in the world. Shorecross had given up without any kind of struggle. In fact, he had been like a deflated balloon when he emerged from the underground room. When Evan came into the station, he found Shorecross in the interview room with a solicitor on one side of him and Watkins and Hughes on the other.

"May I be present, if you don't mind?" Evan asked, and was given a nod, indicating he should take the chair in the corner.

"D.C. Evans has just entered the room," Watkins said into the tape recorder. "Now, Mr. Shorecross, to recap—you had your Scouts build the bunker on the mountain. Is that correct?"

"We were doing a survival training weekend," Shorecross said. "They only dug a primitive shelter. I went back later and finished it."

"For what purpose, sir? Was it built with Miss Price in mind?"

"No, not at all," Shorecross said. "It was only during the last couple of weeks that I learned that Miss Price now lived locally."

"Then what was your intention, sir?"

"I don't think that's any of your business." Shorecross looked at his attorney. "I don't have to answer, do I?"

"Not if you feel it incriminates you further."

"Then I choose not to answer."

"I have an idea," Evan said, making the others look around at him. "Hillary Jones. It was you, wasn't it? You were her stalker. You fantasized about holding her prisoner."

"But I wasn't really going to do it, you stupid boy," Shorecross snapped. "It was all play-acting. Fantasy. You can see for yourself that the bunker was never used."

"So where did you take Shannon Parkinson?" Watkins asked.

"Who?"

"Shannon Parkinson. The girl who disappeared on the mountain last week. If you didn't take her to the bunker, what did you do with her?"

"The girl who disappeared on the mountain last week? I know nothing about her," Shorecross said angrily. "I offered to help you search for her, remember."

"You offered to help us search for Miss Price," Evan said.

"But the first offer was genuine. Why would I want to kidnap some girl from a mountain? Besides, I was in my office at the bank when it happened. Everyone will vouch for me."

"I suppose we have to be satisfied with that outcome," Watkins said wearily as they left the interview room later that night. "I'm not thrilled about his pleading insanity, but at least it will ensure that he spends the rest of his life locked away."

"In a nice parklike setting, not a cell like the place he kept Bronwen," Evan said bitterly. "But I've got Bronwen back safely and that's really all that matters, isn't it?"

"Do you think he was telling the truth about Shannon Parkinson?"

"I'm inclined to believe him," Evan said.

"In which case, we're back to square one where she's concerned."

They walked together to the canteen and Watkins shoved a pound coin into the beverage machine. "In the good old days we'd have had real cups of tea all night," he said. "Not this bloody dishwater."

"Better than nothing," Evan said, putting his own coin in.

"You'd better get home to bed," Watkins said. "You look a wreck."

"I'm all right now," Evan said. "It's like coming out of hell."

"I'm glad for you, son," Watkins put a hand onto Evan's arm. "We're all glad for you."

Evan looked away and cleared his throat. They sat in the semidarkness at a Formica table, waiting for the tea to be cool enough to drink.

"I don't quite know what else we can do about Shannon Parkinson," Watkins said. "We've had divers search the lake. We've had people check mine shafts. Someone must have taken her."

"Unless she went of her own free will," Evan said, stirring his tea with a plastic straw.

"Meaning what?"

"She could have staged her own disappearance. What if she was fed up with her current boyfriend and she'd met somebody new? Or what if she was fed up with the tight restrictions her family placed on her? She could have come down the other side of the mountain, even caught the train down, and gone off on her own for a while."

"In which case no crime has been committed and we're off the hook." Watkins took a sip of his tea, made a face, and put it down again. "Tastes like piss water," he said. "But I don't like to walk away like this, especially with her family waiting for news of her. You know how you felt when we didn't know where Bronwen had gone."

"I do," Evan said. "Why don't we go and talk to her family and friends. Maybe one of her friends knows something, a secret she hasn't shared until now."

"It's worth a try," Watkins said. "Go home and get a good night's sleep and we'll head for Liverpool in the morning."

Evan stopped at Bronwen's bedside at the hospital first thing in the morning, to find her bed surrounded by flowers and her parents already in residence. He stood at the entrance to the ward feeling strangely superfluous until Bronwen looked over at him and her face lit up in a radiant smile.

"Evan," she said, holding out her hand to him.

"How are you feeling?" he asked and bent to kiss her.

"Absolutely fine."

"That's wonderful. I was so worried."

"I know."

"You were so brave."

"Survival instincts kicked in."

"I hope you have that bastard securely behind bars and you aren't going to let him out on any amount of bail," Bronwen's father said.

"Don't worry. He's not going anywhere. He's pleaded not guilty by reason of insanity."

"Insanity—I should say insanity!" Bronwen's mother said, smoothing back her daughter's hair. "It's too bad we don't have the death penalty any longer."

Evan shook his head. "We're talking about a man who handed out his own death penalty to anyone who crossed him. He killed his own father because his father despised his musical talent."

"And my friend Penny," Bronwen said. "He killed her, too. He put a trip wire across a path so she tumbled from her horse and broke her neck. And he was going to kill me." Her voice wavered. "I still can't believe it really happened. It's like a film I was watching. All the time he was so civilized, offering me a cup of cocoa . . ."

"That cup of cocoa had enough drugs to make sure you went to sleep and didn't wake up," Evan said.

"What turns a person into a twisted monster like that?" Bronwen's mother asked.

Evan shrugged. "Maybe some people are just born that way."

He paused and looked up as a doctor entered the ward. "I thought you were supposed to have peace and quiet," he said to Bronwen, and then he glared at Evan, "and you were supposed to come back to have that shoulder X-rayed properly."

"What happened to your shoulder, Evan?" Bronwen asked.

"It's okay. I hurt it when I fell into the bunker."

"What bunker?"

"The bunker where I thought he was hiding you," Evan said. "He pushed me in and then shut off the air supply."

Bronwen reached out and took his hand. "Oh Evan, how awful for you."

Evan smiled. "Lucky I had a squad car and it was parked where it could be seen from the road or neither of us might be here right now."

"I do hope you won't have to wear a sling for the wedding, Evan," Bronwen's mother said. "It will spoil the pictures."

"Mother!" Bronwen glared at her. "Damn the bloody pictures."

"Bronwen!" Mrs. Price said.

Evan grinned to himself.

Chapter 28

An hour later he was riding beside D.I. Watkins, joining holidaymakers in the Sunday mass exodus from Wales.

"You'd think our economy should be booming with all this tourism, wouldn't you?" Watkins said.

"Most of them have their own caravans, look you," Evan said. "They probably bring their own food as well and all we get out of them is the occasional ice cream or drink in the pub."

"You're a cynic, boyo, you know that."

"I haven't exactly been through the happiest of times, have I?" Evan said. "It's going to take a while to get over this."

"Of course it is," Watkins said, "but I've no doubt a wedding will cheer you up."

"I still can't believe that it's less than a week away," Evan said. "I hope Bronwen will be well enough."

"How did she seem this morning?"

"Remarkably bright."

"She's a tough girl, Evan. Many women would have cracked after what she's been through."

"I still can't come to terms with Shorecross getting off so lightly," Evan said. "Do you think the judge will buy the insanity defense?"

233

"Oh, I'd say he was clearly round the twist, probably has been all his life."

"So he'll wind up in some cushy insane asylum where they'll let him stroll the grounds and play his piano. It doesn't seem fair, does it?"

"Isn't that the first thing you realized when you joined the police force?" Watkins asked. "Life's never bloody fair. Good people get their heads bashed in. Bad people walk away free. It's only very occasionally that we actually see justice done." He slapped on the rim of the steering wheel. "I hope to God we find out what happened to Shannon. I don't like leaving it not knowing."

"I agree," Evan said.

The motorway skirted to the north of Chester and soon they were crossing the Mersey into Liverpool. Shannon Parkinson lived in one of those faceless suburbs that sprawl out from every major city. Neat semi-detached houses built before World War II, front gardens with gnomes and birdbaths, men outside polishing cars and mowing pocket handkerchief–sized lawns, children riding scooters. The house and garden were well kept although there was no sign of life and the curtains were drawn. Evan suspected that the family might be away and was surprised when he knocked on the front door that it was opened quickly by a middle-aged woman, smartly dressed in a summer suit and heels.

"Can I help you?" she asked warily. "We're just off to church. If you're from a newspaper, we're not talking to anyone."

"It's Inspector Watkins and D.C. Evans, North Wales Police, madam," Watkins said, stepping forward. "I take it there's been no news on your daughter then?"

"How can there be when the likes of you haven't done a damned thing?" she snapped, her face contorting with bitterness. "She may not be an important case to you, but she's all we've got. Our precious joy." She put her hand up to her mouth and turned away.

"Now, Mother, don't distress yourself again." A tall, gaunt man, dressed in his Sunday suit, came out of the living room behind her. "Did I hear that you're policemen? You've nothing to tell us, have you?"

"I'm afraid not, Mr. Parkinson," Watkins said. "But I don't want you thinking that we haven't done everything we could. We've searched the whole mountain several times, we've had divers in the lake where we found her glove . . ."

"Glove? I didn't think she took gloves with her. I told her to and she said it was the middle of summer and I always fussed too much."

Watkins glanced at Evan.

"Paul Upwood identified a glove we found as Shannon's," Evan said. "Bright red wool."

Mrs. Parkinson shook her head. "She never wore gloves. She's one of those young people who never seem to feel the cold. Even in winter she'd go out without a coat. Her father told her she wanted her head examined, but she never listened to us, did she, Father?"

"Too headstrong by half." Mr. Parkinson nodded agreement. "We weren't exactly happy with her going on this trip but she went anyway."

"Why weren't you happy?" Evan asked.

"I didn't trust him," Mrs. Parkinson said. "He wasn't the right young man for her."

"He seemed like a nice enough bloke," Evan said. "Well mannered, attending the university."

Mrs. Parkinson shook her head. "There was just something about him I didn't like. Shannon changed after she started going out with him."

"You're not suggesting that he had something to do with her disappearance, are you?" Watkins asked.

The Parkinsons looked at each other, then Mr. Parkinson shook his head. "He worshipped the ground she walked on, I'll say that much for him. He'd not have let Shannon get hurt."

Mrs. Parkinson glanced at her watch.

"Sorry, you were on your way to church," Watkins said.

"That's all right, if there's anything else we can do to find our Shannon," Mr. Parkinson said, looking at his wife's face. "The wife doesn't like to be late usually."

"Is there anything else we can tell you?" Mrs. Parkinson said. "We've been over everything with the local police, so I really don't know what to say . . ." Her voice trailed off into hopelessness.

"By all means, go ahead to church then," Watkins said. "But maybe first you could give us the names and addresses of Shannon's best friends. Sometimes young girls will confide something to a best friend that they keep from their parents."

"Like what?" Mrs. Parkinson looked perplexed.

"If she was planning to run off somewhere on her own maybe? Go into hiding for a while?"

Evan saw a great wave of relief flood over her face as she realized her daughter might still be alive. "Why would she want to run off and put us through all this worry?"

"Because you disapproved of her young man, maybe?" Evan suggested.

"You think it was all a plot and she's off somewhere now with that Paul?"

"It's possible."

Mr. Parkinson shook his head violently. "No, she'd never put us through all this worry. She's a good girl at heart. She cares about her mum and dad."

"Shannon's best friend was Amy Illingsworth," Mrs. Parkinson said. "She lives round the corner on Milton Drive. I think it's number twenty-eight. It has a monkey puzzle tree in the front garden. I can never understand why people plant those things. Ugly as sin, aren't they?"

Evan noted the number.

"Thanks very much for your help," Watkins said. "I can tell you now that for a while we thought she'd been captured by a madman. We discovered a bunker, you see. Only it turns out he had nothing to do with her disappearance. So now we can put out feelers all over the country and hope for better news, can't we?"

"Oh yes." Mrs. Parkinson's face glowed. "I do hope so."

"I hope we haven't raised her hopes too high," Evan said as they drove away. "If someone's not found after a week, the outcome isn't often good."

"If she's run off anywhere, the friend will know," Watkins answered. "All we have to do is persuade her that it's in Shannon's best interests to tell us."

Amy Illingsworth's house was indistinguishable from the Parkinsons', except that the front garden was paved over and a motorbike was parked there. An unkempt woman, still in her housecoat, opened the door.

"Yeah? What do you want?" she demanded. "And it better not be bloody Jehovah's Witnesses again."

"North Wales Police, madam," Watkins said. "We'd like to speak with your daughter Amy, if we may."

"Amy? She's not done anything wrong, has she? I told her she was asking for trouble, staying out all hours at those bloody clubs."

"She's not done anything wrong, Mrs. Illingsworth," Watkins interrupted. "We understand she is Shannon Parkinson's best friend. We hoped she might help us in our search for Shannon."

"Oh. Right. But I don't know how she can help you. She's been that worried." She went to the foot of the stairs. "Amy!" she yelled in a voice that would cut metal. "Get yourself up and down here. We've got policemen wanting to talk to you."

A few minutes later a bleary-eyed girl, her face bearing the smudged remains of last night's makeup, came into the room.

"It's Sunday morning. Only time I get to sleep in all week," she complained, flopping into the nearest armchair. "Anyone got a fag?"

"I'll make us all a cup of coffee," the mother said, and disappeared tactfully to the kitchen.

"Have you heard anything about Shannon yet?" Amy asked.

"Nothing. That's why we came to see you," Watkins said. "We wondered if she'd maybe confided something to you about her plans."

"Plans?"

"Such as running away from too strict parents?"

Amy looked surprised. "They're not too strict. They spoil her rotten. Give her everything she wants, they do. Not like my mum." She lowered her voice for the last phrase.

"Paul Upwood claims that they forbade her to see him and watched over her like jailers," Evan said.

Amy's lip curled in a sarcastic smile. "He said that, did he? He's a bloody liar, then. The only one who watched over her like a jailer was him."

"Paul?"

"Yeah. He was too bloody possessive by half. Told her what to wear, wouldn't let her put on makeup, that kind of thing. She turned into a zombie after she started dating him. We had a falling out over it. He wouldn't let her see me anymore 'cause I'm too common, apparently. I said to her, 'You choose, it's either him or me.' And she said, 'You know I can't go against him.' But I tell you what"—and she leaned forward in the chair—"she was getting right fed up with him. In fact, I think she'd met someone else she fancied more."

"So you think she might have run off to be with another bloke?" Evan asked.

Amy considered this. "Yeah. It's possible. She'd want to hide out for a while so that Paul couldn't come and find her."

"You've no idea who this other bloke was, have you?" Evan asked.

She shook her head. "Like I said, we weren't speaking much before she went on holiday. I only saw her the once and I told her it was daft, going away with him. 'You hate walking and fresh air and all that healthy stuff,' I told her. And she said that Paul had set his heart on it and she didn't want to let him down. 'But it will be the last time,' she said."

"What did she mean by that?" Watkins asked sharply.

Amy shrugged. "I expect she'd made up her mind to dump him for that other bloke."

"And you've no idea where she met the other bloke?" Watkins asked. "A local, is he?"

"Like I said, we haven't been talking much. Paul cut her off from all her old friends. So I've really no idea. It's not likely to be anyone from school. She liked older men." She attempted to smooth down her unbrushed hair. "So, I'm sorry, I can't really help you. I wish I could."

Watkins and Evan made their exit before Amy's mother appeared with the coffee.

"We should pay a call on the local police and have them interview Shannon's school friends," Watkins said as they drove away. "Maybe she confided about the new boyfriend to someone else. But she could have met him anywhere."

"Too bad it's the summer holidays," Evan said. "If anyone is away from home at the moment, it will be assumed that he's off on holiday. Shannon could have arranged to meet him and faked tiredness on the mountain as an excuse to get away from Paul without a fuss."

Watkins nodded. "That does seem the most likely scenario. We'd better get onto the media again and have her picture shown. She'll have to have surfaced somewhere."

"Funny about the glove, though," Evan said. "Why would Paul lie about it?"

"Unless he was trying to place her somewhere that she hadn't really been," Watkins said thoughtfully.

"And why would he do that?" Evan asked.

Watkins paused for a long moment before he said, "What if she'd told him she was leaving and going off with someone else? It might have been a way of salvaging his pride, or of punishing her."

"Seems like a ridiculous length to go to," Evan said. "If we hadn't scoured the whole mountain, I might have thought that he'd got rid of her himself and planted the glove to hint that it was an accident."

"But then her body would have turned up in the lake."

"That's true."

They drove on in silence. Evan played through the scenes in his mind. Paul had seemed distraught and yet certain things didn't make sense. He had claimed he was much fitter than she was and she couldn't keep up with him. And yet he had puffed and panted when Evan took him back up the mountain. Evan shut his eyes, picturing the scene again for himself. Even if Paul had come down the Pyg Track quicker than Shannon, the mountain was bare for most of the way. He'd only have had to look back and he'd have seen her. What if they hadn't been on the mountain at all?

"What's on your mind, Evans?" Watkins asked. "How do you see this?"

Evan took a deep breath. "You know what I'm thinking, sir? I'm wondering if they ever went up Snowdon. Paul Upwood was out of breath by the time we'd gone over the first crest when I took him up with me, and yet he claimed they had words because she couldn't keep up with him. So how about this: what if she told him she was planning to leave him? We know he worshipped the ground she trod on, according to her parents. We know how possessive he was. What if he wasn't prepared to let her go? What if he killed her and has hidden the body somewhere else—somewhere far away from Snowdon?"

"That would be looking for a needle in a haystack, wouldn't it?"

"I'm not so sure," Evan said. "They didn't have a car with them, so they could only go where the Sherpa bus and their own two feet would take them. We know they were staying at the youth hostel and both were seen at breakfast that morning. The bus driver doesn't remember them on his route, so they must have walked. The question is, in which direction?"

"We did put up some posters and nobody came forward to say that they'd seen her that day," Watkins reminded him.

"Of course. He would have deliberately chosen a less traveled route, probably one with some trees, and not too steep either, the way he panted."

"We'll take a look at the map when we get back, but in the meantime I don't know about you, but I'm starving. Fancy a fry-up at the transport café?"

"I never say no to a good fry-up," Evan said. "Especially since I'm about to embark on a life of healthy eating with Bronwen."

"Your last meal, like the condemned prisoner's, then." Watkins chuckled.

"Sorry, but I find it hard to smile about last meals at the moment. I hope to God we find Shannon Parkinson's body if he did kill her. I don't want another man getting away with murder."

"We'll find her. As you said, he wasn't much of a walker. And he can't have had time to bury her properly. We'll have the dogs out again and she'll turn up, sooner or later."

They pulled into a transport café called the Traveller's Rest and walked away from the counter with plates piled high with eggs, beans, chips, sausage, bacon, mushrooms, and fried bread.

"Enough cholesterol to kill an ox," Watkins commented as he dipped the fried bread into the egg yolk, "but it looks wonderful."

Evan was just putting the first forkful to his lips when he stopped. Yolk dripped down onto the rim of his plate.

"Hang on a minute," he said. "I was just remembering that first time that Paul Upwood showed up at my cottage. He wasn't at all out of breath. You know the climb up to the cottage, don't you? It's steep enough to make even Charlie Hopkins pant a little. So that must mean that Upwood hadn't come up the hill at all. He'd come down from above. You know there's a path that follows the stream up between the Glydrs and Mynedd Perfedd. I think he could have managed it without too much difficulty."

"Any woods up there?"

Evan paused to think. "Not many trees, but plenty of rocks, oh, and there's that little reservoir on the other side."

"Right," Watkins said. "As soon as we've finished this, I'll have men up there. And I suppose I'd better call out the divers again." He sighed. "We better find a body. HQ is going to nail me for going over budget this month."

Evan looked up from his meal. How often they made light of tragedy in their profession. Finding bodies was just part of the job. But now he'd had his own personal brush with tragedy, he found he couldn't smile at Watkins's quip. Finding the body meant a lifetime of grief for a family. He'd never forget that again.

Chapter 29

Before the day was out, Shannon Parkinson's body had been found, tangled in a clump of reeds at the edge of the small lake. A warrant was issued for Paul Upwood's arrest. Evan was annoyed that he hadn't been allowed to join in the search to look for Shannon, but by the end of the day he had to admit that his shoulder would not have appreciated the hike. In fact, the stress and exhaustion of the last two days suddenly caught up with him, so that he was fast asleep in a chair in the duty room when Watkins came to find him with the news.

"Well done, chaps." D.C.I. Hughes poked his head around the door. "I just heard the news. It's always satisfying to write case closed on something, isn't it?"

"Not so satisfying for her parents," Watkins said gravely. "Her mum was so hopeful when we left her. I don't envy the local Bobby who has to break that news to her."

"I hope Bron's parents realize how lucky they are," Evan said. "I certainly do."

"You've been through an ordeal this week, Evans," Hughes said, with uncharacteristic kindness. "Why don't you take a few days sick leave. Give you a chance to prepare for the wedding."

Evan's brain raced quickly though seating plans, flower arrangements, his mother's sausage rolls, Mrs. Williams versus the caterer . . . "I don't think I'm actually that sick, sir," he said. Watkins chuckled.

The wedding morning dawned bright and clear. Evan's mother appeared at an indecently early hour, clucking and shaking her head. "You know what they say about fine before seven, rain by eleven, don't you? I hope you've got a nice big umbrella so that Miss Price doesn't ruin her headdress."

"Don't be such a pessimist, Mam," Evan said. "And I must say I'm glad you'll finally have to call Bronwen by her first name after today. Or are you going to call her Mrs. Evans?"

"Don't be silly," Evan's mother pushed past him. "I'll welcome her into the family. It's only Christian charity, isn't it? Of course, if you were both real Christians, you'd be getting married in the chapel here in the village, not traipsing down to some high-faluting Church of Wales. They'll probably be swinging incense and praying to statues and all those heathen kinds of things."

Evan laughed. "It's a simple wedding ceremony, and we've asked the minister at Capel Bethel to come and say a blessing, too. Now are you satisfied?"

Mrs. Evans searched for a long moment for something else to complain about, then shook her head. "At least you've got plenty of sausage rolls so that the guests don't go hungry," she said as her parting shot. Then she paused in the doorway and came back. "Your da would have been proud of you," she said quietly. "I just wish he was here to see this day."

"I wish so too, Mam."

"Right," she said, with a deep sigh. "Can't stand around here chatting. There's work to be done. All those pastries to get down from Mrs. Williams's house to the tent. See you in church then, eh, son?"

"See you in church, Mam."

Evan glanced at his reflection in the speckled glass mirror as he left the cottage. An unfamiliar figure in a dark suit, silk tie, and neatly combed hair stared back at him. "Oh well, then, no sense in hanging around," he said to the reflection. "Better get it over with."

He arrived at the church to find Mrs. Price fussing around. "Oh, thank goodness you're here, Evan. And where's your best man? He's not here yet, either."

"He'll be here," Evan said, glancing at his watch.

"He won't have been called out in an emergency, will he?" Bronwen's mother asked anxiously.

"I'm sure he'll make it," Evan said and wished she'd go away.

Guests arrived and were seated. Mrs. Williams and Evan's mother were seen carrying trays of food over to the large tent. Caterers scurried to and fro. The inhabitants of Llanfair, all good chapelgoers, glanced at each other with apprehension as they entered the church, expecting to be struck on the spot by the wrath of God.

"It will all be very Papist, I'm sure," he heard Mrs. Powell-Jones say loudly to her husband, the minister. Evan grinned to himself. At least they'd come. He wished Bronwen was here beside him at this minute. It all felt very strange and unreal. Why had they let themselves get caught up in all this?

At the last minute a police car screeched to a halt and Inspector Watkins jumped out, straightening his tie as he hurried toward the porch where Evan was waiting.

"Sorry about that, boyo," he said. "I hope I didn't give you a fright."

"I knew you'd get here," Evan said. "Something came up, did it?"

"It did. I got a call that a man's body had been located by the Parks Service in a wild area on Cader Idris. Single gunshot wound. A suicide note was on the ground beside him."

"Paul Upwood?" Evan asked.

Watkins shook his head. "Rhodri Llewelyn," he said. "Your instincts weren't wrong, after all. Apparently he had been quietly embezzling from the bank for years. He thought we were onto him and he couldn't face the consequences."

"I must say it did cross my mind that Shorecross had done away with him too," Evan said. "So he took his own life."

"He wanted to save his mother from any embarrassment, so the note said."

"Right." Evan paused in the doorway. "Well, that's that, then. We'd better get inside before Bronwen's mum gets hysterical."

"Got her knickers in a twist, has she?" Watkins put a hand on Evan's shoulder. "This is it then, boy. Last moments of freedom. Good luck."

"I'm not going to the gallows, you know," Evan answered with a grin. "This is supposed to be the happiest day of my life."

But he fought back the sick feeling in his stomach as he walked down the aisle to take his place. It wasn't just wedding nerves, either. The news about Rhodri Llewelyn had startled him. His actions had caused another man to take his life. The man had committed a petty crime, to be sure. He deserved to be caught, but were a few pounds here and there worth a life? It was tough being a policeman. Sometimes they got it right and sometimes they didn't. Simple as that.

He looked up as the organ broke into the opening prelude and the two bridesmaids came down the aisle. Then Bronwen's sister as matron of honor and her son, dressed in a minute kilt, as pageboy. Then he saw her, silhouetted against the fierce sunlight, and the organ changed to "Here Comes the Bride." She started to walk forward and Evan felt a lump in his throat. He had never seen anything so lovely in his life.

"You got through it without fainting," Bronwen teased as they emerged from the church after the ceremony. The sun had disappeared behind a cloud and a wind had sprung up, streaming her veil out behind her.

"Over this way, everybody," Mrs. Price called. "The weather doesn't look too promising. Let's get all the major group photos before it starts to rain and then we can do the individual shots and the more intimate couple portraits inside the church if we have to."

She started herding people to the church porch like an efficient sheepdog.

At that moment Evan's mother appeared. "They've hidden my

sausage rolls," she said angrily. "Thought they weren't good enough, I expect. Well, I'm just going to find them again and put them out in a place of honor, too. And if they've thrown them away, heaven help them! Who hired those caterers, that's what I'd like to know. They must be foreigners, English people no doubt."

"Bronwen, do you want to touch up your makeup before the photos?" Mrs. Price called. "You do still look a little pale. Understandable, of course, but you want to glow in the pictures, don't you?"

Bronwen squeezed Evan's hand again. "You have that rabbit-in-the-headlights look about you. Do you hate this as much as I do?"

Evan nodded.

Bronwen leaned closer. "Look, they've got plenty of food and drink and music. They don't really need us there, do they?"

"What are you saying?" Evan asked.

"I was thinking that maybe we'd let them take the group photos and then somewhere between here and the marquee we could slip away."

"Bronwen! We couldn't do that," Evan exclaimed.

"Why not? It's our wedding. We can do what we like." Bronwen gave him a wicked smile.

"But think of all those people who've come a long way to be here. Think of your mum and dad. They'd be so disappointed."

"Evan, why are you always such a Boy Scout?" Bronwen demanded.

"Sorry. You know what I'm like and you still married me." Evan pushed her veil back from her face as the wind snatched it. "Look, we'll go in, have a glass of champagne, cut the cake and then say we've a plane to catch, which is true. Is that all right for you?"

Bronwen slipped her arm through his. "I suppose it will have to be."

At that moment the rain started. Guests rushed to the shelter of the tent, attempting to cover posh hats with their hands. Evan grabbed Bronwen's hand and they sprinted across the grass. An hour later they were driving south, heading for the airport, Switzerland, and a new life.